SLEEPERS

A JOHN MILTON THRILLER

MARK DAWSON

ALSO BY MARK DAWSON

John Milton

The Cleaner

Saint Death

The Driver

Ghosts

The Sword of God

Salvation Row

Headhunters

The Ninth Step

The Jungle

Blackout

The Alamo

Redeemer

Beatrix Rose

In Cold Blood

Blood Moon Rising

Blood and Roses

Isabella Rose

The Angel

PART I

SOUTHWOLD

1

Leonard Geggel spent the drive to Southwold thinking about CHERRY. It had been a year since Geggel's retirement from MI6 and he hadn't spoken to his old agent since then. Indeed, they had not parted on the best of terms. Pyotr Ilyich Aleksandrov had always been a cantankerous man, but, as the Russian grew older and more resigned to the fact that he would never be able to return home, he had become more and more frustrated. The two of them had argued during their last meeting. Aleksandrov had said that he needed an increase in his stipend so that he could move to a different house. Upon investigation, Geggel had found that Aleksandrov and his neighbour had fallen out over the folk music that Aleksandrov liked to play late at night as he drank himself into a stupor on the Moskovskaya Osobaya vodka that he had imported from Poland. Geggel had not even taken Aleksandrov's request up the chain; he knew that it would be rejected and agreed that rejection would have been the right response. He had told Aleksandrov that there was to be no more money, and that he should make it up with his neighbour. The suggestion had provoked a foul-mouthed tirade against him, MI6 and the British state, followed by the angry suggestion that his work was not valued and that he should never have defected in the first place.

That had been the last time that they had met. It had come as a surprise, then, that Aleksandrov had made contact. He had called Geggel on his personal number and insisted that he must come to Southwold at once. Geggel had asked the reason for the urgency, but Aleksandrov would not be drawn on it. Instead, he had reiterated that it was of critical importance and that it simply could not wait. Geggel had reminded Aleksandrov that he was retired, and that it would be more appropriate to contact the woman who had replaced him as his handler. Aleksandrov had dismissed the suggestion, saying that Ross was young and incompetent. There was sexism there, too: Geggel knew that Aleksandrov did not hold truck with the idea that women could run male assets, and that he thought their value in intelligence-gathering was to 'open their legs and listen carefully.' Aleksandrov had added that he would only deal with someone that he knew and trusted. That, in the Russian's world, was as close to a compliment as one would ever likely get, and, after considering the request for a moment, Geggel said that he would come.

In truth, Geggel had been looking for something interesting to take his mind off the mundanities of his forced retirement. He hadn't wanted to leave the Service, but there had been an unfortunate incident where one of the agents he had been running in Tirana had been blown, and the shit had rolled downhill to him. Geggel still did not understand how the agent had been revealed to the SVR; he had always been scrupulously careful, and the agent—a secretary in the prime minister's office—had been so cautious that it had been almost impossible to arrange face-to-face meetings. Geggel's conclusion was that the source had been blown by way of a leak from inside MI6. He had suggested it to his line manager but, after a week of lip service about an investigation that Geggel knew had never got started, it was suggested that the error was down to him and that, perhaps, it was time for him to think about calling it a day.

He had dabbled with lecturing, but teaching others about geopolitical events just reminded him that he no longer had any role in shaping them. He had retreated to his garden, clearing out a messy bed and replacing it with a polytunnel where he could grow vegetables all year long. He had found some peace there, but when he lay awake at night, his le Carrés and Ludlums finally laid down on the bedside table next to him, he would close his eyes and imagine the life that he had once led. There was no point in pretending otherwise: he missed it.

Geggel had been on the A12 for almost all of the journey. It was a poor road, and, as soon as he was beyond Ipswich, it became a single carriageway prone to delays as cars queued behind the tractors that rumbled between the mirror-flat fields that made up the East Anglian landscape.

He looked down at the phone that he had dropped into the cupholder and wondered, again, whether he should call the River House and tell them about Aleksandrov's contact. He had wrestled with that choice ever since they had spoken and, ultimately, had decided against it. He knew what would happen. The details of the call would be passed to his replacement and it would be she who went to speak to Aleksandrov. Geggel and the old agent disagreed on many things, but they did share some common ground. Chief among them was a disdain for the woman—Geggel remembered her name, Ross—and, more to the point, the things that she represented.

It wasn't that she was a woman, at least not for Geggel. It was that she was part of the new influx of SIS staff, those who responded to the vulgar advertisements in the newspapers that promised a fulfilling life as a 'spy.' Geggel and his old colleagues had shared a laugh over one particular advert that they had seen in the *Times*. *'If the qualities that made a good spy were obvious, they wouldn't make a very good spy.'* The whole thing was preposterous. These bright young graduates, fresh out of university, were selected with psychometrics and then fast-tracked. It was to the detriment of the old sweats who had been there for years and knew how things *really* worked. The change in culture was the reason Geggel had not fought against his enforced retirement. Aleksandrov had chuckled at Geggel's annoyance, but had then suggested that he had heard through the grapevine that Yasenevo was not so different, either. The old warhorses, like them, were being put out to pasture in the Center just as they were in Vauxhall Cross. This was a brave new world, moving too fast for them to keep up. Aleksandrov had poured two tumblers of Moskovskaya and they had toasted their obsolescence together.

He continued north, passing the turn for Walberswick, and then approached the road that led to Southwold.

2

Pyotr Aleksandrov glanced out of the front window and looked up at the sky. It was clear, suggesting that the forecast for sunny and warm weather was going to be accurate. He went through to the hallway, collected his jacket, and picked up the briefcase with the documents that he had printed out last night. Anastasiya had emailed him the sample schematics and he was confident that he would be able to parlay them into everything that they needed to bring her safely back to him.

He opened the briefcase and withdrew one of the pages, looking at the technical drawing and daydreaming for a moment. He had long since given up the possibility that he might be reconciled with his daughter. They had parted on such bad terms. He had been in the gulag for four years, and his ex-wife had spent that time dripping her poison into Anastasiya's ear: he was a traitor, he was selfish, he was greedy, he cared only for himself. He had seen her once after his unexpected release and had offered to bring her with him to the west, but she had refused and, at the culmination of the argument that followed, had told him that she never wanted to see him again. Her recent email had come out of the blue, and had allowed him to dream of a reconciliation.

He just had to persuade Geggel to help him.

He slid the schematic back into the case and closed the clasps. He zipped up his jacket, opened the door, and stepped out onto the street. He was surprised to find that he was nervous. This was not the first time that he had met with Geggel to sell intelligence. They had done it for ten years, and it had made him several hundred thousand pounds and had secured this life, shabby and tedious though it might be. He was well acquainted with Geggel; his old runner was the nearest thing that he had to a friend. But times had changed. Aleksandrov was no longer operational and Geggel was retired. They had argued, too. He didn't know how the meet would play out, and that made him feel unsettled. He reminded himself that he hadn't arranged this rendezvous for his own benefit. He was doing it for Anastasiya. She was in hiding, somewhere between Lake Baikal and the Pacific, and Aleksandrov knew that the FSB's bloodhounds were out looking for her.

He needed Geggel's help to save his daughter's life. That was why he was anxious. He didn't know what his old handler would say, and the stakes had never been higher.

3

Nataliya Kuznetsov watched through the front window. Aleksandrov's cottage was at number one Wymering Road. The cottage that they had rented was diagonally across the street at number five. The place had been a fortunate find. Southwold was a popular destination for tourists who wished to enjoy its quaint 1950s atmosphere, and while many of the houses and cottages were available for tourists to rent, demand was high. Someone at the Center had found this one on Airbnb and, after sending someone from the embassy to check that it was suitable for their purposes, they had booked it for a month using the credit card in the name of Nataliya's legend, Amelia Ryan.

An advance team had been sent from Moscow to equip the property. The two technicians were from Line OT, the Directorate responsible for operational and technical support for agents in the field. They had installed tiny cameras in the ground- and first-floor bay windows that provided continuous coverage of the house across the street. They had set up an IMSI-catcher, a complicated piece of equipment that mimicked a wireless carrier cell tower in order to force all nearby cellular devices to connect to it; the catcher allowed them to monitor Aleksandrov's cellphone. They had located the telecoms junction box and, under cover of darkness, installed devices that routed all voice calls and broadband data to a server that they had set up in the front room.

They had been here for two weeks as the Ryans, here for a break and the fresh sea air. Their marriage was real, but their identities were not. Thomas Ryan's name was Mikhail and he was from Almetyevsk. Mikhail and Nataliya had met at School No. 101 outside Chilobityevo; the school had previously been known as the Red Banner Institute before it had been renamed the Academy of Foreign Intelligence. They had studied together, had been recruited into Directorate S together, and had been placed in the United Kingdom together as *operupolnomochenny*, or operations officers. This was just the latest in a long line of operations that the couple had undertaken for the motherland over the course of their decade's worth of service. It was also, according to their handler, the most important.

There had been plenty of time while they had watched and waited, and Nataliya had used it to become familiar with the old man and his daughter. MI6 had disappeared the spy after his exchange ten years earlier. The SVR had been unable to find him and, given his lack of importance at the time, had decided it was not worth the investment that would have been required to track him down.

But that was before his daughter had gone missing with a terabyte of data on the new Su-58. Anastasiya Romanova, née Aleksandrova, had disappeared and the Center wanted to find her again. It seemed reasonable that she might reach out to her exiled father. Aleksandrov had been located by an

SVR mole in MI6 and the two of them had been sent to put him under twenty-four-hour surveillance. They had sat on his phone calls and internet traffic. They had followed him on his daily walks into town and established his routine. They had put a beacon on his car and broken into his house to place miniature listening devices in the front room, kitchen and study. The first week had been a bust, and then the second was the same; it had taken fifteen days before they had lucked out with the interception of an email sent from daughter to father.

They had reported back to Yasenevo and waited for instruction. And then, the following day, they had eavesdropped the conversation between Aleksandrov and his old handler. A rendezvous had been agreed and, after reporting the development to the Center, they had received their orders. They were to observe the meet and then eliminate them both. In the meantime, another sleeper had visited the handler, a man named Geggel, and had pressed a beacon underneath the right-rear wheel arch of his car. Nataliya and Mikhail were able to follow the tracker on an app on their phones. Geggel had set off two hours earlier. Traffic looked clear and he hadn't stopped en route; they estimated his arrival in Southwold within the next ten minutes.

Nataliya saw movement on one of the two monitors. Aleksandrov had opened the front door and had stepped out onto the street. He paused outside the door, looking left and right, the old spy's instincts still firing after all these years of inactivity.

Nataliya clipped her microphone to her collar and opened a channel to her husband.

"Aleksandrov is on the move," she said.

Mikhail's voice sounded in her earpiece. "*Acknowledged.*"

Nataliya watched the screen. Aleksandrov had moved

away from the house; she stood and parted the slats of the blind just a little, enough so that she could see him as he walked by the house on the same side of the street.

"Dark jacket, carrying a briefcase. Heading east, into the town."

Mikhail acknowledged the information. Nataliya collected her jacket from the back of the chair and took her handbag from the table. She unzipped it and checked inside: she saw the dark glint of the pistol with its long, tubular suppressor. She zipped the bag, slung it over her shoulder and made her way to the door.

She stepped outside and looked to the left. Aleksandrov was near the end of the road, just before it took a sharp ninety-degree turn to the left. She let him turn the corner and pass out of view. She would follow as backup, out of sight and able to take up the surveillance when Mikhail called for the switch.

Aleksandrov was an old field agent with experience, but he had lived here—in boredom and safety—for ten years. He didn't take the proper precautions. He wasn't especially careful. His tradecraft was lacking. It would cost him.

Mikhail Timoshev was sitting on a bench on the promenade overlooking the sea. A Styrofoam cup of coffee rested on the arm of the bench and he had a copy of the *Times* on his lap. He looked down at the name that had been scrawled across the top of the front page: RYAN, 5 WYMERING. He had been to the newsagent at the end of the road and requested that a copy be delivered every day during their stay, and the paper always arrived with his name and address on it to help the paperboy remember. He had been Thomas Ryan for so long that he often had to remind himself that that was not his real name.

Aleksandrov's pattern was usually to go into town at around midday. He would collect a newspaper from the shop on the High Street and then take it to the pier where he would buy a cup of coffee and a cheese scone and find a seat where he could gaze out to sea. Mikhail or his wife would observe him, at a distance, never close enough for him to notice them. Today, though, had been different. Nataliya had reported his route as she tailed him.

He took out his phone and watched the glowing dot that represented the beacon on the bottom of Leonard Geggel's car. It had followed the High Street and then Queen Street before arriving at the Common. There was a place to park cars there—a line of bays that had been painted onto a wider than usual stretch of the road—and it looked as if Geggel was going to leave his car there.

Mikhail looked down at his paper as an elderly couple walked by, arm in arm. This was what he lived for. The jolt of adrenaline. The anticipation of action. The sudden release after days of careful surveillance. This was his purpose in life. It was what they had been trained to do. He was better at it than at anything else.

"Aleksandrov has gone into the Lord Nelson," Nataliya said. *"I'll wait outside."*

"Geggel is here," he reported. "If they're meeting there, he'll come this way. Stand by."

Mikhail took a sip of his lukewarm coffee and replaced it on the bench next to him. He held the paper up, flipping the pages, and, as he did, he saw Geggel. Mikhail looked down, glancing up just as the man went by. It would have been possible for Mikhail to reach out and take the sleeve of his overcoat if he had so chosen. It was definitely him. They had been given a photograph of the old SIS spook and there was no question that it was the same man: six feet tall, mousey hair, old acne scars on his cheeks, heavy black spectacles.

Mikhail took another sip of his coffee, shuffling around in his seat just a little so that he could observe Geggel as he proceeded to the north. He waited until he was at the junction with East Street before he collected the coffee and stood up. He dumped the cup in the bin, folded the newspaper and stooped to pick up the plain leather bag that he had placed next to the bench.

"I'm on the move," he said into the microphone.

He followed Geggel northwest as he climbed East Street. He reached a pub—the Lord Nelson—and stopped outside the entrance. Mikhail paused alongside a van with two kayaks strapped to its roof, conscious that he wouldn't be able to wait for long if he wanted to avoid being made as a potential tail. Mikhail and Nataliya had not lasted as denied area agents for as long as they had without being careful. Their normal operating procedure would call for them to abandon a mission if they received even the slightest hint that they might have been compromised, but the orders that Vincent Beck had passed on from the Center had been different. They had authorisation to take greater risks than would otherwise have been the case.

Dealing with Aleksandrov was important enough to justify risking their exposure.

Geggel opened the door to the pub and went inside.

Mikhail updated Nataliya and followed.

G eggel made his way into the pub. It was an old building, with plenty of character. The bar was to his left, complete with rows of pumps carrying the idiosyncratic badges of the ales from the local Adnams brewery: Ghost Ship and Old Ale. Metal tankards and glass pint pots were hung from hooks on the ceiling, and the two members of staff—a man and a woman—passed around each other with difficulty in the cramped space. There was a door to the kitchen and the day's menu was written out on blackboards that were screwed to the wall. Drinkers conversed at the bar and diners had taken all of the chairs around the pub's few tables.

Aleksandrov was waiting at the bar. He acknowledged Geggel and waited for him to come over.

"Pyotr," Geggel said.

"Leonard. Thank you for coming."

"It's been a while."

"You still like ale?

"Of course."

"Go and get a table. I'll bring one over and we can talk."

Geggel slid between the clutch of drinkers waiting to be served at the bar and crossed the saloon to a table that had just been vacated. He took a seat against the wall so that he could look into the room—old habits died hard—and waited for Aleksandrov to come over with their beers. The Russian set the glasses down on the table and dropped into the other chair.

They touched glasses and then drank. The ale was hoppy and not unpleasant.

"How are you?" Aleksandrov said once they had finished their first sips.

"Can't complain. You?"

Aleksandrov sat down. "I am very well, thank you. How is retirement?"

"Truthfully? A little boring. I miss our work."

Aleksandrov laughed. "As do I," he said. "I miss my country, too. But I will never be able to return."

Geggel's heart sank; had he come all this way to suffer one of Aleksandrov's rants? The Russian had been prone to black moods and had made it his habit to regale Geggel with wistful tales of the glory days of the Rodina and what he had sacrificed for British intelligence whenever they met. Geggel had eventually concluded that Aleksandrov believed MI6 were obliged to provide him with a sympathetic ear to listen to his complaints. Their meetings had quickly become tiresome and Geggel had not looked forward to them. But he had blanked out those memories after he had received Aleksandrov's cryptic telephone call. He had been too excited to allow the past to dampen his enthusiasm.

"I wasn't expecting to hear from you," he said, trying to move the conversation along.

"I was not expecting that I would have to call." Aleksandrov took another long swig of his beer. "You are wondering why I did not speak to your replacement?"

"Not really," Geggel said. "I know you didn't get on with her."

"She is a baby," he grumbled. "She does not take me seriously. She does not know the work that we did together."

"How could she? She was still in school."

"Precisely," the Russian said, slapping both hands on the table. "That is precisely it. How old is she? Thirty?"

"I don't know."

"She has no experience. She does not value the intelligence that I provided. The risks I took, *the price I paid*—she has no idea. All I am to her is an old spook. Washed up and irrelevant, sent to this place to be forgotten until I die."

Geggel knew he needed to wrestle Aleksandrov back to whatever it was that he wanted to talk about, or he would lose half an hour to a sullen tirade.

"Well, Pyotr," he said, "I'm here. I came when you asked and I'm listening. What can I help you with?"

The Russian's mood changed as at the flick of a switch. "No, Leonard, it is the other way around." His lips turned up in a self-satisfied smirk. "It is *I* who can help *you*."

THE PUB WAS BUSY. Mikhail had found a space at the bar where he could watch Aleksandrov and Geggel. He had hoped he might be able to hear them, but the noise in the room—the sound of conversations competing with the commentary from the football that was showing on the room's single television—made that impossible. The two men leaned across the table, their faces just a few inches from each other, Aleksandrov punctuating the conversation with excited stabs of his hand. He reached into the briefcase that he had brought with him, took out a piece of paper, laid it on the table and then drilled his finger against it. Mikhail clenched his jaw with frustration. He had orders to find out what they might discuss, and now they were going to have to find that out with a much less elegant solution.

"You want a drink?"

He turned around. The publican was looking at him.

"I'm sorry," Mikhail said with a smile.

"You want to watch, you'll need to buy something."

It took Mikhail a moment to realise that the man meant the television and not the clandestine discussion that was taking place at the table.

"Pint of bitter," he said.

"Which one?"

There were half a dozen pumps, each advertising a different beer. Mikhail picked one at random, gave the man a ten-pound note, collected his change and then sipped at the warm, flat beer. It was not to his taste at all. He kept watching, observing, looking for anything that might be helpful, but it was no use.

He took out his phone and put it to his ear, pretending to make a call. He spoke into the microphone instead.

"It's too busy. I can't get close enough."

"What do you want to do?"

He took a moment, watching as Geggel said something and Aleksandrov reached across the table to take his hand.

"The orders are clear. One each, then meet at home once it's done."

"Copy that."

6

Aleksandrov reached down for a briefcase that had been resting against the chair legs. He entered the combination on the locks that secured the two clasps and popped the lid open. He reached inside and took out a single sheet of paper. He handed it across the table and Geggel looked at it. It was some sort of schematic.

"What is this?"

"You've heard of the Su-58?"

"The aircraft? I know the Su-57. The new fighter Sukhoi was working on—they shelved it."

"The Fargo," Aleksandrov said with a nod. "No. That was a distraction. All the while, they were working on the 58. NATO doesn't even have a designation and now they have completed a successful design." He laid a finger on the paper. "That is a schematic of the underside missile port. The Su-58 can be equipped with the new variant of the Ovod cruise missile. Sukhoi were given the task of producing a plane that could shoot down the Americans' F-22s and F-35s. They have succeeded."

Geggel looked down at the page and then back up to Aleksandrov. "Where did you get this, Pyotr?"

"Do you remember my daughter?"

Geggel found the information was surprisingly easy to recall. "Oh," he said. "I see. She worked for Sukhoi."

The recollection triggered a little spill of excitement. The possibility of using the father to turn the daughter had been tantalising back then, but, as Geggel recalled, Aleksandrov had shut down the possibility as soon as he sensed SIS's motives. Anastasiya was a patriot, a dedicated servant of the motherland, and she had seen her father's defection as the most heinous of betrayals. She had disavowed Aleksandrov in disgust. Geggel and Aleksandrov had had many late-night conversations about it; Aleksandrov had been crushed by her reaction.

"She was assigned to the research division in Komsomolsk," he said. "They are developing the Su-58 there. There is a treasure trove of intelligence waiting to be taken. Anastasiya had access to everything."

"I also remember that the two of you were not exactly on speaking terms."

"We were not."

Geggel noted the use of the past tense and tapped his finger on the schematic. "But she sent you this."

"Things change. My defection was bad for her career, as you would expect. But her reaction to it—her hatred of me —persuaded the GRU that she is trustworthy. They always knew that she was smart and hard-working, and, once they were satisfied that she was patriotic, that she hated me, she was given responsibility again."

Geggel sat a little straighter. He might have been retired, but his instincts were still sharp and he knew, immediately, that this conversation had the potential to be one of the most important of his life. "That's not enough," he said. "Something else must have changed."

Aleksandrov nodded. "She was married five years ago. His name was Vitali Romanov and he was a nice man, from what I understand. An oil and gas trader—very successful, rich. I do not know the details, but he was convicted of financial improprieties and sent to Sevvostlag. Anastasiya says he was innocent, but that the state would not listen to her. He died in the gulag. They said it was a heart attack, but Anastasiya said he was well before he was sentenced. She says that they murdered him for his money." He sipped his beer. "Oligarchs with connections to the Kremlin. It happens often. Anastasiya sees this as the second betrayal of her life, but this one is worse than the first. What happened to him has given her the opportunity to consider what I did in a different light. She sees that perhaps the Rodina is not the utopia that she once thought."

Geggel glanced around the room. The pub was busy, but he couldn't see anyone who looked as if he or she might be paying them any special attention. The hubbub around them was welcome; if he was wrong, and someone was watching them, it would be too noisy for them to eavesdrop.

"What does she want?"

"To defect," Aleksandrov said. "She wants to come here with me."

"And she knows she'll have to give us something to make that happen?"

Aleksandrov nodded, his expression a little bitter. "She knows that she cannot rely on your kindness, yes. I have taught her that much. She knows that she will have to buy her passage, but that is fine—she has something *valuable* to sell." Now it was Aleksandrov's turn to lean forward. He rested his elbows on the table and spoke quietly. "This schematic is just the start. She can provide you with every-thing: blueprints, timelines, Gantt charts, evaluation crite-ria, production schedules, subcontractors, tender information. Data on airborne radar and weapons control systems. *Everything*."

"I'm listening, Pyotr."

Aleksandrov grinned. "Your aerospace industry will see it as a goldmine. It is unprecedented. The value in this intel-ligence... it is incalculable."

Geggel tapped a finger on the piece of paper. "Do you have the rest?"

Aleksandrov shook his head. "Pass that to your old friends on the river and ask them to investigate. My daughter wants you to respect her—this is how she proves that she is worthy of that respect. SIS should confirm that this information is good. When they have done that, we can discuss how she can be exfiltrated."

"Where is she now? Is she safe?"

"She is in hiding. The FSB questioned her after Vitali's death. She told them how she felt—she is hot-blooded."

"Like her father," Geggel suggested.

Aleksandrov smiled. "She knew that she went too far, and disappeared before they could come back to bring her in. They are looking for her now. She is frightened. Exfiltra-tion will not be a simple thing. She knows that—but she *also* knows that what she will bring with her is worth the effort."

"So how do we contact her?"

"It must be through me. She will not speak to anyone else." Aleksandrov reached across the table and grasped Geggel's hand in both of his. "Will you help?"

Geggel knew that he had no choice: the information that Aleksandrov was offering was so valuable that it would be tantamount to treason to pass up the opportunity of acquiring it, but even more than that it was a chance for him to remind his old superiors that they had erred by treating him the way they had. He could bring the opportunity to them as a demonstration that the old ways were still better than the new, that an old hand like him was still worth something even when held up against the up-and-comers like Jessie Ross and the other youngsters who had replaced him.

Aleksandrov squeezed his hand. "Leonard?"

"Yes," Geggel said. He disengaged himself from Aleksandrov's grip and glanced down at the piece of paper that lay on the table between them; it had been stained by a splash of spilled ale. "I'll need this."

"Of course."

"I'll show it to them. They'll have questions."

"I am sure they will. But they must work through you, Leonard. I trust *you*. I do not trust anyone else."

Geggel stood. He took the paper from the table, folded it neatly, and slipped it into his pocket. Aleksandrov stood, too, and Geggel took his hand and shook it.

"I'll contact you as soon as I have word from London. Don't contact her again unless you have to."

Aleksandrov kept hold of his hand, clasping it in both of his. "Thank you. This is a very good thing that you do. My daughter will be grateful. As am I."

Geggel smiled, and Aleksandrov released his hand.

"Be careful, Pyotr."

"And you."

7

Nataliya had taken up a position on the promenade. She could look north toward the pub where Aleksandrov and Geggel had met, or, by turning to the west, she could see the street where Geggel had parked his car. There was nothing out of place, and nothing that gave Nataliya any cause for concern.

She heard Mikhail's voice in her ear. "*They're both coming out.*"

She gazed up the street. Aleksandrov came out first, pausing beneath the pub's sign until Geggel joined him. The handler extended a hand and Aleksandrov took it, drawing Geggel into a hug. They exchanged words—Nataliya was much too far away to be able to hear what was said—and then they parted. Aleksandrov turned right and Geggel turned left.

"They've split up," Nataliya said, turning her head away from an approaching couple. "Aleksandrov has gone north. Geggel is heading to me."

She saw Mikhail exit the pub. "*Take Geggel,*" he said. "*I'll take Aleksandrov.*"

Nataliya pushed herself away from the railings and turned toward the car park. She followed the promenade as it traced its way along the top of the cliff. She glanced down at the row of beach huts, the lower promenade, the stony beach and then the sea, the high tide breaking over a set of wooden groynes. She walked quickly, but not so fast as to draw attention to herself, and, as she walked, she opened her handbag and reached her fingers inside until she could feel her lock pick.

She arrived at the common, an area of grass that had been yellowed by the hot summer's sun. She crossed it and saw the line of painted parking spaces on Park Lane. She had been sent a picture of Geggel's Citroën, and confirmed that the registration was the same. It was the large seven-seat Grand C4 SpaceTourer, with plenty of space in the back. She reached the vehicle, took out her pick and, after checking around her, knelt down by the lock. The pick had already been coded, and she slid it into the keyhole, unlocked the door, and slipped inside. The seats were arranged in a two-three-two pattern. She closed the door and dropped down into the footwell between the rear and middle rows.

She waited for Geggel to arrive.

Geggel hardly noticed his surroundings as he made his way back to his car. He had a spring in his step. Aleksandrov's reason for the meeting had been unexpected, and Geggel found that he was more excited than he had been for years. He reached up and slid his fingers into the inside pocket of his jacket; he felt the sharp edge of the folded square of paper and thought of the schematic that was printed on it. He took the piece of paper out and unfolded it on the bonnet of the Citroën. He took out his phone and snapped it, taking two pictures to be sure, and then emailed both to himself. Better safe than sorry.

He knew what he would have to do: contact Raj Shah, get the intelligence checked out, and then work out how he could involve himself in the operation to exfiltrate Anastasiya Romanova. He was confident that he could do it. Aleksandrov had made it plain that he would only deal with him; he would make that very clear when he made contact. He knew that his replacement, Jessie Ross, would protest, and he had some sympathy for her, not that that would make any difference. This was his achievement. He would bring it in, and he would take the plaudits. It was remarkable. He was on the cusp of landing the biggest intelligence coup for years. It didn't matter that he was retired; this would be the crowning moment of his career.

He opened the door and lowered himself onto the seat. He started the car, reversed out of the bay and set off, following Godyll Road as it sliced between the green space of the town common. He picked up the A1095 and followed it toward the main trunk road that would lead back to London.

He took out his phone, plugged it into the USB port and then took out his wallet. He removed the credit cards and tossed them onto the seat next to him until he found what he was looking for: a plastic card, like the credit cards he had just filleted, with a government logo on the back and a phone number beneath it. He typed the number into the phone three digits at a time, switching his attention between the screen and the road ahead. He finished, but didn't dial the number. His finger hovered over the screen; he didn't even know whether it was still current. He pressed dial.

"Vauxhall Cross," the woman at the other end said over the speaker. "How can I help you?"

Geggel felt something hard pressed up flush against the side of his head. He looked up into the mirror and saw a woman behind him; the hard point he could feel against his temple was the muzzle of a handgun.

"End the call," she said in a quiet, firm voice.

Geggel gripped the wheel a little tighter.

"Hello? This is Vauxhall Cross. How can I help you?"

The woman pushed the gun, hard enough that he had to put his head against his shoulder. "*Now*," she said.

Geggel reached forward and pressed the screen, killing the call.

"Thank you," she said.

Geggel looked back in the mirror. The woman was dark haired. She wore glasses, had earrings in both ears, and wore a Led Zeppelin t-shirt.

"Who are you?"

"Keep driving," she said. "I want to ask you some questions."

8

A leksandrov made his way home, stopping in a delicatessen on the High Street to buy olives and cheese and then continuing on his way. Mikhail followed, leaving a sizeable distance between them. He knew where Aleksandrov was going; he didn't need to see him every step of the way, and so he drifted into and out of shops, looking for all the world like an idling tourist enjoying a lazy Sunday afternoon. Aleksandrov turned onto Wymering Road and Mikhail turned, too; by the time Mikhail reached Aleksandrov's house he was already inside. Mikhail saw movement through the sitting room window.

There was no reason to wait. Mikhail's orders were clear. He checked that the road was empty and crossed the short path to the front door. It was set back in an arch that would hide him from the other houses on the street; he would only have been visible to those directly behind him, and the only thing there was the garden of a bungalow that was being refurbished. The builders were not there today; no one could see him.

He reached into his jacket and pulled the Beretta from

its holster, hiding it against his hip as he knocked on the door with the knuckles of his left hand. He heard the sound of footsteps and then the sound of a key being turned. Mikhail took a step back, still within the shelter of the arch. The door opened enough for Aleksandrov to look outside.

"Hello?" he said.

Mikhail kicked the door, hard, and then followed immediately with his shoulder. Aleksandrov was caught off balance; the edge of the door slammed into his face and he stumbled back into the hall. Mikhail followed in quickly, the gun pointed ahead. Aleksandrov had tripped and fallen, and was on his backside, scrabbling to get away. Mikhail closed the door with his foot and then closed on Aleksandrov, the gun pointing down at him.

"Get up," he said.

Aleksandrov held a hand up before his face.

"Up," Mikhail said, reaching down with his left hand and hauling Aleksandrov up so that he was on his knees. He pressed the muzzle against his forehead, smearing the blood from the cut the door had made. "Up—*now*."

Aleksandrov reached a hand out for a console table and used it to help him to get to his feet. He was unsteady. Mikhail knew the layout of the house and knew that the kitchen could not be seen from outside the house. He turned Aleksandrov around, put the gun against the back of his head, and impelled him to the back of the house. The kitchen was neat and tidy: white goods down one side, a breakfast bar with stools, and a small two-person settee. There was a kettle on the hob, just starting to whistle, and Russian folk music played from a speaker on the work surface.

"Turn around," Mikhail said.

Aleksandrov did. He stared at the gun.

"Don't," Mikhail said, shaking his head.

"Who are you?"

Mikhail pushed the muzzle of the gun against Aleksandrov's forehead again and, eyeing him, switched to Russian. "Do you have to ask?"

Aleksandrov didn't respond; instead, Mikhail saw his larynx bob up and down as he tried to swallow down his fear.

"We need to have a talk, Pyotr," he said. "Do you mind if I call you Pyotr?"

Aleksandrov shook his head and reached up to wipe the blood that was running into his eyes.

"Sit down."

Mikhail took the pistol away and flicked the barrel in the direction of the settee. Aleksandrov backed away, his eyes on the muzzle, and sat. The kettle started to whistle loudly, and Mikhail, still training the gun on Aleksandrov, reached over, took it from the hob and put it on a metal trivet.

Aleksandrov gawped at him, as if confounded by the contradiction of the gun and this gesture of domesticity. "Why are you here?" he asked, taking a seat on the settee.

"You don't know?"

"No, I don't understand. I have been retired for ten years. I served my time—I paid for my crimes. I'm still paying for them."

"Really? How is that?"

"Because I cannot return home. They would kill me if I tried, so I have to stay here."

"I'm not here because of what you did before. There would have been no reason for me to come if you had stayed retired, as you should have. But you haven't stayed retired, have you, Pyotr? You want to get back into the game. Now— try again. Tell me—why do you think I am here?"

Aleksandrov swallowed again. "Because of my daughter."

"That's right. Your daughter—Anastasiya. It would appear that the apple has not fallen far from the tree."

"What do you mean—"

"Like father, like daughter. Treachery. Treason. Do you need me to explain?"

Aleksandrov stared at the gun; a single bead of sweat formed on his brow and Mikhail watched as it rolled down into the thick white hair of his eyebrow. "I can't help you."

"Can't, Pyotr, or won't?"

"You want to know where she is. Yes? But I don't know. She hasn't told me."

Mikhail had seen the emails between father and daughter, and Anastasiya had not revealed her location.

"Where do you think she might be, Pyotr?"

"Please—I'm not fooling with you. I don't know."

"Guess."

He swallowed again. "Komsomolsk, perhaps. But she could be in Khurba, Amursk, Malmyzh. She could have gone as far south as Vladivostok. She could be in Moscow for all I know. She didn't tell me, I swear."

"Let me ask you another question, then. What did you say to Leonard Geggel this afternoon?" Aleksandrov's mouth gaped open. "I was there, Pyotr. I was in the pub with you—I saw it all. What did you say to him?"

"Anastasiya wants to leave Russia. She wants to offer information to MI6 so they can get her out and make her safe. I told Geggel—what she had, what she wanted for it."

"And what did he say?"

"He said he would contact MI6 for me. He would try and arrange it."

"The information—what does she have?"

"The new Sukhoi fighter. She has been working on it."
He looked almost apologetic. "She has everything."

"What did Geggel say? Did he think they would be
interested?"

Aleksandrov closed his eyes, swallowed again, and
nodded. "Yes," he said.

Mikhail leaned forward. "Where is she, Pyotr? Tell me
how to find her. She is not at her home. Where would she
go? Does she have a friend she would trust?"

"I don't know," he said again, desperation straining his
voice. "I haven't spoken to her for years. I know nothing
about her life—*nothing*."

Mikhail had been in these situations before and trusted
his judgment. He could tell when someone was lying; a gun
pointed at the head had the useful consequence of eliciting
the truth, and, when it did not, there were other ways. He
watched Aleksandrov's performance now—pitiful, begging
—and doubted that he was lying. They had intercepted the
emails. They had monitored his phone calls. There was
nothing to suggest that he was holding anything back, but
he had to ask the questions. Now, though—now that he had
the answers, and believed them—there was nowhere left
to go.

"You should have said no," he said, standing. "You
should have told her to hand herself in. It would have made
things much easier for you both."

He raised the pistol, aimed it, and fired a single round.
The suppressor muffled the report, the shot punching into
Aleksandrov's head flush between the eyes. He jerked back
and then fell to the side, his face pointed up at the ceiling,
one leg on the floor, one arm draped over the side of the
settee. Blood pulsed out of the hole and dripped down onto
the carpet.

Mikhail raised his arm so that he could look at his watch. He had been inside the house for five minutes. He set the timer for an additional five minutes and then, without sparing a second look at the dead man on the settee, he started to search the house.

9

They passed over Buss Creek, through Blackwater and then across the fields, the wide-open spaces, flat for as far as Nataliya could see. She was in the middle of the three seats behind the two seats in the front. She had lowered the pistol, reaching ahead so that she could press it into Geggel's ribs. The old spy drove carefully, a steady fifty, both hands on the wheel just as Nataliya had instructed.

"Who are you?" he asked, looking back in the mirror. Nataliya saw the fear in his eyes. He was an agent runner, not an agent. He might never have had a gun pointed at him before; he might never have seen a gun.

"It doesn't matter who I am," she said.

His voice was tight with tension. "So what is this to do with?"

"Why did you come here, Mr. Geggel?"

He glanced back again. He could have tried to deflect, to say that he had visited for the sea air, but, to his credit, he didn't. He must have known who she was and who she represented. It wouldn't be difficult to join the dots from there.

"To see my friend," he said. "It's about him, isn't it? Aleksandrov?"

"We know why he wanted to see you, Mr. Geggel. We've been watching him for several days. We heard his telephone call to you. We've been reading his emails."

"So what do you need me to say?"

"Did he tell you about his daughter?"

"He did."

"And?"

"He said she wanted to defect."

"In return for what?"

"She has schematics for a new Sukhoi fighter that she said she was prepared to sell in exchange for our help. He wanted me to speak to Vauxhall Cross."

"And you said?"

"I said that I would." He looked up at her in the mirror. "But I don't have to do that."

"Do you have the schematic?"

"Yes," he said.

"Give it to me."

She gave the pistol a little shove to remind him that it was there and waited as he took his left hand from the wheel so that he could reach into his jacket. He took out a piece of paper and held it up so that Nataliya could take it. She kept the gun where it was and took the paper in her left hand, unfolding it and taking a quick glimpse. She didn't know anything about aviation, but she recognised that it was a cross-section of a piece of aeronautical equipment.

Geggel put his hand back on the wheel. They had reached the junction. He indicated, turned right and then joined the A12.

"What did he say about his daughter?"

"Not much." He left it at that until she poked him with the gun again. "She used to love Russia and hate her father. Now she hates Russia and hopes he might be able to save her. He said something about her husband being murdered. Sounds like your people fucked up."

The attitude was unexpected, and she saw that he was watching in the mirror as he delivered it. She didn't know what he hoped it might achieve.

"You want to know where she is?" he suggested, still watching in the mirror.

"Did he say?"

"He did. What do I get if I tell you?"

"Perhaps you don't get shot—"

Geggel took his left hand off the wheel and stabbed down for the gun. Nataliya had been distracted for a moment by the suggestion that Geggel might offer Anastasiya Romanova's location, and what she could offer him to divulge it, and wasn't able to move the gun away before he was able to grab her wrist. The gun jerked down, the sudden movement forcing her finger back on the trigger, and the weapon discharged. The Citroën swerved right and then left, narrowly missing oncoming traffic. There was a lay-by next to the road, a barbed wire fence marking its boundary along the lip of a slope that descended into the field below. The Citroën raced over the lay-by, crashed through the fence, continued over the lip and then bounced down the slope. Nataliya wasn't wearing a belt, and braced herself against the seat, all thoughts of covering Geggel with the gun temporarily suspended. She caught a glimpse of the land ahead of them: a wide margin of scrubland, a fringe of trees and then an expanse of mudflats.

The car was still moving fast. It reached the bottom of

the slope and now it was racing through a gap in the trees. It continued on, bumping and bouncing over the uneven ground until it reached the mudflats. Nataliya braced for a sudden stop. The back end jerked up as the bonnet plunged into the mud. Nataliya was thrown forward, her head cracking into Geggel's headrest.

10

M ikhail returned to the house across the street, unlocked the front door of the house that they had been using and went inside. There was a mirror over the occasional table, and he turned to look into it. The disguise was one that he had used before: the unruly beard, wild hair and thin metal-framed spectacles had always reminded him of Molodtsov, the garrulous teacher who had taught both him and Nataliya English at the KGB Academy in Michurinsky Prospekt. The likeness was so similar that Mikhail referred to the disguise as 'The Professor,' and it had become something of a standing joke between him and his wife. The Professor had always been reliable, and it was with some regret that he had decided that he would have to retire him from now on.

He went into the downstairs bathroom and stood in front of the mirror above the sink. He reached up to behind his ear and found a loose edge where the beard had not adhered perfectly to his skin. He slid his fingers beneath the backing and pulled until the beard came away. He dropped it into the bin, removed the pins that held the wig in place and then put them and the wig into the bin, too. He took off the glasses and rinsed his face in the cold water, removing all traces of the adhesive. He took the bag out of the bin and carried it back to the kitchen. There was an open refuse sack on the counter; Nataliya had already emptied the fridge. He put the bag inside the sack, knotted it, and took it to the front door. They would take their rubbish with them.

He looked at his watch and set another timer, this one for ten minutes. He needed to move fast. He went into the front room and disconnected the cameras and computers. He unplugged the hard drives and slid them into a sports bag so that they were ready to be removed. He collected all the paper that he could find, dumped it in the grate and lit it. He hurried upstairs. They had unpacked only what they needed, and so he stuffed the used clothes back into the bags, bagged up and added their toiletries, zipped the bags up and slid them down the stairs. He checked each room, one by one, moving quickly but methodically, and satisfied himself that they were leaving nothing behind that might compromise them. He made his way back downstairs and, after checking that the road was quiet, he transferred all the bags into the back of his car. He locked up, got into the car, and checked his watch.

Eight minutes.

Time to go. He started the engine, pulled out, and left Wymering Road—with the dead traitor still undisturbed in the kitchen across the street—and headed north.

NATALIYA TOUCHED her fingers to her forehead and looked at them: they were stained with blood. She must have cut herself on the edge of the headrest when she banged into it.

Her neck felt sore and her back was stiff. She wiped the blood away and looked around: the car had come to rest at the edge of the estuary, left at an angle as the front had ploughed into the start of the mudflats. The back end was off the ground and the wheels were still spinning. The road was behind them, elevated above the flats, but it looked as if the car would be partially hidden by the line of trees.

She took out her phone and called Mikhail.

"Yes?"

"Where are you?"

She heard the sound of a car. "On my way," he said. "Are you all right? You sound—"

"He crashed the car," she said. The words were slurred, as if they were too large for her mouth.

"Are you hurt?"

"Banged my head."

"I'll come back. Where are you?"

"Just after the turn-off to the town."

"I've got you," he said. Nataliya knew that he would be able to find her with the GPS tracker on her phone. "I'll be there in five minutes."

Nataliya put the phone in her pocket and pushed herself upright. A bolt of pain radiated out from her neck. Whiplash. She found the piece of paper that Geggel had given her and stuffed it into her pocket. She slid across the cabin, opened the door and lowered herself down. The ground was boggy, her feet squelching as she went ahead and opened the passenger door. She climbed back inside and looked at Geggel. He was slumped against the deflating airbags, his breath wheezing in and out, shallow and faint. There was blood on his thigh; she pulled his jacket back and saw a wide patch of blood on his shirt. The shot that Nataliya had fired had hit him below the ribs and behind his belly, in the area of his left kidney. He was bleeding out.

"Help me."

Geggel's voice was weak, barely audible. He had turned his head to look at her; he mouthed the words again.

She reached down for his leg and yanked it, dragging his foot off the accelerator so that the engine's hopeless whining ended. She reached inside his jacket pocket and found his wallet and phone, put them on the dash and, covering her fingers with her sleeve, opened the glovebox. It was full of junk: a box from an old satnav, a collection of phone charging cables, and the litter of crumpled-up receipts and empty crisp packets. She filtered through the mess but found nothing of interest.

She took the pistol and pressed the muzzle of the suppressor against his head.

"Where is Anastasiya Romanova?"

He tried to speak, but all she could hear was the wheezing of his breath.

Her head pounded and she felt blood running down into her brow. "Where is Anastasiya Romanova?"

"I..."

She shoved the pistol, bending Geggel's neck away, forcing his head over onto his shoulder. *"Where is she?"*

"I... don't... know."

Nataliya pushed the door open with her foot and stepped out again. Geggel turned his head, resting it against the wheel. He looked back at her with desperation in his eyes; it looked as if he didn't have the strength to speak again.

Nataliya aimed into the cabin and shot him again. The report, although muffled by the suppressor, still rang out over the estuary; a flock of black-headed gulls clattered out of the reeds and took to the air. Geggel's head jerked to the side, jerked back again and finally slumped forward against the wheel.

Nataliya followed the track that the car had left through the damp ground and clambered up the slope. Purchase was difficult and she was unsteady on her feet; she drove the heels of her boots into the scree to stop herself from slipping back down again. She reached the top. A car sped away to the north. It didn't stop; there was no reason why it would. Even if the driver had noticed her as she struggled over the lip of the slope, he or she would have concluded that she had just been caught short and had gone to relieve herself.

A car approached from the south. Nataliya recognised it, and as it drew nearer, she saw Mikhail. He went by, braked, indicated right, and then used the Southwold turning to loop around. He drew up in the lay-by and reached across to open the passenger door. Nataliya dropped inside.

"Your head," he said.

Her thoughts were cloudy. "Banged it. Might be concussed."

"Geggel?" he asked her.

"Dead."

"Anything?"

"He doesn't know," she said.

Mikhail put the car into first, checked the mirror, and pulled out onto the road. Nataliya opened the glovebox and took out a bottle of painkillers. She shook out two, put them in her mouth and then washed them down with water from the bottle that Mikhail had left in the cupholder. If it was a concussion, it was a mild one, but it wouldn't have made a difference; a doctor was out of the question. She reclined the seat and leaned back against it. She knew the drill: Mikhail would conduct a careful dry-cleaning run to shake out any tails. She had a few hours to relax before they got home.

Mikhail took out his phone and made a call to Vincent to report the outcome of their afternoon's work. Nataliya closed her eyes and let the sound of the tyres on the rough tarmac lull her to sleep.

LONDON

11

V incent Beck had a flat on the twelfth floor of the Lannoy Point tower block in Fulham. He had lived here for fifteen years, ever since his wife had passed away. He had made it his own in that time: it was comfortably furnished, nothing too expensive, with his one extravagance being his Rega turntable. He loved classical music, and there was nothing he enjoyed more than to put a record on, sit at his small dining table and look out and enjoy the view over west London.

The flat was pleasant and there was a strong sense of community in the building, but neither of those benefits had influenced Beck's decision to purchase it. His one requirement, when he had been looking at the sixties tower blocks that dominated this part of the city, had been that the flat that he settled on be on the top floor. The reason was simple: his burst transmitter had a clear line of sight to the satellite right out of the windows.

He went into his bedroom and dropped down to his hands and knees. He kept his encoder hidden in the false bottom of a suitcase that was, in turn, hidden away beneath his bed. He opened the case, prised back the panel, and took out the encoder. It was the DKM-S model; twenty years old, but it had always been reliable and—even though he generally had no time for superstition—Beck was loath to ask for a replacement. The DKM-S was a compact device that was about the size of a small paperback book, its electronics housed within a lightweight grey Hammerite aluminium case. There was a sixteen-button keypad on the front panel; Beck composed his classified *zapiska* and checked the output via the LED display. The burst transmission allowed for only a limited amount of characters, and so he had to be brief.

Both neutralised. House closed down. Assets left area safely. Meeting assets tonight. Will report.

The encoder would compress the message and then broadcast it at a high data signalling rate, reducing the chances of it being intercepted. He pressed the button to send the message, waited until it had gone and then imagined Nikolai Primakov's reaction. The message would be translated and delivered to him at his desk in his expansive office overlooking the forest at Yasenevo. Beck knew that Primakov would be pleased. This assignment, more than any of the others that he had overseen for the deputy director, had clearly been weighing on his mind. Its flawless execution would be a relief.

Beck switched off the encoder and replaced it in its hiding place. He stood up, stretching out the kinks in his back, and went through to the sitting room. He had a journey to make later tonight, and he needed to start the preparations.

12

John Milton sat on a wooden bench in the gardens outside the hospital building. He was too afraid to go inside. It was more than just fear, though: there was guilt and shame, too. The numbing hangover didn't help, either.

Milton had taken the Tube to Mile End station, and then walked the rest of the way. It was just before seven on a sunny Sunday evening, and the Mile End Road had been quieter than would have been the case during the rest of the week. Milton had followed the details he had written down on the back of his hand, turning onto Bancroft Road and then making his way through the grounds of the hospital to the Burdett Centre. It was a new building, single storey and surrounded by a pleasant and well-tended garden. There was a lawn and a fountain and a row of tall elms that swayed in the gentle breeze. Milton had found the bench and sat down; it offered a vantage point to watch the other men and women as they arrived and made their way inside. He had counted a dozen, three of whom had returned outside to smoke. He didn't know how many people would attend a meeting. He had never been to one before, and, save what he had been able to read on the internet that morning, he had no idea what to expect.

Milton wanted to join them. He had made his way here because he knew now, beyond any doubt, that he needed help. But that was all well and good; knowing that something was wrong was one thing, but admitting to himself that he was out of control and helpless to his compulsion was something else entirely. He didn't know if he would be able to do that.

There was another reason for his reticence. Control would not look kindly on him if he knew that he was here. It would speak of weakness, for one thing, a feebleness that would have him suspended and fast-tracked to an appointment with the Group psychiatrists who would prod and poke him until they had diagnosed the cause of his mental ailment. More than that, Control would know—as Milton knew—that the meetings that Milton was considering encouraged a frank and open sharing of the reasons why the attendees resorted to the bottle. Milton's particular profession required the utmost discretion, and even a hint of negligence in that regard would have him placed under house arrest, at best.

He was taking a risk.

He had just come off a job. Control had assigned a file to him: an MI6 analyst called Callaghan had been found poking through files that had no connection to his work. He had accessed the SIS network from his home computer and had been traced by his IP address. He had been put under surveillance and had been followed to Brick Lane in East London where he had been observed removing a small object from a cleft in the wall of an alleyway behind an Indian restaurant. It was a dead drop, and when agents investigated it they discovered that he had left behind a USB drive that, upon analysis, was found to contain intelligence on an active SIS operation in Eastern Europe. The follow-up investigation attributed more than two dozen disappearances of local sources to Callaghan's perfidy.

The traitor's flat was searched and the details of a hidden bank account containing fifty thousand pounds were recovered. The dead drop was put under surveillance but no one ever returned to it. The SVR agent, thought to be a Directorate S agent, either had a preternatural sense for self-preservation or he or she had been tipped off. The decision was made that they would not arrest Callaghan for fear of what might come out during a trial; instead, Milton was given the green light to interrogate him and then make him vanish.

The memories rushed over him and, even though he closed his eyes, he couldn't stop them. He had broken into the man's flat and waited for him to return from work. He had found a bottle of gin in a kitchen cupboard and had had his first drink then, two fingers to silence the spectres in his head, the wails and shrieks of the phantoms who were hungry for another to join their number. Callaghan had arrived. Milton had hidden behind the door and met him with his Sig pressed to the back of his head. Callaghan had confessed to everything, had answered Milton's questions and then gone beyond them. He had volunteered information on his recruitment, on the intelligence that he had supplied, on the intelligence the SVR had requested of him. There was no need for what the CIA euphemistically described as 'enhanced' techniques; Callaghan had spilled his guts as soon as Milton had sat him down and told him how it was going to play out. Milton had recorded his *mea culpa* on a digital recorder and then, with the wailing pounding in his head, he had pressed the suppressor against the back of Callaghan's crown and put a 9mm round into his brain. He had called it in, requested clean-up, and left.

After that? He could remember fragments, and then nothing: he had taken a taxi to Chelsea and had started drinking properly. He remembered The Crown, The Pig's Ear and Riley's. He remembered the dream, vivid and real: Callaghan visiting him while he was on his hands and knees in a filthy toilet cubicle. Milton saw the hole in his head and the blood still dripping down onto his face. After that, though, there was nothing. Milton had woken up with a black eye, a vicious bruise all the way down his ribcage, scraped and bruised knuckles and someone else's blood on his shirt. He couldn't remember how it had got there.

"Hello?"

Milton looked up. It was one of the men who had been smoking outside the building. The man was in his forties, dressed in clothes that suggested a reasonable income and a care for his appearance, with skin that bore all the hall-marks of a fake tan.

"Hello," Milton said.

"Are you here for the meeting?" The man's teeth were a little jagged, and Milton could smell stale smoke on his breath when he spoke.

"I'm fine," Milton said, suddenly wanting to be left alone again.

"Is it your first?" The man had an effeminate quality. He didn't wait for Milton to answer his question and, instead, he sat down next to him on the bench. "I remember my first, too. Nervous as hell. My throat was so dry I could barely speak. I still get nervous now, so I pushed myself out of my comfort zone and volunteered to be secretary here. My name's Michael."

He put out his hand for Milton to shake, but, instead of taking it, Milton stood up. "I'm just enjoying the sunshine," he said. "I'm not here for a meeting."

"Of course," the man said gently. "But if you were, and if you changed your mind, you could just come and sit at the back and listen. You might find that's what you need."

Milton found himself conflicted: his head was shouting that he should walk away and never come back, while his heart told him that Michael was right, that this was what he needed, that he had come here for a reason, that he could take a seat at the back of the room and just soak it all in, get a feel for the meeting so that he could decide whether it was for him. He was caught there, pinned by wariness and indecision, but, just as Michael was about to speak again, Milton's phone buzzed in his pocket.

He turned away from the bench, took out the phone and looked down at the screen. The caller was Global Logistics.

Milton tapped to accept the call and put the phone to his ear. "Hello?"

"Smith?" The caller was using Milton's usual legend for when he was in the United Kingdom: John Smith, a sales rep for the company.

"Yes," he said. "Tanner?"

Tanner was Control's private secretary: ex-army, infantry, like Control and all of the other operatives in the Group. He sounded nonplussed and a little annoyed.

"Where are you?" Tanner asked.

"In the city," Milton said.

"Something's happened. We need you."

Milton gritted his teeth.

"I'm sending a car to pick you up now. Where are you?"

Milton reached a brick wall and sat down on it. "Mile End."

"What are you doing in Mile End?"

Milton had no interest in answering that. "I can be at the Tube station in fifteen minutes."

"Very good. The car is on its way."

There was no point in arguing. Milton looked back at the building. Michael was just going inside, with the other two smokers following him. A wedge was removed from underneath the door and it swung closed.

"And Smith?" Tanner was still on the line.

"What?"

"You're going to need to be sharp. We have a situation. You'll be briefed en route."

13

Jessie Ross woke up to the sound of her phone buzzing in her handbag.

She had been out in Camden last night. It had been a typical Saturday: they had started in the Good Mixer, staggered up Parkway to the Dublin Castle, watched a terrible band and then danced to the same music they always danced to until the late lock-in finally came to an end at three. She had told herself that she wouldn't stay out all night but, already half cut, her resistance had been pathetic. They had picked up a greasy kebab from Woody's Grill and taken it back to Fuzz's house to eat it.

The phone.

She sat up and found that she wasn't alone in bed. She remembered. There was a man next to her. He was lying on his front, his head angled away so that she couldn't see his face. The sheets had been dragged all the way down to his knees and she could see that he was naked. She knew who he was: his name was Peter and he was one of Izzy's friends from Fort Monckton, the facility that served as the SIS field operations training centre.

She got out of bed, took her dressing gown from the hook on the back of the door and put it on. She found her handbag beneath the piled clothes on the floor and took out her phone. She looked at the display and saw that the call was from Raj Shah and that, much worse, she had already missed four calls from him. She groaned. He was calling on a Sunday? It must be serious.

She took the call and put the phone to her ear. "Hello?" she said quietly as she stepped out of the bedroom and into the kitchen diner of her flat.

"I've been calling you for the last thirty minutes," he said.

"I'm sorry," she said. "The phone was on silent."

"Where are you?"

"At home. What's happening?"

"I need you to get to Southwold as quickly as you can."

"Southwold?" She wrinkled her brow as she tried to remember where that was. "Norfolk?"

"Suffolk. I'm sending a car to pick you up. There'll be a briefing in the back—you need to be up to speed by the time you get there."

She looked down at the dirty dressing gown and then at her reflection in the window. Her hair was a disaster and she was still wearing last night's make-up. She was a mess. "Give me half an hour," she said.

"Can't do that. The car will be with you in five minutes. Don't fuck about, Jessie. This has the potential to be very serious."

Jessie thought about her son; Lucas was with her parents, and she was supposed to be going over to pick him up later. She was going to have to call them to see if they could keep him for a little longer. She went back into the bedroom and opened the wardrobe, hoping against hope that she had something suitable to wear.

"Jessie?" Shah said curtly.

"Yes, sir," she said, taking down a skirt that would just about do the trick. "It's fine. Can you give me an idea what this is about?"

"Pyotr Aleksandrov is dead. He's been shot. I don't need to tell you what that means."

"Hey," said the man on the bed.

"Shot?" Jessie hissed. "By who?"

"Get in the car. I'll see you there."

Shah ended the call.

"Hey," the man on the bed repeated.

Jessie turned around. She could see his face now. He was blandly handsome, in the sort of emaciated indie musician fashion that she found annoyingly attractive. Last night was the first time that they had met; Izzy had set it up as a blind date and Jessie had decided that he was someone it might be useful to know.

"Hey," he said for the third time. "Come back to bed."

"You have to go," she said, taking off the dressing gown and pulling on the only clean underwear that she could find.

"Don't be mean," he said.

She found his jeans and t-shirt on the floor and tossed them at him. "I'm serious. Get dressed. I have to go to work."

He must have heard the determination in her voice and, grunting, he sat up and started to work his legs into his trousers. Jessie picked up her blouse, saw it was dirty, found a clean white shirt and teamed it with the skirt.

"I had fun," the man said.

"Great," she said, going through into the bathroom and quickly sorting out her hair and make-up.

"So can I see you again?"

She wanted to say no, but she was ambitious and you never could tell how people might prove to be helpful down the road. No point in burning bridges when they didn't need to be burned.

"I'll call you," she said. She reapplied her make-up, then took a bottle of aspirin out of the cabinet and swallowed down two tablets with a double-handful of water.

"You're not just saying that?"

Jesus. Why were men all so insecure these days?

"Maybe we can get lunch next week. When are you in the River House again?"

"Thursday."

"So give me a call."

She was just checking herself in the mirror—better, not great, just about presentable—when she heard two short blasts of a car horn from outside. She couldn't wait around any longer.

"I've got to go," she said. "Let yourself out."

She grabbed her jacket, keys and phone and left the flat.

A black BMW was idling at the side of the road. She hurried over to it, opened the back door, and slid inside. There was a man sitting there already. He looked to be of average height—five eleven or six foot—and looked as if he might be muscular without it being obvious. His eyes were on the grey side of blue, his mouth had a cruel kink to it and, as he turned to look at her, she saw that he had a faint scar that ran from his cheek to the start of his nose. His hair was long and unkempt, with an unruly frond that curled across his forehead like a comma.

"Hello," he said.

"I'm sorry," Jessie replied. "I don't think we've met."

The man put out his hand. "John Smith," he said. "Nice to meet you."

14

They raced south under blue lights, the Sunday evening traffic parting before them. Smith was wearing a pair of jeans, a black polo-neck shirt and a scuffed leather jacket. Jessie looked down at her own clothes—the skirt was creased and she spotted, to her horror, a small red wine stain on her shirt—and felt a fresh surge of irritation.

She took out her phone and typed a quick message to her mother, telling her that she had been called away on urgent business and asking whether she would be able to look after Lucas for another couple of days. Her parents lived in Southampton, and ever since Lucas' father had betrayed her, they had taken her son on alternate weekends so that he could maintain something of a life. They were besotted with the boy, as Lucas was with them, and the arrangement had proven to be invaluable. Jessie argued with her parents often, usually prompted by their unsubtle suggestions that she had been single for too long and shouldn't a young and attractive woman like her have found someone suitable to settle down with rather than going out with her friends... but, despite their disagreements, Jessie knew that they worried about her for all the right reasons and that, without them, her life would be so much more difficult.

She fidgeted, unable to settle. She looked over at Smith: he was skimming through a sheaf of papers and, perhaps aware that she was looking at him, gestured to the seat back in front of her.

"One for you, too," he said, pointing to a bundle of papers in the seat back pocket.

"Thank you," she said.

Smith looked back down at his papers.

"How long will it take to drive there?" Jessie asked.

Smith looked up again and smiled at her with forced patience. "Where?"

"Southwold."

"Who told you we were driving?"

"We're not?"

"The plan changed."

Jessie looked out of the window and noticed, for the first time, that they were heading south.

"Southwold's east."

"It is," Smith said as the driver carved through a gap on the Old Street roundabout.

"But—"

"We're flying there. Helicopter."

"Oh."

"You flown before?"

"Not in a helicopter."

"We'll be there in forty minutes. It'll take two hours if we drive. Apparently, this"—he tapped a finger on the dossier —"is fast moving and they need everyone there yesterday."

He looked down at the papers again.

"I'm sorry," Jessie said. "I don't think you told me what you have to do with this."

"I didn't," Smith said. And then, when he realised that she was still staring at him, he added, "I'm your military liaison."

"Why on earth do I need that?"

"You might not," he said. "But it's better to have something and find you don't need it, than not have something and find that you do. Read the briefing."

Smith looked back down at his own briefing document. She had exhausted his patience; it was clear that he had no wish to continue the conversation. She looked at him a little more carefully. He looked a little rough around the edges: his face was stubbled with five o'clock shadow and there were dark pouches beneath his eyes. He looked like she felt.

Jessie fished her briefing pack out of the seat back and started to leaf through it. It began with an MI6 summary of CHERRY's case file. It had been signed off by 'LG'; Jessie knew that was Leonard Geggel, her predecessor. CHERRY had a reputation for surliness, and, as she flicked through the reports that had been filed by Geggel—a man famed within the River House for a similar level of crabbiness— she saw repeated references to how unhappy the retired spy was.

CHERRY's given name was Pyotr Ilyich Aleksandrov, although they had resettled him as Vladimir Kovalev. He was born in St. Petersburg in 1950, had served in the Soviet Airborne Troops and had then been co-opted into military intelligence. An impressive career had followed, and he had been a prize catch when he had been turned by Geggel while he was operating out of Athens Station. Aleksandrov had allowed them to mine a rich and valuable seam of information; he had reached the rank of colonel in the GRU and provided MI6 with lists of active Russian operatives and other organisational information. He was venal, as was often the case, and jealous of the perceived lifestyles of his counterparts in London and Langley. More than that, though, was a feeling of underappreciation that had quite clearly been with him all his life, a feeling that had not been assuaged since his defection.

Aleksandrov had had a good run. He had lasted nine years before he was blown and would have lasted longer if it were not for the unwise extravagance of spending some of the £100,000 a year he earned from MI6 on a brand-new BMW. The FSB had investigated him, then arrested him, and after a two-week spell in the bleak dungeons of the Lubyanka, they had broken him and extracted a confession. He was convicted under Article 275 of the Russian Criminal Code for high treason in the form of espionage and sentenced to thirteen years in a high-security detention facility, whilst also being stripped of his military rank and decorations.

His liberation had come with the capture of a cadre of Russian spies in New York. An offer had been made to exchange the Russians for five double agents who had been working for MI6 and the CIA. The offer had been accepted and, on a snowy bridge in Prague in a scene reminiscent of exchanges in the depths of the Cold War, the swap was made. Aleksandrov had asked for asylum in the United Kingdom and MI6 had acceded to his request.

But his useful years were long past. Aleksandrov had been out of the game for years and hadn't been able to offer them anything useful since he had been exchanged. He was old and washed up, homesick and embittered by every slight and grievance that demonstrated, he argued, that MI6 was ungrateful and had forgotten the service that he had provided.

And now he was dead.

15

M ilton flicked through the briefing pack, but, after a moment, he found that his attention drifted back to the woman whom they had picked up. She looked frazzled, as if she had only very recently been woken up, and he got the distinct impression that she—like him—was only really pretending to study the notes. She bore the very faint smell of alcohol and sweat, and that reminded Milton of his previous lost night, his memories sunk somewhere within his blackout, the evidence of his misdeeds in the aching of his ribs.

"Here we are," the driver said.

They were in Battersea, the curve of the river ahead of them. The heliport was a commercial operation, but SIS occasionally chartered flights that took off from here. HQ was just up the road, after all, and they had no facilities of their own. A wire mesh gate was rolled out of the way and the driver took them all the way out to the landing pad. There was a helicopter waiting for them. It was an AS365 Dauphin, one of the Airbus line that was typically used as a medium-distance executive shuttle. Another car was waiting alongside the AS365. It was similar to their own, one of the MI6 pool cars that ferried staff around the country on occasions like this. Milton opened the door and stepped out, the wind from the river tousling his hair.

The rear door of the second car opened and two men stepped out. Milton recognised the first: it was Tanner. He had never seen the second man before. He was middle-aged and Asian, slightly overweight and dressed in a tatty suit that was beginning to look a little shiny at the elbows and knees.

Milton left Ross in the car and went across to Tanner.

"Evening, Milton," Tanner said.

"Evening."

"We need to get going," Tanner said. "We have a major situation. Did you read the file?"

"Yes," Milton said. "It's just background. I'll need more than that."

"You'll be read into it properly in the air."

Milton turned and gestured back toward the car. Jessie Ross was making her way across to the second man. She called out to him; it was evident that they knew each other. "You know her?" he asked.

"She's MI6," Tanner said. "An agent runner."

"The other guy?"

"That's Raj Shah. Runs counter-intelligence."

Milton nodded over to where Ross and Shah were talking. "Do you know anything about the girl?"

"Probably not much more than you," he said. "She's young. File says she's ambitious. She's been overseeing Aleksandrov and the other ex-pat Russians who've ended up here."

Milton was going to say something else when Tanner

glanced over his shoulder; Ross and Shah were on their way over to them.

She strode ahead of her boss and went to Tanner. "Hello," she said.

Tanner put out his hand. "David Tanner," he said.

"Jessie Ross. SIS. You work with Mr. Smith?"

"I do."

"Military liaison?"

"That's right. Better to have something and find you don't need it—

"—than not have something and find that you do. I know. He said the same thing."

Shah took Milton's hand. "I'm Raj Shah. Good to meet you."

"And you, sir," Milton said.

The pilot jogged out from the ready room and indicated that they should get into the cabin. "We've got clearance," he said.

Tanner opened the door and held it for Ross, Shah and Milton to embark. The interior was plush: four leather seats faced each other in opposing rows, with small tables separating each pair. There was fake wood panelling, overhead reading lights and wide windows on both sides of the cabin. Tanner climbed in awkwardly—he had lost half of his leg to an IED outside Kabul—and then pulled the door shut. They put on the headsets that rested above the seats.

"Strapped in?" the pilot radioed back.

"Good to go," Tanner said.

"Flight time is thirty-five minutes," he said. "I'm going to push it."

16

R aj Shah spoke loudly, having to compete with the sound of the engine despite the headphones that they were all wearing.

"All right, then. I'll assume you've read into the file. This is a very fast-moving situation, and it's evolving all the time. What we know now will likely be out of date by the time we land, but I'll do my best."

The helicopter banked sharply as the pilot curved around onto a new vector, racing low across the city.

Shah waited until the helicopter had straightened out again and then continued. "Pyotr Aleksandrov has been living in Southwold for ten years, for almost as long as he's been in the country. We gave him a new legend: Vladimir Kovalev, retired businessman, came here to marry an English woman now deceased. All fairly standard. He's not been operational since he's been here. He's consulted for us now and again, and he's done some work for OpSec and Intelligence companies in the city, but nothing of particular importance. His knowledge of the SVR is historic. He's been spending his time writing a history of Soviet military intelligence, from what I've been led to believe." He turned to Ross. "That, and moaning about how badly he's been treated since we brought him over."

"Only met him a couple of times, sir," Ross said. "But that's my understanding from reading into the file. I believe my predecessor found him difficult."

"That he did," Shah said with a smile. "They were quite a pair." Shah paused as he looked down at his notes. "This is what we have. At approximately five o'clock this evening one of Aleksandrov's neighbours reported seeing him on the floor of his kitchen. The neighbour's kids were playing football and the ball went over the fence. The neighbour went and got it and saw him. They called an ambulance which attended at 5.12 pm. The crew broke into the house and found him. He was pronounced dead at 5.16 pm."

Ross had taken out a pen and was scribbling notes on the back of the briefing document from the car.

"Cause of death was a single gunshot wound to the head," Shah said.

"Fuck," Ross breathed to herself, and then, aware that everyone had heard her, she added, "Sorry."

Shah ignored her and carried on. "The first police officer was on the scene at 5.30 pm. He requested a PNC check on Kovalev. We have an alert on his name, just like we do for all the other defectors we've got here, and, in the event that anything happens to any of them, SIS gets pinged."

"What's the working assumption?" Milton asked.

"He had no real enemies over here that we could ascertain. He was living a quiet life. We're assuming that he was assassinated. That's the only conclusion to be drawn."

The helicopter raced over the M25 and kept going. Milton glanced around the cabin. Shah was finished, looking at the others just as he was. Tanner was pensive, his hands clasped in his lap. Ross looked both excited and anxious.

"Questions?" Shah said.

"What about Geggel?" Ross asked.

"Who?" Milton asked.

"Leonard Geggel," Shah said. "He was Aleksandrov's handler before Jessie."

"They were friends," Ross said.

"That might be exaggerating it," Shah said. "Aleksandrov didn't have friends. Geggel doesn't either, to be fair."

"But it might be worth speaking to him."

"I agree," Shah said. "I'll make sure he's called."

"What about the situation on the ground?" Tanner asked.

"The street is locked down. Police are holding it for us."

"The intelligence assessment?"

"Do you mean who do we think might have done this?"

Milton nodded.

"We don't have anything concrete yet, but common sense points to Moscow. We don't know why they'd go after an old hand like Aleksandrov, but it seems most likely."

"Moscow has form for similar attacks in the past," Tanner added.

"They do," Shah said, "and whatever the motive turns out to be, it's most likely something from Aleksandrov's past with them."

"You said we didn't have anything concrete," Ross said. "What *do* we have?"

Shah looked as if he was weighing up whether to say more. "This is classified," he began, "but it's relevant and so I'm going to read you in. We think the Russians are operating illegals in London. Have you heard of Directorate S?"

"Sleepers?"

Shah nodded. "SIS has intelligence that suggests we might be looking at multiple enemy assets who may have been in place for years. I wouldn't be in the least bit surprised if it was them. We have one man under heavy surveillance—we think he might be a runner for the others. He's been careful so far, nothing to give us anything to go on, but they'll know that what's happened to Aleksandrov will make a lot of noise."

"Who?" Jessie asked.

"Details are on a need-to-know basis, and it might not be relevant. He's in London. We have a team on him. We'll see if he makes a mistake. We see some unusual activity, something out of his ordinary routine—if we see that, maybe we get a break. Maybe."

Ross was quiet and Milton had nothing else to ask. He had been involved in situations like this before, although never in this country. The facts were essentially fluid in the hours following an incident. Fresh evidence would emerge to disprove previous hypotheses and new witnesses would be found to open up different avenues of investigation. Shah was right; they were better dealing with the incontrovertible basics rather than indulging in speculation that would already be out of date by the time they landed. But Milton agreed with much of the assessment. The Russians had the best motive for taking out a defector whom they would see as a traitor. The Kremlin was most likely.

Milton closed his eyes and tried to blank out the muffled roar of the engine. His hangover ached and he could taste the old vomit in the back of his throat. He didn't want to be here, but he knew he had no choice. This was already a big deal, and, if they could track down the people responsible, he knew that there was a good chance he would be deployed to bring them in or take them out. The thought of it brought back flickers from the previous night, of Callaghan on his knees begging for his life. It nauseated him, and reminded him that he needed a drink. He would find peace at the bottom of a glass, a means to forget.

MOSCOW

17

I t was eight thirty in the evening when Deputy Director Nikolai Primakov was chauffeured through the Borovitskaya Gate in the western corner of the Kremlin. It had been drizzling intermittently all afternoon, and the wipers of his official BMW scraped as they sluiced the run-off from the windshield. Primakov gazed out of the wet windows as the driver took him past the Grand Palace and the Cathedral of the Archangel, and then turned into the vast open space of Ivanovskaya Square. The chauffeur slowed the car so that he was able to slip it between the narrow walls that offered access to the courtyard of the Senate building. Primakov gazed thoughtfully out of the window as the car drew to a stop. The driver opened his door, collected an umbrella from the trunk, and opened it to offer shelter as Primakov stepped out.

"Thank you," Primakov said.

He took the umbrella and made his way across the slick cobblestones until he reached the entrance to the building. Primakov was anxious; there was no point in pretending otherwise; the Security Council was one of the most powerful bodies in Russia, and, more than that, today's meeting would be chaired by the president himself. Primakov intended to present the meeting with a subtly amended version of what had just taken place in the United Kingdom. He knew that there was a chance that the president might see through the tissue of lies that he would weave in order to direct attention away from the real reason for the operation. They all knew it: the president's intuition bordered on the clairvoyant, and Primakov had seen many men, in situations like this, crumble under the most seemingly benign of questions. He had to guard against that as best he could.

The meeting was held in a vast room that was dominated by a long table that ran down the centre. It was large enough to accommodate forty people, with their aides and secretaries seated at additional tables that were spaced around the walls. The room was opulent, with a magnificent chandelier suspended from the barrel ceiling, and with a series of decorative marble columns spaced around the room. Primakov took his usual seat. He was one of the last to arrive. The president would be last of all, summoned when everyone else was in place, and Primakov looked at his empty chair at the head of the table and felt the usual knot of fear at the prospect of reporting to him. He turned away, looking at the others who had gathered. The attendees were the *knyaz'ki*, the Kremlin power brokers who exercised total control over the Russian state. There was the Chairman of the Government, the Manager of the Presidential Administration, the Chairwoman of the Federation Council of the Federal Assembly, together with the ministers for defence, foreign affairs, and internal affairs and the directors of the external and internal intelligence agencies.

The agenda for the meeting had been distributed in

advance, and copies were set out on blotters around the table. Primakov picked up the sheet of paper on his own blotter and glanced over it. His report had been scheduled as the first item; he would be expected to leave as soon as that point of business had been concluded.

The doors at the end of the room were opened by uniformed officers, and the president stepped inside. His chair was flanked by the flags of the Russian Federation and, as he stepped forward, his aide drew back the chair for him to sit down.

The president opened the meeting. He was curt, avoiding pleasantries, and moved straight to the top of the agenda. Primakov started to speak but found that his throat was dry; he reached for a glass and filled it with water from a carafe. He was painfully aware that everyone was watching him. He swallowed the water, ignoring the clammy sensation beneath his arms and in the small of his back, and cleared his throat.

"Thank you, Mr. President. I realise that not everyone has been briefed, so I will summarise what has happened today. Ten years ago, a former GRU colonel who was convicted of spying for the British was exchanged for several Directorate S agents who were arrested by the Americans. This man—Pyotr Ilyich Aleksandrov—was relocated in the United Kingdom. We recently received intelligence that Aleksandrov was seeking to sell classified information to MI6. The president authorised Directorate S to mount an operation against Aleksandrov and that operation was successfully concluded today."

"I've received a briefing," said major-general Alexei Nikolaevich, the First Deputy Director of the *Federal'naya sluzhba bezopasnosti Rossiyskoy Federatsii*, or FSB, the internal security service. "The means deployed were unusually... flagrant."

"That is correct," Primakov said. "We didn't see the point of disposing of him stealthily."

"Even though this will bring attention to us?"

"The decision was taken that we should make a point. We want our involvement to be deniable, of course, and my colleagues in Line PR are already seeking to cast doubt on our involvement, but it will be obvious to those who need to know. The British, for one. The other Western governments who need to be reminded that we are not a country to be pushed around. And, most importantly, the other dissidents and defectors who have settled in the west. We want them to know that the SVR has a long reach, and that there will be no forgiveness for continued treachery. We believe that this will have a sobering effect on anyone who might otherwise have sought to follow Aleksandrov's example. Our course of action was agreed to in advance, of course."

He glanced at the president; his face was as impassive as a Sphinx. His pale blue eyes were locked onto him and, once again, Primakov felt that his lies were being stripped away like the skin of an onion, layer by layer by layer.

"This intelligence," the Minister for Internal Affairs said. "What was Aleksandrov trying to sell?"

Primakov swallowed and fought the urge to look back at the president. He needed to be convincing.

"Aleksandrov told his old handler at MI6 that he was in possession of a list of all of the SVR's active agents in Western Europe."

"And did we believe him? Where could he have come across such a document?"

"We do not know," he said. "It is possible that he made contact with a source within the Center." The president was watching him with those limpid eyes, seeing everything. "Line KR has initiated an operation looking into that as a matter of the utmost importance."

"Thank you, Deputy Director Primakov," the president said, his voice as smooth as silk. "There will be political repercussions from this operation, but I am satisfied that the benefit outweighs the cost." He smiled, just a little, his mask shifting.

"Who carried out the operation?" Nikolaevich asked.

"Directorate S agents," Primakov said. "They remain in place. We will monitor the investigation. If we feel that there is a risk that their involvement has been detected, we will recall them to Moscow at once."

"Where I shall be delighted to meet them," the president said. "They have performed a great service for the Rodina today. They are to be commended. Thank you, Deputy Director."

The president said no more, and, instead, looked down at his agenda. Primakov knew that the ordeal was at an end. He slid his chair away from the table and stood, noting, to his alarm, that his legs were weak. He nodded his acknowledgements to the colleagues around the table; Nikolaevich smiled and gave him a wink. Primakov buttoned up his jacket and made his way to the exit. He held onto the balustrade as he descended the staircase and hurried to where his chauffeur was waiting for him. He had forgotten his umbrella and was quickly soaked in the growing downpour that hammered against his car and on the cobbles of the courtyard. His chauffeur opened the back door and Primakov collapsed inside. He closed his eyes and scrubbed the rain away from his face. The driver swung the car around and they passed through the Borovitskaya Gate once more. Primakov looked back at the tower, layered like the sections of a cake with a spire topped with a single red star. They had plotted to kill Brezhnev here. Assassinations. Death. Primakov couldn't keep such thoughts from his mind.

He wondered what the council was discussing now that he was gone. Primakov thought that he had done enough, but there was no way to be sure. The president sometimes appeared omniscient, and, despite his compliments, Primakov could not help but harbour doubts.

He thought of Natasha. He had taken a grievous risk for her. He had risked his career. His life. He had done it because he loved her, because he was old and she made him feel young. And now he wanted to see her and tell her that her problems were at an end, and to enjoy the gratitude that he knew she would feel.

SOUTHWOLD

18

They arrived over Southwold. Milton saw the black expanse of the sea, the twinkling lights of big oil tankers laid up a mile offshore, and then the brighter lights of the town itself that glowed up at them through the deepening dusk. The lighthouse stood over the town, casting a golden finger of light that flicked out over the frothing waves. The pilot told them to hold tight as he brought them down on The Paddock, a grassy area that formed the inner part of Southwold Common on the town's southern boundary. The wheels bumped once and then settled.

Tanner opened the cabin door, slid it back and hopped down onto the grass. Shah followed, then Ross, then Milton. The downdraft was strong, disturbing rubbish from a nearby bin and forcing them to duck their heads as they scurried away. Milton stayed close to Ross as they followed Shah to the man who was waiting for them just outside the stone wall that marked the boundary of the United Reformed Church. The two men shook hands and exchanged words before Shah turned back to them.

"They've set up base in there," he said, pointing to the church. "The police are briefing everyone in five minutes."

They followed Shah through a gate and into the church grounds.

THE CHURCH HAD BEEN TAKEN over as a central control point for the police and intelligence operation. It was close to the house where Aleksandrov had been found. The church hall was busy. There was a collection of men and women, some of them in suits, others in clothes that suggested that they might have been called to the town at short notice. Milton guessed that the crowd would include detectives and intelligence operatives. Milton, Shah and Ross stood together. There was a tangible buzz in the room, the crackle and pop of electricity, the expectation that something extraordinary was going on.

There was a folding table at the front of the room with two chairs behind it. A second table bore a large television screen. A man and a woman emerged from a room at the back of the hall and made their way through the crowd to the front. The man sat down but the woman remained on her feet.

"Thank you all for coming," she said. "My name is Francesca Kennedy. I'm the Deputy Assistant Commissioner and the senior national co-ordinator for counterterrorism policing in the Metropolitan Police. Suffolk Constabulary has now handed over this incident to us. The Assistant Commissioner is here"—she indicated the man sitting next to her, who responded with a nod of his head—"but I'm going to brief you. As you all already know, the victim was a former Russian spy who had been working for SIS for many years before he was exposed and prosecuted. He's been living here in Southwold under a new identity since his request for asylum was granted. Given that background, his murder raised numerous red flags."

She took out her notebook and flipped through the pages, setting out the timeline. A few additional facts had been added, but it was largely the same situation as the one that Shah had briefed them on in the helicopter.

"Aleksandrov was found at home, as you know. Single gunshot to the head. We've been piecing together his activities this afternoon. He was seen in the Old Nelson public house just after lunch. The publican knew him and said that it wasn't unusual for him to go there for a drink around that time. He normally drank alone, but the publican said that he was with another man today. He didn't get a look at the man and hasn't been able to provide a description or any additional details."

Shah raised his hand, and Kennedy nodded to him. "Raj Shah, SIS," he said. "We have no idea at all who the other man was?"

"No. Not yet. But he's obviously of significant interest. Finding him is the main priority. You got any ideas?"

"Not yet," Shah said. "If we think of anything, we'll share it at once."

Milton noticed Ross lean closer to Shah so that she could whisper something into his ear.

"CCTV?" one of the detectives asked.

"Nothing in the pub—the publican says he can't afford it. There's not a great deal of coverage in the town, either, but local uniform is securing everything they can. We're going through it now—if there's anything useful, they'll find it. We don't know that much at the moment, but we're working as fast as we can to build it up. I'm grateful for the extra help."

Milton doubted that the help would make any difference. They might be able to put together Aleksandrov's last few hours, and they might—eventually—be able to put a name to the men or women who had killed him. It wouldn't matter. Milton knew that if this was a professional job, then the assassins would already be miles away from here. They would be heading for the nearest airport and a flight out of the country. He doubted that they would have the information they needed in time to stop them from leaving. They might already have gone.

Kennedy went on. "Aleksandrov lived on Wymering Road—that's five minutes northwest of here. We've secured the property and moved the neighbours out. We'd rather limit access to the property until the SOCOs are finished gathering evidence and are out of the way. I'm told we're looking at another hour for that. After that, I don't have a problem with small teams going in to look for themselves, but for obvious reasons I'd like it to be under police supervision."

Kennedy brought the meeting to a close. Tanner, Milton, Shah and Ross moved to the side of the room.

"This is all going to be too little, too late," Tanner said quietly.

"I agree," Milton said.

"Where do you think they are now?"

"If they're not on a plane already, it won't be long. We're already five hours behind them."

"A little optimism?" Ross said. "You're not giving up already?"

"It's realism," Milton said. "This sounds like a professional job, probably a state-sponsored one. Men and women like that don't wait around to be caught. They do their job and then they leave. And they have a big head start."

"I'm going to update HQ," Tanner said, taking his phone out of his pocket and turning away.

Milton waited in the church hall and then followed the departing officers out into the alley. The night was cooling fast, and he zipped up his jacket. The high street at the end of the alley was quiet. Milton wondered how long it would stay like this. How long would it take for the news to leak? A Russian spy had been assassinated on the streets of a sleepy English coastal town. It would be a big story. A scandal. They probably had the town to themselves for the night, and maybe for some of tomorrow if they were lucky. After that, it would be pandemonium. They needed to get a lead before then or they never would.

LONDON

19

Vincent Beck was listening to Brahms when his landline rang on the table next to his record player. He picked it up and saw, with a quickening of his pulse, that the caller ID was a number that he recognised.

"Is this Vincent Beck?"

"Yes," Beck said. "Who is this?"

"We believe that you were sold an insurance policy with a mortgage you took out ten years ago. It's sometimes known as PPI. Does that sound like it might be right?"

Beck's throat was arid. "How many years ago did you say?"

"Ten," the man said.

"No," Beck replied. "Not me. I'm afraid your records are mistaken. Goodbye."

Beck ended the call and stared at the phone. It took him a moment to gather his thoughts. He had known that a moment like this would come—it always did, eventually—but he had been here so long without issue that it was difficult to accept it. But the moment *had* come and, now that it was here, he had to make sure that he reacted appropriately. He went to his bedroom, took the small suitcase from underneath the bed and packed a change of clothes. He took his keys from his pocket, lowered himself to the floor and slid beneath the bed far enough so that he could reach the loose floorboard. He used a key to prise up the end and removed the board so that he could reach into the void beneath. He took out his go-bag, scrambled out from underneath the bed and opened it up. The bag contained a burner phone, a passport and driver's licence in a false name, £5000 and a small Glock 26 handgun, together with two spare magazines. The Glock was designed for concealed carry, with a small frame and abbreviated barrel that meant that it was easy to hide anywhere on the body. It was chambered in 9mm, with ten rounds in the magazine and one in the spout. Beck zipped up the bag and put it into the suitcase. He confirmed that the burst encoder was hidden in the suitcase and closed it up.

He took the suitcase to the hall and then quickly passed through the rooms to make sure that he hadn't left anything that might later prove to be incriminating. Satisfied, he went back to the suitcase, extended the handle and wheeled it out of the flat's front door. One of his neighbours was just stepping out of the lift. She was an old woman who spent her days in a pub down by the river. Beck bid her good evening and she did the same, her words a little slurred as usual. Beck put his arm between the doors to stop them from closing and pulled the suitcase into the lift. He hit the button for the ground floor and waited for the doors to close.

He took a moment to compose himself. It had taken him five minutes to clear the flat. That was good. Fast enough. There was no time to spare, and no way of knowing how

serious the threat against him was. If anyone had been
listening to the call that he had received, they would have
concluded that it was from a call centre. It would have
sounded authentic, and that was the intention. However, the
precise wording had been agreed to in advance and the
answer to his question—"ten"—served as the trigger signal.
Each number, from one to ten, bore a separate meaning.
"Ten" meant that Beck and his agents had been, or were at
imminent risk of being, blown.

The lift reached the ground floor and the doors opened.
Beck stepped outside. There was a group of young boys
smoking weed on the scrubby patch of grass outside the
building, but nothing else that made him nervous. Beck was
always careful, but tonight required even more caution
than usual.

It was nine in the evening when he set off and wheeled
his case down to the river, following the route that he took
every day. He followed the gentle curve for a mile, maintaining the same leisurely pace as yesterday, the day
before that, and all the days before that. Beck was an old
man, in his seventies, and, to any normal observer it
would look as if he was just off to catch a bus or a train.
The main purpose of the walk was to help him to identify
surveilling parties and, if necessary, lose them. It was an
SDR—a surveillance detection route—and Beck had
learned it from a retired KGB colonel who had taught a
class at the Dzershinsky Higher School in Michurinsky
Prospekt. Beck had been in his twenties when he had
attended the KGB school, but the lessons were just as relevant today as they had been then. The fundamental art of
espionage was unchanged, despite the advances in technology that had added so many opportunities and perils
to the work. In this case, Beck needed to be sure that he

was black before he met with his agents. The utmost caution was required.

He usually stayed on this side of the river until he reached the Hurlingham Club, but today he carried his case up the steps from the footpath and crossed the water into Putney. He headed south and then continued along Putney High Street until he reached the overland train station. It was a couple of miles from his apartment, and he used all the tricks designed to flush out surveillance: he paused to tie a lace, crossed over the road to look in the window of the Franco Manca restaurant, turned onto Disraeli Road and then quickly turned back on himself. He waited on the platform for a train, scanning the other men and women to see whether any of them were repeats. He had never spotted anything that made him suspect he was under surveillance, but that did not mean that today might not be different. He looked for clothes that he might have seen before, and, when nothing registered, he checked shoes. Clothes were easy to change, but, in his long experience, Western agents never remembered to change their shoes. It was sloppy tradecraft and an easy giveaway but he saw nothing tonight that gave him cause for concern. There were no signs of pursuit: no suggestion of agents leapfrogging each other, no obvious handovers, no one following him along his erratic route.

The train rolled into the station. He climbed aboard and took a seat at the end of the carriage where he would be able to watch anyone else who got on with him.

Beck was too wily to relax. He had years of experience playing this particular game and had deployed the same tactics in any number of denied areas around the world: he had operated in San Francisco, Madrid, Paris, Berlin—on both sides of the Wall—and Washington. His posting to

London had been the longest of his career, and it would be his last. His real name was Vladimir Rabtsevich but he had used this particular legend for so long that now he thought of himself as Beck. He was a retired language teacher at the Znaniye School in Chelsea. He had worked there for ten years to provide the ballast for the legend. A wife had been invented for him; they had used the usual trick, finding a candidate by working their way around Highgate Cemetery until a deceased child of suitable age had been located and then building a persona with the benefit of their birth certificate. Mrs Beck was said to have died, but the fact that she had been British allowed him to stay in the country without a visa. He lived alone with a cat called Lenin, ate microwave meals for one, and occasionally visited the Curzon for the foreign arthouse films that they showed there. He didn't own a mobile phone because, as he said whenever anyone asked him, he didn't like their intrusiveness. The real reason, of course, was because he had no wish for the spooks at GCHQ to be able to track him between the phone masts that prickled across London's streets. He used burner phones and telephone boxes to arrange his business, different ones each time.

Beck got off at Clapham Junction and changed onto the train to Winchester. He looked around at the quiet Sunday night carriage. He was comfortable, still confident that he was black. He looked at his watch. He had an hour until he arrived.

20

"*All units, this is Blackjack. PAPERCLIP is on the move. Minimal comms unless operationally necessary. Out.*"

The earbud was loose, and Michael Pope pushed it in until it was snug. He was sitting in the back of one of the Group Three backup cars; a surveillance expert occupied the driver's seat. They were parked on Fulham Palace Road, waiting for PAPERCLIP's route to be relayed.

PAPERCLIP was the cryptonym of Vincent Beck, an expat Russian who had been living in the United Kingdom for ten years. He was ostensibly a retired teacher of foreign languages, but, as a result of intelligence received from BLUEBIRD, the Secret Intelligence Service had confirmed that he was a senior agent runner working for Directorate S. BLUEBIRD was MI6's pride and joy, an active source buried within the SVR, and the tip about Beck had been just the latest in a long line of valuable intelligence scoops.

Beck had been subjected to round-the-clock surveillance ever since he had been uncovered. His landline had been tapped, his apartment bugged, and he had been followed every time he stepped out of the front door of his house. So far, though, he had revealed nothing except a predilection for long riverside walks, arthouse cinema and the borscht served at Zima Russian Street Food and Bar on Frith Street in Soho.

"This is Alpha. He's going down to the river."

This operation was sensitive and complex enough to warrant the involvement of several of the Groups that comprised the Firm. Group Three was responsible for human surveillance, the teams of agents who coalesced around a target so that it was practically impossible for that person to go anywhere without being observed. In the way that the agents of Group Five—responsible for ensuring the smooth transmission of intelligence among the Groups— were informally referred to as 'postmen' and the cryptanalysts of Group Six were 'hackers,' the agents of Group Three were dubbed 'bloodhounds.' They had earned the sobriquet through the diligence and discretion of their surveillance and tracking and the reputation, hard won, that, once a target was put under their surveillance, it was impossible for them to be shaken off.

The agents of Group Fifteen were referred to as 'cleaners' or 'headhunters.' Pope, as Number Five, was one of its most senior operatives. Pope was emplaced in the event that a decision was taken to interdict PAPERCLIP, or anyone else that he might meet. Control was rotating his agents to keep them fresh; this was the second day that Pope had been on the team, and tomorrow he would be rotated off in favour of Number Six.

"This is Alpha, handing off."

"This is Bravo. Picking up. PAPERCLIP is heading toward the bridge."

The team was extensive. There were ten agents assigned, with none of them staying with him for longer than neces sary. Beck was good, and they were assuming that he had been operational for the entirety of the ten years that he had been in the country. He had never been caught, and that suggested a certain expertise. The sophistication of the surveillance had been ratcheted up in accordance with that.

"This is Bravo. He's going over the bridge. Handing off." There was surprise in the agent's voice.

"This is Foxtrot. Picking up."

"Is that unusual?" Pope asked the female agent driving the car.

"Yes," she said, putting the car into gear and pulling out. "First time over the river since we've been on him. We need to change position."

They drove down Fulham High Street and swung onto Putney Bridge. Pope looked out to the left as they started across the river. Beck was walking on his own, passing beneath one of the outsized lanterns that threw out its warm glow over the water below. He was a big man, solid and healthy despite his years, and he walked with purpose. He was wearing a light jacket and pulling a wheeled suitcase along behind him. There were a handful of other people on the bridge. Pope had no idea which of them were engaged in the operation, but guessed there would be at least three, with one going in the opposite direction in the event that Beck reversed course in an attempt to reveal possible surveillants.

"This is Blackjack. We've checked the origin of the call. There's no call centre. It was a flare. Assume he's running."

The car reached the other side and swung off onto Waterman's Green. The driver continued around the curve until they were out of sight of the bridge and then performed a U-turn, bringing the car to a halt next to a bus shelter.

"This is Foxtrot. He's heading straight on. Handing off."

"This is Golf. Picking up."

Pope had conferred with Control an hour previously and had been brought up to speed on the events in South-wold. The death of the dissident Russian was being attributed to Russian actors, and, as a suspected agent runner, Beck had become of even greater interest. The hope was that Beck's agents might be responsible and that he might inadvertently betray them. And now, on the evening of the murder, Beck was on the move. He had received a warning and he was acting on it. Pope found it hard to believe that that could be a coincidence.

They waited next to the shelter, listening to the chatter over the radio as Beck changed course in what was an obvious attempt to smoke out surveillance. They had enough assets to adapt the coverage so that he didn't see the same follower more than once. Pope listened as Beck was reported as returning onto the main road and continuing to the south.

"This is Golf. I think he's going to the station."

The driver put the car into gear and rolled away from the kerb.

"This is Blackjack to Number Five. Get to the station, please."

"On our way," the driver reported, bullying her way into the traffic and then waiting for the lights opposite the medieval church to change.

Pope felt the tingle of adrenaline. This was not the sort of operation where it was possible to furnish him with clean rules of engagement. There had been no need for him, or any of the other Group Fifteen agents who had been involved in the surveillance, to do anything other than wait for an order to move. But PAPERCLIP's uncharacteristic activity this evening, especially given what had happened on the Suffolk coast, suggested that the operation was approaching a climax. Pope reached down to the service pistol that he had holstered beneath his left shoulder. His fingertips brushed the stippled grip of the Sig and then slid away from it, zipping up his jacket to obscure the weapon.

"This is Foxtrot. He's crossing for the station. Handing off."

"This is Golf, picking up. He's buying a ticket."

"This is Blackjack to Five. You're up. Get after him."

The driver pulled over on the opposite side of the road to the station entrance.

"Go," the driver urged.

Pope got out, waited for a chance to cross and then jogged out between two slow-moving buses.

"Golf to Five. Paperclip is on platform one. Repeat, platform one."

Pope pressed his pre-paid card on the reader, passed through the barriers and made his way to the platform. He saw Beck at once. The old man was sitting on one of the benches, looking up and down the platform. Pope walked on without giving him a second glance. His earpiece was tiny and in the opposite ear; Beck wouldn't be able to see it. He checked the departures board; the first train, due into the station in a minute, was going to Winchester.

Pope was five paces beyond Beck when he heard the rumble of the approaching engine. He kept walking, all the way down to the front of the platform, and waited for the train to arrive. He turned back to see Beck board the third carriage of five. Pope helped a mother to wheel her pram down from the carriage and onto the platform and then boarded himself. The doors closed and the train pulled out.

MOSCOW

21

P rimakov told his driver to take him to the Fourth District. He had him pull up half a mile short of his ultimate destination, told him to take the night off and then waited for him to merge into the traffic and drive away. He walked the rest of the way himself, following the Moskva River through a pleasant park that was lit with reproduction antique lanterns that cast a warm glow out over the water.

They had chosen the usual location for their tryst, the Directorate S safe house that was occasionally occupied by agents who were returning to Moscow from abroad. It was almost always empty; Primakov had confirmed that that was the case today, and that they would have privacy for as long as they wanted it. The apartment was in one of the new blocks that had been constructed here during the last twenty years, funded by ambitious developers who took advantage of the more relaxed rules on the movement of capital to invest in accommodation for the city's burgeoning middle class. These buildings were alike, each thirty stories tall and sleeker than the Soviet-era architecture that blighted so much of the rest of the city.

Primakov opened the door to the lobby, walked past the reception desk without acknowledging the porter, and took the lift up to the fourteenth floor. He knocked on the door and waited until he heard the sound of bare feet slapping against the wood of the hall. The door opened and his lover greeted him with a smile.

"I thought you would never get here," she said.

"The council meeting ran a little late," he said, happy to mention that he had been to the Kremlin because he knew that she would be impressed.

"And?" she said, her eyes wide.

"I think we might have got to the end of the problem."

Her face dissolved into a wide smile and, without even waiting to draw him into the apartment, she placed both hands around his head so that she could draw him down to her level. She kissed him full on the lips.

"Thank you," she said. "You don't know how grateful I am. What would I do without you?"

PRIMAKOV HAD MET Captain Natasha Kryuchkov during a conference that had taken place in the Kremlin six years earlier. He had been there to listen to his boss, the Director of the SVR, speak about the intelligence challenges that had arisen thanks to Russia's increasingly active role in world affairs. The first hour of the symposium had been deathly dull, and Primakov had decided that he would manufacture an excuse to leave as soon as the Director had finished. He had gone to get a cup of strong black coffee to help him stay awake for the second hour when he had bumped into a young, attractive brunette dressed in the green uniform of the *Glavnoye razvedyvatel'noye upravleniye,* or the GRU's Main Intelligence Directorate.

Primakov's wife had died of cancer five years earlier, and, since then, he had resigned himself to a bachelor's life. It had been a bleak way to live. Natasha was attractive and attentive and the two of them had enjoyed an easy rapport. Primakov was not naïve enough to think that she was drawn to him because of his looks; he was thirty years older than she was, and, although he took care with his appearance, he still looked his age. He guessed that she recognised him and was flattered that he took the time to speak to her. He was encouraged by her evident interest and had invited her for a tour of Yasenevo. That had gone well and, ignoring the slight sense of ridiculousness that he was contemplating dating a woman so much younger than himself, he had invited her to dinner the next week.

They had enjoyed a pleasant evening together. She told him all about her career, and what she hoped to achieve. She worked in the Counterintelligence Service (Department), specifically within the Directorate for the Counterintelligence Support of Strategic Facilities. She had enjoyed a rapid rise through the ranks thanks to a tenacious approach, hard work and a fierce loyalty to her country. For his part, he explained how he had come to achieve a position of authority within the SVR, and how things had changed over the years. He admitted that he was disenchanted with how the service had been altered since the death of the KGB, and that he was looking forward to his retirement in five years' time. That he felt able to be so indiscreet with her was, he concluded, a sign that there was more to their putative relationship than might otherwise have been the case. She had invited him to her apartment the week after their first dinner, and they had started seeing each other more frequently after that. They both agreed that their assignations should be clandestine, given that the relationship would be frowned upon by the Kremlin. His colleagues would deride him for an affair which was, they would say, inappropriate and embarrassing; her superiors would conclude that she was sleeping with him because she wanted to advance her career.

Their affair had developed into something different. Primakov could have lived with the suspicion that she was with him for her own career; it was a compromise he could make in return for being with her. But, as time went by, he came to accept that that was not the case. He had done her a few favours, put in a good word here and there, but nothing that would be enough to keep her around. She told him that she loved him and he came to believe that.

And then, a month ago, Natasha had finally turned to him for help. She had been in a blind panic as she explained that a senior engineer working in the Sukhoi factory had disappeared. Her investigation had revealed that the engineer had stolen several terabytes worth of data related to the new Su-58 that was being developed at the factory. The engineer was a woman: Anastasiya Romanova.

The chief of Natasha's Department in the GRU was a man named Klimashin; Primakov knew him by reputation and knew that Natasha's fears were well founded. Klimashin was an ambitious and devious man and would do everything he could to protect his own standing. He would absolve himself of responsibility for the intelligence failure and would sacrifice Natasha and anyone else if it meant that his own career could be saved.

Primakov reviewed the case himself. Natasha had started an investigation to find Romanova but had drawn a blank. The woman had simply disappeared. Her friends had been rounded up and questioned, but none of them had any idea where she might have gone. Primakov put two of his analysts on the case, warning them that it was sensitive and their findings were not to be shared outside of his office. They quickly made progress, revealing a motive for the disappearance. Her husband, Viktor Romanov, had built up a successful business in the oil and gas sector. He had come into conflict with an oligarch who was close to the president and, rather than be prudent and back down, Romanov had brought legal proceedings alleging fraud and embezzlement. It wasn't difficult to join the dots and work out what had happened next. The oligarch made a call, and, within days of the filing of the proceedings, Romanov had been arrested. He was tried and convicted and sent to Penal Colony No. 14 on the banks of the Partsa River in Mordovia. He died six months later. The official account was that he had suffered a heart attack, but Primakov knew that the truth would have been more brutal. Romanov's money found its way to the oligarch, a fraction was funnelled to one of the Stalinist romanticisers who ran the colony, and the Romanov problem was made to go away. His wife had been interviewed after his death and had responded badly. The agents responsible had reported that she blamed the state, and had recommended that she be removed from the factory until her loyalty could be confirmed. But she had vanished before that could happen, and a forensic investigation of her network activity suggested that she had illegally downloaded hundreds of terabytes of restricted information.

Primakov instructed his researchers to delve deeper. Anastasiya Romanova's father was Pyotr Aleksandrov, who had been convicted of treason and then swapped for the illegals who had been captured by the CIA. It appeared that treachery ran in the family and, his instincts aroused, Primakov used EUREKA, the Directorate S agent that they had placed within MI6, to provide him with the father's location. He then directed Vincent Beck to deploy two illegals to put Aleksandrov under surveillance.

It was a gamble, and Primakov had no reason to think that it would pay out. The file said that Aleksandrov and his daughter were estranged, but he still felt it worth the attempt. Romanova was alone, hunted by the state and with secrets to sell; why would she not go to her father? After all, he had experience in selling stolen intelligence and a direct line to decision-makers at Vauxhall Cross.

The fishing expedition was successful. They had intercepted the call that Anastasiya had placed to her father and learned of their plan to bring her out of Russia so that the two of them might be reunited and reconciled. But now Primakov had a dilemma: he couldn't very well go to the Director and tell him that Anastasiya was offering the secrets of the new fighter because that would end up damning Natasha. But doing nothing would lead to the same result. He decided that a creative approach was necessary and, instead of the Su-58, he simply invented something else for Aleksandrov to sell. The phone call between Aleksandrov and his former handler, Geggel, was fortunate in its timing. Primakov amended the transcript and took it to the Director. Primakov's version of the conversation suggested that Aleksandrov had acquired a list of active agents and their legends, source unknown, and that he had contacted Geggel in order to discuss their sale. Urgent action needed to be taken to prevent the information from falling into the hands of the enemy. Anastasiya was not mentioned at all.

The Director had approved the operation with the caveat that Aleksandrov's death must also serve as a warning to anyone else who would be foolish enough to cross the Rodina in this way. They hadn't tried to hide it. It was obvious to anyone with even the slightest passing interest that Aleksandrov had been killed because he had tried to cross the motherland. His death would prevent the spread of the information he was trying to sell while serving as a warning to others on the consequences of greed.

22

Primakov and Natasha lay together in bed, the blinds open so that they could drink in the night-time view of the city. The lights atop towers and cranes sparkled across the horizon, and buildings were crushed together in the oxbow curve of the river. The view always reminded Primakov of how much Moscow had changed in the years since he had first arrived here. The last decade had seen an especially rapid transformation as capital flooded in from newly liberated markets, the president's cronies first in line to shove their snouts into the trough. Primakov had no problem with that. He was a pragmatist. He understood how the system worked and knew that he stood to benefit by demonstrating his fealty and effectiveness to those above him. His policy had been successful so far, and he was keen to ensure that it continued to be so.

Natasha had taken him straight to bed, and it was only now that she asked him about the events that he had set in train for her.

"How did it—" she began.

"It's done," he said, gently talking over her anxiety.

"The father?"

"Dead. The message will be unambiguous."

"But there's nothing on the news."

"I doubt the British are ready to go public yet. They will. And when they do, she will know that it was her fault. She'll stay quiet and, in the meantime, we'll track her down. She can't hide forever."

Natasha rolled onto her back, stared up to the ceiling and exhaled. "I wish this was finished. Worrying all the time —it's exhausting."

He stroked her hair. "It's nearly done," he said. "There's something I didn't tell you: Directorate X traced the IP address for the email she sent to her father. She used an internet café in Komsomolsk. They have CCTV. We have a picture of her paying her bill."

"She's still there?"

"She's changed her hair, but it looks like she is too frightened to travel. I have two men I trust in situations like this. They will find her."

Primakov had been thinking of sending Stepanov and Mitrokhin. He could have spoken to Nikolaevich at the FSB, but he would have needed a pretext to ask for help that would still hide the real reason for the request. Nikolaevich was a wily old fox, and he could make things uncomfortable for Primakov if he joined the dots between Romanova and Aleksandrov. Far better to send his best men. Stepanov had an excellent nose, and people tended to give Mitrokhin what he wanted to know. They made an effective team.

Natasha rolled over again and draped her arm across his chest. "Can you stay tonight?"

"Perhaps. Let me check."

He realised that he hadn't turned his cell phone back on again after deactivating it for the council meeting. He got up and went to the chair where he had left his clothes. He took it out of his jacket pocket, pressed the button and waited for it to boot up. It buzzed in his hand with a series of incoming messages. One of them was marked urgent, and, with a feeling of unease, he scrolled down and tapped his finger on it.

"What is it?" Natasha said.

His face must have given him away. "It's nothing," he said. "Just information on the operation. But I need to go back to the office."

"What information? Something is wrong?"

"Please, Natasha, don't worry. Everything is as it should be. But there are some things that I need to do. Perhaps I will be able to return later."

He dressed quickly, then excused himself and went down onto the street. He wished that he had his car, but he didn't, and he did not want to call his driver to pick him up from the park. Instead, he followed the street to Strogino Metro station. He took out his phone as he waited for a train to arrive and read the message for a second and then a third time. It was from the Center. EUREKA had filed an urgent report to the London *rezidentura* earlier that evening. Vincent Beck, the agent runner responsible for the sleepers in the United Kingdom, was reported as being compromised. EUREKA's order had been passed to Directorate S and, in his absence, his deputy had given the order to exfiltrate both Beck and the illegals who had mounted the operation against Aleksandrov. Beck was on his way to the agents now and the process to bring them out had been initiated.

Primakov put his phone away and tapped his foot impatiently. There was no knowing what the British would find if they were able to capture and interrogate Beck or his agents. He had read Beck's *zapista* confirming that the operation had been successful, but the message was cursory and no substitute for the more detailed report that would follow in due course. It left him with questions: had the assassins spoken to Aleksandrov before they killed him? Had they been able to eavesdrop on any conversations between Aleksandrov and Geggel? If they had, what had they heard? Had they reported anything else to Beck? What would the British discover if they captured the old man and interrogated him? Perhaps they would find out that Aleksandrov was not selling the identities of SVR agents. Perhaps they would know that Aleksandrov was working with his daughter, and that it was the schematic of the Su-58 that Aleksandrov was dangling in order to persuade them to get her out. If the truth was ever uncovered, it would eventually make its way back to the council and the president. His lies would be revealed.

That could not be allowed to happen. There was a gust of wind as the train rumbled out of the mouth of the tunnel. Primakov waited for the doors to open and then stepped aboard.

The agents couldn't be captured. That would herald disaster. He had to bring them home.

WINCHESTER

23

Vincent Beck hoisted his case onto the seat next to him and gazed out at the landscape as it raced by the windows on either side of the train.

He couldn't stop thinking about the call. The source of the information that had led to the warning was not clear. Beck had known that Mikhail and Nataliya would be compromised at some point—it was inevitable, given the nature of the work—but the call had still come as a shock. Still, he thought as he headed out of London, they had had a good run. They had been operational for ten years and they had done good work in that time. There had been a number of impressive coups for which they—and, he supposed, *he*—could claim credit. They had nurtured relationships with men and women inside the intelligence community; they had seduced or blackmailed senior figures within British and American corporations that had led to a flow of top-secret patents and designs; and they had been able to remove troublesome individuals who would have been better advised not to work against the Rodina. One oligarch had been funding opposition parties; he had ended up dead of a suspected heart attack. Another had opened proceedings against an oil company tied to the interests of the president; he had been killed in a fiery wreck after his supercar's brakes had failed on the M25. Still others had been silenced after they had been blackmailed with evidence of their sexual peccadilloes and perversions, that evidence collected during honeytraps filmed in hotel rooms equipped with a barrage of secret cameras.

The assassination of Pyotr Aleksandrov had been carried out in the same exemplary manner as all of their other work. If it was to be their final operation, they could hardly have ended on a more satisfactory note. They had done what they had been asked to do and, once more, had demonstrated to anyone else foolish enough to consider working against the motherland that the reach of the SVR was long, and that nowhere was safe.

"The next stop on this service will be Winchester. Please mind the gap between the train and the platform edge."

Beck got up, lowered his case to the floor, and made his way to the vestibule where he waited for the train to pull into the station. It had been a straightforward journey. There had been only a handful of passengers in the carriage with him, and none of them had given him any cause for alarm.

The train rolled through into the station and he saw the time on the glowing departure board that was suspended halfway down the platform: it was eleven. The train stopped, the doors opened and Beck disembarked. He went over to an empty bench and sat down, taking advantage of his age so that it might appear that he needed to take a breath. He counted ten other passengers who disembarked, but none of them had been in his carriage. None of them were repeats from earlier. He waited until they had made their way through the barriers, waited another minute, and then followed them. It was impossible to be sure, but he was as confident as he could be; he had been thorough and careful, and he had seen no indication that he was being followed.

He was black. It was safe to proceed.

THERE WAS a taxi rank outside the station, with three cars waiting to pick up passengers. Beck opened the rear door of the first car in line and lowered himself inside.

"Where to?"

"King's Worthy, please."

"Right you are."

The car pulled away and Beck allowed himself to relax a little. He had been doing this for years and yet, despite his experience, it never got easier. Nervousness and anxiety were part and parcel of the work, but that was good. It was as he always reminded his agents: nerves kept you sharp. Relaxation was a symptom of complacency, and succumbing to complacency was often the final mistake an agent would make.

It was a little after eleven when the taxi arrived at the house. Beck paid the driver and waited until he had pulled away before he used his fob to open the gates. He walked up the gravelled drive to the front door, thinking about how quintessentially English this all was: the village, the ancient church, the wisteria and roses climbing up the wall of the house, the owl hooting in a nearby tree.

He knocked on the door and waited.

Nothing.

He looked through the letterbox. The hall light was lit,

but, save that, there was no other sign that anyone was home. They would be conducting a thorough dry-cleaning run. They were careful, and that, usually, would have been good. Tonight was different. They needed to get out of the country as quickly as they could.

He took out his key, unlocked the door and went inside to wait.

SOUTHWOLD

24

The SOCOs had finished their work at Aleksandrov's property and Kennedy said that a small intelligence team could now go inside. Tanner stayed behind, but Milton, Ross and Shah were driven in two unmarked police cars to Wymering Road. It was a residential street, entirely unremarkable except for the fact that it had been closed, with two police cars parked nose-to-nose at one end and another two at the other. There was a tighter cordon around the Aleksandrov property and its neighbours, and the only people allowed inside were police, military and security service personnel. The crime scene technicians were gathered outside, next to a plain white van, removing their anti-contamination suits and storing the evidence that they had collected. A team of officers were removing the parts of an evidence tent from the back of a police van. It would be erected around the front door, a temporary measure until the property could be professionally secured to prevent unauthorised access.

The driver of the car told them to wait. "Let me check that they're clear."

Shah's phone buzzed and he stepped aside to take the call.

Milton took out a packet of cigarettes, put one to his lips and lit it.

Ross turned to him. "Can I bum one?"

Milton gave Ross the packet. She cupped the end of the cigarette and Milton lit it for her.

"This has got to be one of the weirdest evenings I've ever had," she said, blowing smoke.

"It's up there," Milton replied.

"I mean, seriously—this is the last thing that you would expect to find in a place like *this*. I know they've hit people in London, but *here?* It's nuts."

"I doubt it makes much difference to them."

She gestured over toward the house. "You think they did it? The Russians?"

"I don't know," Milton said, blowing smoke. "But Aleksandrov was one of theirs for a long time, and he did a lot of damage. The SVR has a long memory."

"Have you dealt with them before?"

"The SVR?"

She nodded.

"Once or twice," Milton said.

"And?"

"And I wouldn't be surprised if we find their fingerprints all over this."

Ross looked like she was going to probe him for more, but the driver said that they could go in. They went inside the front door and were led along the corridor and into the kitchen. Milton took it all in with a practiced, professional eye: it was an unremarkable room, without much in the way of personality, and distinguished only by the fact that a dead body was laid out across the floor. Milton saw the gunshot wound and concluded, from the scorch marks around the entry wound, that the weapon had been fired at close range. There was blood on the floor, already congealing across it and over the grouted lines between the tiles.

Milton looked over at Ross. She was pale and had put her hand down on the counter to steady herself.

"Are you okay?"

"I'm fine," she said.

"First time you've seen a dead body?"

"Yes," she said.

"You'll get used to it," he said.

"I'm not sure I want to."

The police had taken the necessary photographs, but a technician was still in the room with a video camera. He focused on the body and then backed up to take in the rest of the room. Milton took Ross by the wrist and guided her back out into the corridor so that they would be out of his way.

"There's not much for us to do here," he said. "Best to leave it to the professionals."

They went outside. Shah had finished his call and was waiting for them.

"Change of plan," he said.

Ross turned to him. "What is it?"

"Leonard Geggel," he said. "We have a lead."

25

Ross and Milton were driven out of town in the back of an unmarked police car. The cordon was opened to allow them to pass through. A crowd of locals had gathered there to look down the High Street and they gawped into the car as the driver slowly accelerated away.

Shah had explained to them both what had happened. Geggel hadn't answered his phone, and so a junior officer had been sent to visit his house. It was empty; Geggel was a bachelor, and there was no one inside the property that they could speak to. Shah had asked GCHQ to run a trace on Geggel's phone and, to his surprise, they had reported that he had been in Southwold that afternoon, arriving at around two-thirty. They couldn't be precise as to his movements, but his signal was received from a telephone mast close to the Lord Nelson pub. The signal was then detected leaving the town and was last seen transmitting from somewhere near to the junction of the A12 and the A1095.

Ross took out her phone and held it out so that Milton could see it too. She had some sort of custom mapping application and Milton recognised the topography of the area surrounding the town. A circle had been drawn around the junction of the two roads. Milton tried to work out the scale and guessed that the circle had a diameter of around three hundred feet.

"That's where it was transmitting before it went dark," Ross said, laying her finger over a pulsing blue light. "It stopped an hour ago. Either it ran out of battery or it was switched off."

The officer drove them out of town and into the arable fields that surrounded it. Milton watched Ross: she was gazing out of the window, her reflection faint against the glass. She must have sensed that he was looking at her and turned to him. "This is going to be a long night."

"Probably."

"Jesus," she sighed. "I'm going to need something to keep me upright. I'm done in."

"Big night last night?"

"Drinks with friends," she said. "Then I might have stayed out a little too late afterwards." She smiled ruefully. "I might have a small hangover."

"If it's any consolation, I've felt better, too."

Milton could see that she was assessing him. She was attractive. The way she wore her hair, the tattoo that he had seen on her neck when her collar had ridden down low— she was fashionable and hip, all the things that he was not. She was younger than him, too, but that was irrelevant. There was no way that she could be interested in him and, even if she were, he was too professional to allow his thoughts to run away with him.

"What?" he said.

"I wondered," she said with a wry smile. "You have the look of someone who likes a drink."

"I do?" he said.

"Takes one to know one," she said.

Ross's smile widened. She was sharp and prickly and indiscreet and Milton found that he liked her more than he'd thought that he would.

The driver interrupted their conversation. "We're just coming up to the junction," he called back to them.

The driver indicated left and they joined the A12. There were trees on both sides of them, with thick darkness between the tightly packed trunks. Milton looked down at the map on the phone. The land to the north ran down to a wide tidal estuary where the River Blyth meandered out to sea.

"Slow down," Milton said.

The road was quiet at this hour; the driver flicked on his hazard lights and crawled along at ten miles an hour. Milton and Ross stared out of the windows.

"Where is he?" Ross muttered.

Milton looked down at the phone. The blue dot had almost travelled across the whole diameter of the overlaid circle and there was no sign of the car. Milton looked back to the window again. They were a hundred yards from the junction when Milton saw it.

"*There,*" he said.

"I don't see any—"

"Stop the car," Milton said.

They were adjacent to a lay-by on the southbound lane. The officer pulled over into the bay. It was separated from the road by a dotted white line, and then, on its left, by a barbed wire fence that prevented access to a stretch of scrubland fringed with trees. Temporary signs had been planted in the verge: one for production staff attending the nearby Latitude weekend, and the other advertising the

Aldeburgh Festival. Milton got out of the car. He had noticed that one of the fence poles supporting the barbed wire fence had collapsed. It was lying on the ground with the barbed wire loose around it. Now that he was closer, Milton could see that tyre tracks had been left in the dusty median, continuing down the slope and into the wooded area below. He stepped over the barbed wire until he was at the top of the gentle slope. It was too dark to see anything beyond the trees. Ross joined him and looked down as he pointed.

"I think he's down there," Milton said.

"I can't see anything," she said.

Milton turned to the police officer. "Got a torch?"

The man went to the car and returned with a Maglite. Milton lit it and turned its glow onto the trees.

"Shouldn't we wait?" Ross said.

"Call it in," Milton said. "I'm going to check."

"Smith—we've been talking about a state-sponsored assassination."

"I'll be fine." Milton drew his pistol. "Just stay here and call it in," he said. "I'll go down and check it out."

He stepped carefully. A vehicle had definitely been down here. Its passage had dislodged a wide swath of dried earth, and footing was treacherous. Milton planted each foot deliberately, little avalanches of grit and dirt skittering down every time he lifted his boots. He was concentrating on getting down safely when he heard steps above him. He turned his head to see Ross following him.

"I told you to stay up there," he said.

"Fuck that. If that's Geggel, I want to know."

Milton put his foot down without checking, and almost fell as loose gravel scattered. "Fine," he said. "Just stay behind me. And don't touch anything."

Milton reached level ground. He brought up the torch and shone it into the trees. They were sparse here, with more than enough space between the trunks for a car to pass through. He shone the light on the ground and saw the tyre tracks again; they ran ahead, passing between two trees. He followed them, made his way beneath the canopy of leaves, and crossed a stretch of bracken that had been flattened to the ground. He walked for a minute, crossed a clearing with trees dotted around, and then saw the moonlight glittering across the surface of a body of water. It was the estuary that he had seen on the satellite map. The terrain became soft and sticky, and his boots were sucked down as he crossed the start of a wide mudflat. He swung the torch from left to right and saw the light glitter off a pane of glass. He tracked back until the beam was fixed on the object; it was the back of a car, tilted so that it was pointing up at a gentle angle.

Milton closed the distance to the car with Ross following a few feet behind him. The terrain grew boggier as he neared the water. It was obvious what had happened. The car had turned into the lay-by but hadn't stopped; instead, it had crashed through the fence and continued down the slope and through the trees until it had come to a rest here, in the mudflats.

Milton held the Maglite against his pistol and approached the car. He maintained a safe distance as he drew alongside. The front of the car had ploughed into soft mud that fringed the water. The engine was silent; the car must have stalled when it came to a halt. Milton shone the light back so that he could look into the cabin.

Milton stepped closer and looked into the cabin. The torch burned bright, picking out the trash on the floor, the scuff marks that had been left on the carpet by muddy shoes, a can of Diet Coke that had been pushed into the cupholder in the central console. A man was sitting in the driver's seat. He was old—Milton guessed that he must have been in his mid-sixties—and wearing a suit that looked shiny and cheap in the unforgiving glare from the Maglite. He was leaning forward, his head resting on the wheel and a deflated airbag. Milton tracked the beam up to his face and saw that his eyes were permanently open, glassy and unresponsive, and that a gunshot had mangled his head.

"Shit," Ross muttered.

"Is that him?" Milton asked.

"Yes," she said. "That's Geggel."

WINCHESTER

26

There had been no time to get a team to Winchester in time to pick up Beck as he left the station, and so Pope was left with no choice but to risk a single-handed tail. He hoped that Beck's suspicions would have been allayed by the time that he had been travelling without—Pope had to assume—having seen anything that might have given him cause for concern.

Beck had stepped into a taxi and Pope had taken the next in line, telling the driver to follow after thirty seconds had passed.

The village of Kings Worthy was two miles northeast of the city. Beck's taxi stopped and the cabin light came on; Pope saw Beck and the driver settling up. He told his driver to continue on until they were around the corner from the house that Beck had stopped outside. He handed over a twenty and then walked back again.

Church Lane was opposite St Mary's Church and was full of expensive-looking properties. Beck's taxi was pulling away as Pope turned the corner. The old man was wheeling his suitcase along a drive, the wheels crunching against the gravel. The house was accessed by way of a set of white wrought-iron gates that were, in turn, reached by the drive. The perimeter of the property was enclosed by a stone wall with a wooden fence atop it. Pope walked by the closed gates and glanced quickly down the drive to the house, taking in as much detail as he could. The building was constructed of whitened brick elevations with shuttered windows visible on two sides. It had a tiled roof with a single-storey slate-roofed extension to the side. Nothing unusual. A normal property, similar to the others around it. There was a plant pot sitting next to the gate pillar; there was nothing incongruous about it, but it was the kind of item that could be moved to signal danger.

Pope couldn't see the door, but, as he paused by the gate, he heard it open and close. He had no way of knowing how many other people were inside the house with Beck. He would have liked the luxury of more time to assess the property, but his orders were clear. He had to move quickly.

He took out his phone and called the Group. He was connected to the night desk and then patched through to Tanner. He reported the situation, that PAPERCLIP was inside the property and that it would be impossible to continue the surveillance were the target to move on. Pope asked for his orders. He was told to hold his position. Backup was on the way.

SOUTHWOLD

27

Milton and Ross made their way back to the road. Ross took out her phone and reported the news of the discovery. The story had just taken an unexpected turn, and, even as she spoke to Shah, Milton knew that they were nowhere near the boundaries of how far it would expand and what it would eventually encompass. That an ex-spy had been murdered had already alerted the police, the intelligence community, and various Firm agencies including Group Fifteen. The fact that the spy's former handler had also been shot to death, just a short drive from the town in which the spy had been killed, meant that they were dealing with something much more serious. It couldn't have been a coincidence. Aleksandrov and Geggel had met in Southwold and, soon afterwards, both men had been killed. A double murder was certain; the hunt would now focus on finding the perpetrator—or perpetrators—and discovering their motive.

They clambered up the loose bank and returned to the lay-by. The officer who had driven them was waiting for them.

"Find anything?"

"He's down there," Milton said. "Down in the marsh."

Ross finished her call and slipped the phone into her pocket.

"What's happening?" Milton asked her.

"They're sending a team here now." She nodded to the officer. "Close the road. Both directions."

The man went to the boot of the car and took out warning signs and flashing beacons. He set off back down the road and started to arrange them.

Ross breathed out. "This is a fucking *mess*," she muttered.

Milton gestured back down to the marsh. "How well did you know Geggel?"

"Hardly at all. He was an old-timer. Retired a year ago. I was given some of the agents off his book."

"Including Aleksandrov?"

She nodded. "Including him."

"So why did Aleksandrov reach out to Geggel and not you?"

"I don't know," she said tersely. Milton regretted the question; he wasn't surprised that she was so agitated. Why would one of the agents that she was running ignore her and contact her predecessor? It was far from a ringing endorsement.

"I met him a few times," she said after a pause. "We didn't get on. He was old fashioned. I think he thought I was too young. And possibly too *female*."

Milton's phone buzzed. He took it out of his pocket and saw that it was from Global Logistics. He turned away from Ross, took the call and put the phone to his ear. "Yes?" he said.

"This is Tanner."

"Hello, Tanner."

"Report, please."

"We've found the handler."

"Leave it to the police and get back here. We're flying out."

"Why?"

"I'll brief you when we're in the air. The helicopter is waiting. Same place."

He put the phone away and turned back. Ross was waiting for him.

"You okay?" she asked him.

"I need to get back to the town."

LOCAL OFFICERS RELIEVED Milton and Ross from their makeshift cordon to establish something more enforceable, and the two of them were driven back into town.

Milton leaned forward and tapped the driver on the shoulder. "Could you take me to the Common?"

"Yes, sir," the driver said.

"Where are you going?" Ross asked.

"That call," Milton said. "I have to leave."

"Why?"

"I'm sorry," he said. "I can't tell you that."

"Smith?"

The driver brought the car to a stop and Milton stepped out. Ross opened her door and got out, too. There was blood in her cheeks and her eyes flashed angrily.

"Come on, Smith," she complained. "What's going on?"

Tanner was standing by the helicopter. He saw Milton and gave him a nod of acknowledgement. Tanner twirled his finger in the air, the signal that the pilot could start the engine. He stepped over the raised sill of the chopper's door so that he could get inside.

Ross grabbed Milton's arm. He let her, stopped, and turned back. The pilot of the helicopter chose that moment to start the engine and the rotors slowly began to spin.

"Don't ignore me," she yelled over the growing roar of the turbines. "We're on the same side. What the fuck is going on?"

"I'm sorry, Jessie. It's classified."

"Where are you going?"

Milton put out his hand. "I really can't say. But it was nice to meet you."

She left him hanging. "Fuck you, then." She spun on her heel and started to walk toward the church.

Milton turned away from her and ducked his head as he passed through the backwash. He clambered aboard and pulled the door shut behind him.

Tanner was strapping himself into one of the seats. "Everything okay?" he called out.

"Fine," Milton said. He pulled on the headphones and arranged the microphone so that it was over his throat. "I don't think MI6 likes being kept in the dark."

"Control's orders," Tanner said, his voice crackling through the headphones. "We're keeping this one in house."

Milton sat down and buckled himself into the seat. "Where are we going?"

"Winchester."

"For what?"

"We think we know who did this," Tanner said. "We know where they live. You're going to pay them a little visit."

RAJ SHAH WAS in the churchyard, his phone pressed to his ear. Ross strode across the Common toward him; by the time she had opened the gate he had finished his call and was walking across to meet her. The helicopter's engine whined and the rotors whipped up another fine cloud of dust and debris from the dry ground.

Ross had to shout to make herself heard. "Do you know what that's all about?"

"Who's inside?"

"Smith and the other guy... Tanner."

"Where are they going?"

"Wouldn't tell me. You don't know?"

"I have no idea." Shah was a dreadful liar—it was the reason he had never worked in the field—and Ross had never had any trouble reading him. She was sure of her read now: he was telling the truth. He really did have no idea.

Shah put his hand on her shoulder and guided her toward the church.

"I don't know how we're expected to work this case when the right hand doesn't know what the left hand is doing."

"It happens," Shah said. "I know it's frustrating. What did you find?"

"Geggel," she said. "He was here. They got him, too."

"Feels like we're stumbling through the dark at the moment, doesn't it? No idea where we've come from or where we need to go."

She nodded her agreement. "The context's missing. We've got a dead spy, a dead agent runner and no explanation for anything."

28

"How long until we get there?" Milton said over the clamour of the turbine.

Tanner looked at his watch. "The pilot said forty minutes."

"Time's an issue?"

"I don't know whether we've found our killers or not, but, if we have, we've got lucky. They should already have been on their way out of the country by now, but if they are still here, we have to assume that they won't be for long. We think that steps might already have been taken. We'd like to get to them before that can happen."

"So send in counter-terrorism."

"It has to be *us*," Tanner said. "This comes from the very top. Officially acknowledged governmental departments are not to have anything to do with this. Officially, the PM wants to make sure that we behave in accordance with the rule of law. We take the high road when the Russians go low."

"Unofficially?"

"He doesn't want to be hamstrung by protocol or propriety. You have carte blanche on this, Number One. We'd like to bring the bad guys in, but if that's not possible, you're cleared to take them out. Them and anyone else you decide might be connected."

Milton nodded his understanding and hoped his nausea wasn't obvious.

"I can tell you a little more," Tanner said. "We think this is Directorate S."

"Sleepers?"

"It looks that way."

Milton had to agree. They had never been able to trace the agent for whom Callaghan had left the data stick at the dead drop. Milton had grilled Callaghan, but it was obvious that he knew very little. There was a description, but it had been dismissed as worthless given that Russian agents were well known for their aptitude in disguising themselves when they had to meet sources on a face-to-face basis. He had said it was a man, that his name was Tom, that he spoke in unaccented English, and that he had seduced him at a nightclub in Brighton after Pride last year. But that was it. Nothing more that they could work on.

"One of them was working Callaghan," Milton said. "You think it could be the same team?"

"I think it's possible," Tanner said. "We're still waiting for the full assessment, but we've already got a decent amount to go on. We've been following a man who goes by the name of Vincent Beck. He's retired—used to work as a teacher. He's been under suspicion for a while; we've had full spectrum surveillance on him—a big team, all the talents. He's always been careful. We haven't seen anything that made us think that he was involved. Until today, that is. We might have got lucky today."

The helicopter settled at cruising altitude and the whine of the turbines dipped a little.

"Beck went out tonight and we followed him. He ended up in a house near Winchester. We pulled Land Registry records—the house belongs to Thomas and Amelia Ryan. Here—this is them."

Tanner took out his phone and showed Milton two photographs. Two pictures were displayed, side by side: they were passport snaps of a man and a woman, both in their late thirties or early forties. Nothing about them stood out on Milton's first inspection.

"These came from the Border Force," Tanner said. He reached across and swiped the screen. The pictures were replaced by a second set of two, these looking as if they had been taken at an airport immigration desk. "These were taken at Heathrow last year. The two of them had just come back from Talinn. They made it look like a working holiday to Estonia but we have reason to believe it was cover for a hop across the border to Russia."

"So they're SVR?"

"We think they might be," Tanner said. "Immigration reports that the two of them came to London from Belfast twenty years ago as students and stayed here. We think the woman's real name is Nataliya Kuznetsov. She was born in Volgograd. Her mother was a party organiser and her father was a senior KGB agent runner based in the Nigerian embassy. She came to London to study at UCL. That's where she met Thomas—at least that's the story they've sold."

"And him?"

"Real name Mikhail Timoshev. We don't know as much about him as we do about his wife. At some point they adopted new legends as the Ryans and set up an online property brokerage. It's a very good front. Property transactions give the SVR a simple line into them. A Russian oligarch sells his Chelsea townhouse; the Ryans act as go-betweens between him and his buyers; the buyers are given funds in Russia to buy at above market value; the Ryans pocket an inflated commission. Neat and tidy."

"And Callaghan?"

"He said that his runner was six foot tall and reasonably well built. Timoshev fits that. Everything else is unreliable given that he would've been in disguise every time he met him. But how many sleepers could they have? There can't be *that* many."

"You'd hope not," Milton said.

"Maybe we'll find out tonight," Tanner said.

Milton grimaced. "This is all circumstantial. A man we *think* might be an SVR agent handler goes to a house in Winchester on the same day Aleksandrov is assassinated. We *think* the couple he's going to meet are Directorate S sleepers. None of that counts as evidence. I'd feel a lot more comfortable if we had a little more to go on."

"We do have more," Tanner said. He swiped on the screen again to bring up another photograph. "This was taken from a camera inside the Barclays on Southwold High Street. Look."

Milton examined the image. The camera was pointing out of a lobby so that pedestrians passing on the street outside were in view. There was a man in shot. He had a heavy beard and wild, untamed hair. Tanner swiped left and right and then repeated it again, swapping between the still from the CCTV and the images of Mikhail Timoshev from the Border Force.

Milton squinted. "You saying that's the same man?"

"Heavily disguised, of course. The hair, the beard, the glasses. We've run the biometrics. The techs are confident."

"How confident?"

"*Confident.*"

"I only ask because sending me into their home might mean that they die tonight. I'd like a little more than 'confident' before I do that, Tanner."

"This is the best we can do. MI6 has a source in the Center. He's been asked to confirm that Kuznetsov and Timoshev are the Ryans, but that's not going to happen tonight and we don't have time to wait. They'll be gone and it'll be too late."

"Jesus," Milton swore.

"It's as good as we're going to be able to do," Tanner offered with a shrug. "If that's not good enough, you'll have to take it up with Control."

Milton stared at the screen and the image of a bearded man walking by the camera. He felt a clamminess, sweat beading on his brow, and turned away to look out of the window.

He saw Callaghan's reflection in the glass, mocking him.

He turned back. "What does Control want me to do?"

"Bring them in. Find out why the SVR would take such a big risk to assassinate an old spy who hasn't been operational for over a decade."

"And if I can't bring them in?"

Tanner drew his finger across his throat. "You know."

Milton felt the nascent throb of a headache. "Who else?"

"Five's on the surveillance. He's there now."

Milton was pleased with that, at least. Number Five was Michael Pope, and he was the nearest that Milton had to a friend in the Group. They had known each other for twenty years, ever since they were in the Royal Green Jackets. They had been in the Gulf together, although in different battalions, but, upon returning to the United Kingdom, Pope had transferred into the same battalion and had then been assigned to B Company, the same as Milton. They had been sent to South Armagh and Crossmaglen, bandit country that was very much in the pocket of the Provos. They had both joined the SAS and then Pope had followed Milton as he was selected for the Group.

"Anyone else?"

"Ten is on her way—we'll meet her when we land. And Ziggy Penn is in charge of intel. I know, before you moan, that he's annoying. But he's also brilliant."

"Yes," Milton groused. "He is. Right on both counts."

"We're investigating the house and the area as subtly as we can. There'll be three of you, fully armed, and we don't think they know they've been blown. They don't know that you're coming. You go in, grab them or put them down, then get out."

"You make it sound so easy."

"I have unshakeable confidence in you, Milton," Tanner replied, a wry smile bending his lips.

PART II

WINCHESTER

29

P ope had taken up position in the churchyard of St Mary's Church. It was open, with a lych-gate that stood alone as if the wall it had once offered access through had been removed at some point in the past. There was a path to the building that cut between the graves and several large shrubs had been planted along it; these offered excellent cover from the house and the occasional car that passed by, while also allowing Pope a good view of the entrance to the driveway. He checked his watch. It was 12.30 am. He had been watching the house for ninety minutes. The temperature had dropped quickly and he wasn't really dressed for a long stake-out. Never mind. He would be busy soon enough.

Another five minutes had passed when the van with the BT Openzone logo came around the corner. It continued around the bend in the road until Pope couldn't see it any longer. He waited a moment to check that no one was watching from the drive and, happy that he was still undetected, cut between the bushes and shrubs and followed the van. He walked for three minutes until he reached a car park that served the Itchen Motor Company. There was a one-storey building set back from the road with enough parking spaces for six or seven cars. The spaces were empty save for the van and a vintage Jaguar that Pope guessed was waiting to be serviced. Pope heard the buzz of an engine and, as he approached the van, he saw a drone detach from the roof and lift off into the night. It had eight mini-propellers and a suite of cameras was cradled beneath the airframe. The drone climbed almost noiselessly and then proceeded toward the house.

Pope reached the van. The driver's compartment was empty. Pope went around to the other side of the vehicle where he couldn't be seen from the road. He tapped on the door and, after a pause, it slid open.

The interior was not what one would have expected to see from the outside. It had been fitted with a console along the opposite wall. There were two monitors, one of them displaying the feed from the discreet 360-degree periscope that poked up from the top of the van and the other showing aerial footage from the drone. There were digital recording devices, a directional antenna that was sensitive enough to discern the details of conversations from distance and a microwave receiver. There was a man at the console.

"Evening, WATCHER," Pope said.

"Good evening, Five."

WATCHER was the operational codename for Ziggy Penn, the hacker from Group Six who was on long-term loan to Group Fifteen. Ziggy was short and wiry with untidy ginger hair, a messy thatch that had not seen a comb —or, Pope guessed, shampoo—for some time. His eyes seemed to bulge from their sockets, sitting above puffy bags that suggested a lack of sleep. His skin was pale, thanks, Pope knew, to a life spent inside staring at computer screens. His face was sallow, the skin on either side of his nose pitted with old acne scars. Pope had worked with Ziggy on a previous occasion and had found him mildly annoying, although the irritation was alleviated somewhat by the fact that he was unquestionably talented at what he did.

The van's ceiling was low, and Pope had to crouch.

"You took your time," Pope said.

Ziggy indicated the van. "It's not really built for speed," he said. "Got here as fast as I could."

"What do you have?"

"Not as much as you'd like," Ziggy said. "I've got the estate agent's plans from the last time the house was sold." He nodded to one of the screens with a plan of the property displayed on it. "And I just put a drone up."

"I saw it," Pope said.

"It's equipped with a day/night camera and a thermal camera. Here." He indicated the screen with the overhead footage and pushed a button; an infra-red shot replaced the feed on the screen. Pope saw the church and, using that as the waypoint, found the house and the van that they were in. Ziggy smirked with self-satisfaction. "I'll station it over the house. I'll take a close look before you need to go in."

"Anything else?"

"Well," he said, stroking his chin. "They've got a standard domestic broadband connection that I should be able to hook into. I'll have a look for alarms and cameras and, if they have them, I'll see if I can take them out. And if—" Ziggy was interrupted by movement in the drone feed. "Wait a minute," he said. His fingers flashed across the keyboard and the display focused on the car. It had already turned off the road and was rolling into the property. Pope saw its brake lights flash as it rolled to a stop.

"Can we get a better look?" Pope said. "I want to see who's driving."

Ziggy moused over and clicked a button. The drone swung several feet to port, opening up an angle so that it could look down at the car as two occupants got out. He froze the footage, drew boxes around the two people—a man and a woman—and zoomed right in. The software corrected the digital artefacts that would otherwise have spoiled the image, lightened the shot and presented an acceptable view of both people.

"That's them," Ziggy said. "Timoshev and Kuznetsov."

"Send it to HQ," Pope said. "And call Tanner for me, please."

Ziggy swivelled in his chair, picked up a headset with an attached microphone and handed it to Pope. He put it on and waited as Ziggy placed the call and then directed it to Tanner.

The call was noisy, with the sound of a powerful engine making it difficult to hear what Tanner was saying. "*Hello?*"

"It's Number Five," Pope said. "We've had a development."

"*Report.*"

"WATCHER has forwarded pictures to you."

"*Hold on,*" Tanner said, then, "*They're downloading now.*"

"I followed PAPERCLIP to Winchester, as reported. He took the train and then got a taxi from the station to an address in Kings Worthy."

"*He doesn't know you're there?*"

"I don't believe so."

"*You don't believe so?*"

"High level of confidence."

Tanner exhaled impatiently. "*These pictures. What am I looking at?*"

"The male and female at the property two minutes ago. WATCHER is running the registration on the car."

"It's registered to a Mr. Thomas Ryan," Ziggy interceded. "The Land Registry has him down as joint owner of the property. The other owner is an Amelia Ryan. Biometric match confirms—that's them. It's Timoshev and Kuznetsov."

"Anything else?" Tanner asked.

"I'm running a full script on them now," Ziggy reported. "I'll have more when it's done."

"As fast as you can," Tanner said. *"What's your recommendation, Five?"*

"There's a lot we don't know. There are at least three adults in the house now: PAPERCLIP, Timoshev and Kuznetsov. Might be more—no way of knowing unless we get closer."

"We're going to need you to take them. That comes directly from Control."

"I'll need backup. Five or six agents would be ideal."

"We don't have five or six. Most of our strength is tied up outside the country. You can have two."

"That might not be enough."

"It'll have to be. I'm two minutes away with Number One. Ten is on her way, too. Hold your position. We'll be with you soon. Report if anything changes. Tanner out."

30

It was twelve-thirty when Beck heard the sound of footsteps approaching on the gravel and, a moment later, a key turning in the lock. The door opened and Mikhail came inside.

He saw Beck and stopped. "Vincent," he said. "Shit. What's the matter?"

"Where's Nataliya?"

Mikhail stepped aside and his wife came through the door, closing it behind her. She stepped into the light and Beck saw that there was an ugly contusion on her forehead. There was a cut from her left eyebrow to the scalp above her right eye and it was picked out with a trail of dried blood. The skin on either side ran from deep black to purple to blue.

"What happened?" Beck said.

"Geggel crashed his car," she said.

"Are you all right? Your head—"

"I'm fine," she said, allowing him to reach up and gently run his fingers down her cheek. "Mild concussion at worst. I had a couple of hours' sleep in the car. I'll be okay. I have a headache, that's all."

"Why are you here?" Mikhail asked.

"Come inside."

Beck ushered them into the front room. He sat down on the sofa.

"Well?" Mikhail said.

"We've been compromised."

He shook his head. "After today? No. That's impossible. We were careful."

"No. Not after today—it might not even be because of you. The Center has confirmed it—we've been blown. They signalled me this afternoon. There's no question."

Mikhail's anger flared. "What the fuck?"

"Calm down," Beck said. "Just relax. You're certain you're black now?"

"Of *course* we're black," Mikhail snapped. "You think we'd come home if we weren't? We're not amateurs. We've been driving for hours."

Beck concentrated on maintaining his *sangfroid*. "I know you're careful," he said. "We just need to be sure."

"We're sure," Nataliya said, more evenly than her husband. Her voice was quiet. She sounded tired. "We took our time. That's why we're late. No one is following."

"What do you mean we've been compromised, Vincent?" Mikhail pressed, his temper up. "How did they *fucking* find out?"

"Please, Mikhail. We need to address this rationally. Please—sit down."

Mikhail was cool most of the time, but he had a propensity to lose his temper when things had gone wrong. Nataliya, on the other hand, never wavered; she was collected at all times and, even now, Beck was not surprised as she reached over and laid her hand on her husband's shoulder. He sat down on the other sofa and Nataliya sat down beside him.

"We have to think about what's next," Beck said. "Working out what happened can come later. The Center will get to the bottom of it."

"They'd better," Mikhail snapped, although some of the anger was gone from his voice. "I'm telling you that we did not mess up. It's nothing to do with us."

Beck nodded solemnly. "This is what I know. I got a flare this evening. The British have breached our security and we need to shut down. We're about to be exposed and we need to shut everything down and get out of the country."

"How could they possibly know that?"

Beck held out his hands. "I don't know, Mikhail. It was just a flare—no detail. I've heard rumours that there might be a leak within the Center. There's no evidence to suggest that a traitor has access to Directorate S, but it can't be ruled out, especially now."

Both husband and wife were pale-faced when he finished.

"So what do we do?" Nataliya asked him.

"We go."

"Tonight?"

"Right away."

They didn't protest. Beck wasn't surprised; there had been close shaves before, but this was of a different order entirely. The British would unravel every strand of their fake lives until there was nothing left to unpick. Their property business would be shuttered and then every deal that had been done would be forensically examined for links to Moscow. Their friends would be interrogated. They would visit the restaurants they enjoyed, the tennis club that

Nataliya had been attending for five years, the running club that Mikhail ran with every Tuesday night. The Ryans knew that they were burned. They were good at hiding, at blending in, but no one could stay out of sight forever, and not when the spotlight was shining as brightly as this.

"We've had bad luck," Nataliya said. "Losing Callaghan was a blow. This—it feels like they have someone inside."

"Maybe. Callaghan was a pity, but we did well with him for as long as we could. He was never going to listen to us forever. He was too impatient. Took too many risks."

"He was an operational nightmare," Mikhail said.

"You ran him well, Misha. That wasn't your fault, and neither is this. But you're burned. It is what it is. You've done enough. It's time to go home, where the president will present you with medals for the sacrifices you've made. For the things you've done for the Rodina."

Nataliya nodded decisively and stood. "Fine," she said.

"I'll load the car," Mikhail said.

"I'll help," Beck offered.

They made their way upstairs. Beck followed Mikhail into one of the bedrooms. He took down a suitcase from on top of the wardrobe and opened it; it was already packed with clothes.

Beck realised he hadn't even asked about the operation. "How was this afternoon?"

"They met," he said. "They talked."

"Did you hear what they said?"

"No," he said. "I couldn't get close enough."

"And?"

"Aleksandrov is dead, isn't he?"

"And Geggel?"

"Dead," Nataliya said, coming into the room.

"Well done. Excellent work. The Center will be pleased."

Mikhail could be hot-headed, but that was not surprising given the stress that he and Nataliya were under. They had been covert for twenty years. Maintaining their secrecy while undertaking work for the Center was difficult and dangerous. It was claustrophobic. Beck had two main functions: he delivered orders to Mikhail and Nataliya and placated them when they complained about what they had been asked to do. And now a third had been added: get them out of the country before they could be caught.

31

The helicopter swooped low over Winchester and continued to the north. The pilot located a football field adjacent to a sports and social club and descended quickly. As the helicopter settled on its skids, the noise from the turbines dropped from a roar to a whine and then a murmur. Tanner opened the door and hopped down to the grass below. Milton followed. The rotors were slowing down, gradually drooping over the helicopter. Hot exhaust gases vented from the back of the fuselage, causing the air to shimmer in the glow of the helicopter's range lights.

There was a car waiting in the dirt car park next to the field. Milton and Tanner made their way across to it. The engine switched on and the lights flicked to life. Tanner opened the door for Milton and he got in. There was a woman sitting in the driver's seat. Milton recognised her.

"Number Ten," he said.

"Hello, Number One."

Her name was Conway. Milton remembered her file: she had served for several years in the Special Reconnaissance Regiment, and had extensive experience related to covert surveillance and denied area operations. She had been seconded to the MI6 team in Yemen to train Yemeni forces fighting al Qaeda and to identify targets for drone strikes. She had been tagged as a potential recruit to Group Fifteen by her MI6 handler during that operation, and Milton had been impressed enough during her selection to recommend her file to Control. Her work had been excellent so far: efficient, decisive, and, when the need arose, ruthless.

Tanner stayed outside.

"You're not coming?" Milton said.

"It's down to you now," Tanner said. "It's your operation. I need to get back to London."

Tanner slammed the door and slapped his palm on the roof.

Ten pulled away.

CONWAY DROVE them into the village and pulled up in the car park of the Itchen Motor Company. Milton and Conway got out of the car and crossed over to the van that was waiting there. Milton knocked on the door, stepped back, and waited until it was unlocked and pulled open. Light shone out of the interior, enough for Milton to see that Michael Pope had opened the door.

"Evening," Milton said.

Pope reached out a hand and Milton clasped it. "Good to see you," he said.

Pope shuffled aside so that Milton and Conway could clamber into the van. Milton looked around, blinking to allow his eyes to adjust to the wash of light that was emanating from the various pieces of equipment. Ziggy

Penn was sitting at a control desk; he swivelled around in his chair.

"Hello, Number One," he said. "Shut the door, would you?"

Milton slid the door closed again. Much of the space in the back of the van had been taken up by the equipment, and it was cramped for the four of them.

Ziggy turned to Conway. "Number Ten?"

Conway gave a short nod of acknowledgement.

"Then the gang's all here," Ziggy said. "Let's get down to it."

"What have you got?" Milton asked.

Ziggy swivelled his chair so that he was facing the console. "Quite a bit," he said. "I've got a drone over the property."

Milton examined a high-definition overhead image of a house and the surrounding area. It was large, with two wings, several outbuildings and the bright blue square of a swimming pool. The northern boundary of the garden was marked by the curve of a private road that offered access to a collection of similarly large houses. The road that they had taken to get to the van marked the southern boundary.

"The property was last on the market four years ago. I found a cached copy of the plans—here."

Milton looked at the screen to Ziggy's left. It was a brochure from a local estate agent advertising a large house. Ziggy swiped two fingers down on the console's trackpad until he had the plan.

"It's big," he said. "Six thousand square feet with the outbuildings. The Land Registry records the sale to the Ryans for just over one and a half million pounds."

"Business must have been brisk," Pope said.

Ziggy tapped a finger against the screen. "Three floors,

eight bedrooms, three large reception spaces and a cellar. Multiple ways inside. You've got doors in through the annex sitting room, kitchen, utility room and study. That's on top of the front door that opens into the hall."

"There," Milton said, turning to Pope and Conway and then resting his finger on the screen. An annex had been built off the eastern wall of the house. There was a double garage, then a bedroom and then a sitting room. "One of us goes in there."

"I'll take it," Conway said.

Milton nodded. "Five—go in through the front door here. Clear the drawing room and the sitting room."

Pope nodded his agreement.

"And I'll go in through the study door here and work up into the kitchen. We clear the ground floor, meet in the hall and then take the stairs up. Have we seen any movement inside?"

"Nothing," Ziggy said. "A couple of lights on, but that's it."

Milton paused to give them a moment to suggest a change to the plan, but both Pope and Conway were silent.

He turned back to Ziggy. "What about security?"

"I've found an agreement with a firm in Winchester. I got into their files and dug out the contract. The Ryans went for the full package—motion detectors inside the house and access alarms on the doors and windows. The alarm rings a monitoring service and also the local police station."

"Can you do something about it?"

Ziggy looked almost insulted that the question needed to be asked. "Of course," he said. "I'll override it. Just say when."

"Anything else we need to know?" Milton asked.

"Not from my perspective."

"Do you have equipment for us?"

Ziggy reached up to the racking that had been installed on the partition that separated the driver's compartment from the cabin and took down three radios and their accompanying holsters. The units were around five inches by three inches, slabs of metal that were worn beneath their arms. The radios had small control fobs with two buttons. One opened a channel to speak and the other broadcast a solid tone for when silence was required: rapid clicks for target moving, three clicks for yes, two for no. Ziggy gave one unit to Milton, one to Conway and one to Pope. Milton put on the holster, clipped the microphone to his collar and pressed the earpiece into his ear. Pope and Conway did the same.

"Put them on channel two," Ziggy said. "Usual protocol. Comms check when you're outside, please."

"You're monitoring signals?"

"Yes," Ziggy said. "Calls and data going into or out of the house."

"And the police frequency?"

"I'll let you know if there's any chatter."

"Weapons?" Pope asked.

"Over there."

There was a large canvas flight bag pushed up against the partition that divided the cabin from the front seats of the van. Pope stooped down to collect it, dumped it on a seat and unzipped it. He took out three UCIWs, the compact variant of the tried and tested Colt M-16. It was 22 inches from front to back and weighed less than six and a half pounds. Each weapon was equipped with a red dot sight on the front accessory rail and Surefire suppressors. Pope handed one to Milton and the second to Conway and took the third for himself. He reached into the bag again, collected six thirty-round standard M-16 magazines and handed them around.

Milton ejected the seated magazine and checked it with the two spares, pressing on the top rounds with his thumb to ensure that they were charged, then pulled back on the charging handle on the top of the upper receiver to ensure that there was a round in the chamber. He released the handle so that the bolt carrier group could travel all the way forward and hit the forward assist to ensure that the weapon was good to go. He slid the original mag back into the magwell, giving it a tap on the bottom so that it was engaged, and then pulled it down to check that it was properly seated. He put the spares in his pockets, one left and the other one right.

"Ready?" he said.

Pope stood, ducking his head against the low ceiling. "Ready."

Conway nodded.

"Let's go get them."

32

P ope pulled the handle and slid the door back. All three of them jumped down. Milton closed the door and turned to the road and the property beyond. They crossed over to the pavement on the opposite side. There was no need to say anything else. They all knew what they had to do. The three of them were experienced operatives, well equipped and benefiting from the fact that the Russian agents inside the house should be oblivious to the danger that they were in.

Milton pointed to the left and held up two fingers. Pope and Conway nodded their acknowledgement, turned and jogged away in that direction. Milton waited until they were out of sight around the bend and then turned and made his way to the east, looking for a spot where he could scale the wall without being seen. It didn't take long to find. There was a stretch of fence that had collapsed. A large tree had pushed through it, splintering the boards. The wall was lower here, too, and the gap was open apart from the bushes and small shrubs that were spilling out onto the pavement.

Milton's radio crackled. "*Group, Group,*" Ziggy said. "*This is WATCHER. Requesting comms check. Over.*"

"WATCHER, WATCHER," Milton said. "This is One, strength ten. Over."

Pope's voice came over the radio. "*WATCHER, WATCHER. This is Five. Also strength ten. Over.*"

"*WATCHER, WATCHER. This is Ten. Strength ten. Over.*"

"Group, Group," Milton said. "Synchronise watches. I have twelve-fifty-seven in three... two... one... synchronise. Over."

Conway and Pope both radioed back that they had the same time.

"Group, Group, I'm going into the garden now," Milton said. "Radio when you are in position and ready to breach. Out."

Milton walked past the opening in the fence, turned back and then dawdled in front of it, holding the compact machine gun to his side as he waited for the car he had heard approaching to carry on by. Headlights lit up the buildings on the other side of the road as the car hurried around the bend, its taillights disappearing as it went on its way. Milton took a breath, clambered onto the low wall and forced his body into the slender gap with a brick pier on one side and vegetation on the other. He found a crease between the branches and pushed through it as quietly as he could.

33

Nataliya opened the wardrobe all the way, unhooked the metal rail that held her dresses, and deposited it, and the clothes, on the floor behind her. She pressed her right hand against the edge of the rear panel, pushing it back enough so that she could slide the fingers of her left hand beneath it. She yanked, hard, and worked the false panel away so that she could get to the void behind it. She took out a bag full of banknotes in all denominations and two passports issued in the names of their emergency legends. She handed Mikhail one of the passports and he flicked through it to refresh his memory: he was to be Johan van Scorel and Nataliya would be his girlfriend, Francine Claesz. They were Dutch, from Rotterdam, and they had been in the United Kingdom for five years.

She and Beck descended the stairs to the ground floor. There was enough moonlight from outside for them to navigate around the island.

"Are you sure you're all right?" Beck asked her.

"I'm fine, Vovochka," she said, using the diminutive of Vladimir, his real name. "A headache. Nothing more."

"I would like you to see a doctor," he said.

"And how am I going to do that?"

"When you get to France. I will arrange for someone to be there."

"I'd rather just get back home. It's been a long time."

Mikhail came back from the garage.

"The bags are loaded," he said. "Are we good to go?"

"We are," Beck said.

"Where are we going?" Mikhail asked.

"There's an airfield at Popham. There'll be a pilot with a light aircraft waiting for us."

"And then?"

"France. Calais. We'll drive to Charles de Gaulle and fly to Moscow via Luxembourg. Everything being well, we'll be back in Yasenevo by this evening. Any issues with that?"

"None," Mikhail said. "All good."

"Let's get going."

CONWAY AND POPE MOVED BRISKLY. The streets were quiet, but that was both a blessing and a curse: on the one hand, there would be no one to witness them breaking into the property; on the other, any passing police patrol would immediately consider the two of them, out late in this kind of rich residential area, as suspicious. There was the small matter of the submachine guns, too; they both carried them held against their bodies on the side farthest from the road.

The road to the north of the property was The Paddock. It was marked 'Private Road – Residents Only,' but there was no one around to notice them as they jogged along it and followed the fence that marked the boundary of the target address. Tall leylandii had been planted to restrict the view over the fence, but one of the trees was sickly and had died back. Conway put her hands on the lip of the fence and, after taking a breath, she put her foot against Pope's linked hands and allowed him to boost her up and over. She was in the garden, hidden from view by a line of shorter shrubs that had been planted in front of the leylandii. Conway crouched down low and scoped her immediate surroundings: she saw a large outbuilding and then, beyond that, a courtyard and the garage block. She looked up. The sky was black, and if the drone was up there, she couldn't see or hear it.

Pope vaulted up now, his boots scraping against the panel until he was over the fence. He dropped down next to her.

She held up her thumb to indicate that the way ahead was clear. She waited another beat, listening intently, and then, hearing and seeing that nothing was out of the ordinary, she jogged across to the outbuilding. Pope followed. The garage was north of their position. The study, where Milton would breach, was one hundred yards to the east.

They exchanged looks. Pope held up his fist and then raised one finger, then a second, then a third.

They split, jogging carefully and quietly to their entry points. Conway had to pass through an open area, but she stayed in the undergrowth at the side of the garden, crouching down low. She reached the garage block. There were two large roller doors; she guessed that Ziggy would be able to hack them, but they would make a lot of noise as they opened. Instead, she followed the wall around until she found the door at the back of the structure that she had seen on the plan. It was uPVC, with a glass inset panel. She knelt down to examine it and saw a simple mortice lock.

Her earpiece buzzed and Milton's whispered voice came over the channel. *"Group, Group. This is One. Are you in position? Over."*

Conway pressed to speak. "This is Ten. In position."

"This is Five. Also in position. Over."

There was a pause. Milton was double-checking his strategic assessment.

"WATCHER, WATCHER. This is One. Report."

"No activity visible," Ziggy said. *"The alarm is disengaged. I'm working on the cameras. Over."*

Conway felt the usual emptiness in her gut. Nerves. She didn't mind. Nerves kept you sharp. On your toes. Comfort led to complacency, and, in their line of business, being complacent was a good way to get yourself killed.

"This is WATCHER. Cameras are offline. Clear to breach. Over."

She took out her lock picks and knelt down at the door. The lock was old and corroded. It would be easy to force.

Nataliya went into the kitchen and was about to open the door to the annex when something caught her eye. There was a monitor on the counter, the screen split into six panels to show the feeds from the cameras that had been installed around the property. There were cameras up high on the corners of the house and all of them were equipped with infra-red so that they could be used at night. Nataliya paused and stared at the screen. A man was standing next to the outbuilding, his back pressed against the wall. The camera was too far away to offer useful detail, but the image was good enough to show that the man was cradling something in his hands.

"*Mikhail,*" Nataliya hissed. Her husband came across and watched the screen. The man dropped down low and, after looking around the corner of the outhouse, he set off toward the main house. The camera was fixed and the man passed beneath it and out of its field of vision.

And then, as they watched, the screen suddenly went black. All six cameras tripped out at the same time.

"Fuck," Mikhail swore. "They cut the feed."

Beck was biting the inside of his cheek.

"How many do you think?" she whispered.

"More than just him," Mikhail hissed back.

"Do you have weapons?" Beck asked.

"Yes. In the garage."

"Nothing else in the house?"

Nataliya reached over to the knife block and pulled out two knives: a long bread knife with a sharp point and a serrated edge and a chef's knife. She gave the chef's knife to Mikhail and kept the bread knife for herself.

"The car's ready," he said. "We need to go now, before they breach. We'll need the guns."

Mikhail clasped the chef's knife, crossed the room and opened the door to the annex sitting room. The quickest way to the garage was through there, and he led the way. They passed through the sitting room and then the bedroom and approached the partition door that opened into the garage. Mikhail paused against the door, listening carefully, and, satisfied that there was no one on the other side, he opened it.

The garage was dark. There was a window in the opposite wall, but it was up close to the garden fence and only a little moonlight was able to filter through. They kept all their junk in here: cardboard boxes that they had still not unpacked after they had moved in, tins of paint, an old tumble dryer. The equipment for the pool had been fitted here, too, with a bulbous pump and a large boiler to clean and warm the water. There was a car in the middle of the space. It was a new Porsche Cayenne, boxy and powerful.

Nataliya went to a large wooden wardrobe that had been left in the corner of the garage. It was used to store tools and equipment for the garden. She opened the door, reached inside, laid her palm flat against the right-hand edge of the backing panel and pushed down. It was the same as the wardrobe in the bedroom: a false back. The panel squeaked as the loose edge rubbed up against the carcass of the wardrobe, moving back enough for the left-hand edge to come forward. She slipped her fingers into the newly opened gap and yanked the panel out, standing it on its side against the wall. The hidden space was ten inches deep and had been rigged up as an armoury. There was a selection of weaponry there: pistols, two stubby MAC-10s, a combat shotgun and an AR-15. She took one of the submachine guns.

"Shit," Mikhail cursed.

"What is it?" Nataliya said.

"I left the passport on the kitchen counter," he said, cursing for a second time.

"I'll go back," Nataliya said. "Start the car."

"I'll go," Beck said. "You're not well."

"I'm fine," she said sternly. "Stay here, Vincent. I'll be quick."

35

Milton had already picked the lock, and now he pushed down on the handle and stepped into the study. The room, like the rest of the house, was dark. There was a computer on a desk and the standby light cast just enough of a glow to show a collection of papers and a wireless keyboard beneath it. There was an armchair on one side of the room and a bookcase on the other. Milton recalled the layout of the house from the plans Ziggy had shown them: the study led into a downstairs cloakroom with Jack and Jill doors that, in turn, opened into the hall. From there, Milton would clear the sitting room and then move into the kitchen. Pope was to the east, at the front door. He would already be inside and clearing the drawing room and sitting room. Conway would come in through the garage and clear the annex. They would meet in the kitchen and then take the stairs to clear the floors above.

Milton gripped the UCIW, swivelling the barrel across the room as he cleared it. It was empty.

He moved deeper into the house.

CONWAY WAS BUZZING WITH ADRENALINE; she took another breath and rested her hand on the handle of the garage door. She pressed down and the door opened, swinging into the dark space beyond.

"*This is Five. Drawing room is clear. Out.*"

It was dark. Conway didn't have a torch, and she wouldn't have wanted to light one even if she did. She waited inside the doorway for her eyes to adjust, waiting as the shapes of the things around her started to clarify in the dim moonlight that came through the open door: a rack of shelves against the wall, cardboard boxes stacked in rows of two, a large SUV in the middle of the space.

"*This is One. Study is clear. Out.*"

She sensed movement before she saw it. She felt someone behind her and, as she stepped forward and started to turn, she saw something moving through the darkness. She moved just in time to see the dim light from outside catching on the blade of a knife that was swinging toward her. She blocked up with her right hand, catching the blade against her forearm, and felt the sharp edge bite through the sleeve of her shirt and into her flesh. Pain flashed up her arm, a jagged bolt of electricity that burned into her brain. The machine gun was in her hand and she tried to pull the trigger, but the impact had jostled her finger out of the trigger guard and, as she slid it through again, she felt a strong hand around her wrist, forcing the gun away and then up toward the ceiling. She managed to slide her finger back around the trigger and the gun fired, three loud reports that echoed around the confined space. A shower of dislodged plaster fell down onto her.

Her assailant was male. He had his left hand locked

around her right wrist, and, as Conway tried to force the gun down again, the man yanked her closer and stabbed at her again. There was nowhere for her to go. The edge of the knife slid into the soft flesh of her gut and was then yanked up, ripping through the wall of her stomach. She felt the strength drain out of her and the gun slipped from her fingers, vanishing into the darkness. She dropped down onto her knees.

The man with the knife followed, and, as he passed through the weak shaft of light from the open doorway, Conway saw his face: it was Timoshev. His expression was determined. Pitiless.

"You've been burned," she muttered through the rending pain. "Give up. This won't help."

Timoshev didn't respond. He stepped out of the light and into the darkness again, his face dissolving into the gloom as he drew closer to her. He was behind her before she could say anything else. He knotted her hair in his fist, pulled her head back to expose her neck, and sliced the blade across from one side to the other. She gasped, unable to draw breath, and, as she saw the blood spray out from her severed throat, she knew that she was done.

Her radio had a panic button and, with the last ounce of her strength, she reached up and pressed it.

36

M ilton had just cleared the sitting room and was working his way back to the cloakroom when he heard the gunshots. He froze, and, a moment later, his earpiece buzzed. Someone had pressed the panic button on their radio.

"This is One. Report."

"*I'm here,*" Pope said. His voice was as tight as a drum. "*Did you hear that?*"

"Ten," Milton said. "Report. Repeat: Ten, *report*. Out."

There was no reply.

"*Shots fired,*" Pope said.

Milton turned toward the cloakroom and started to move. "WATCHER, WATCHER," he radioed. "Ten is not responding, likely down. Over."

"*Acknowledged. I heard gunshots. Over.*"

Milton went into the cloakroom, cleared it, and passed through into the hall. The door to the kitchen was ahead of him. It was open. He thought of Conway, likely compromised, likely dead, and felt the familiar tremor of weakness.

No.

Not now.

Not here.

He paused, breathed in and out, then crossed the hall and stopped again to aim up the stairs to the first floor. It was dark up there, and he couldn't see anything. He moved on and paused in the doorway. There was another door directly opposite him. He saw, just in time, the shadow standing there, half hidden in the gloom.

"Hands!"

The shadow paused.

Milton aimed the submachine gun.

"*Hands!*"

The shadow took a step back and, in so doing, moved into a shaft of dim moonlight from a window in the room beyond. Milton could see more now. It was a woman. Milton fumbled for the trigger.

Callaghan was sitting on the breakfast bar, kicking his heels. There was blood running down his face. You going to do it again? he asked him. You going to kill her, too? Milton looked down at the gun in his hand, at the blood on the floor, blowback smeared on his skin.

His arm fell a little and, as if waiting for the opportunity, the woman pointed a stubby MAC-10 at him. Milton snapped back just in time, falling back into the hall as a fusillade of nine-millimetre rounds streaked across the space. She had fired quickly, and her aim was off. The door frame detonated in a volley of tiny explosions, fragments of wood and paint and plaster stinging Milton's skin.

The pain banished the dream. "I'm taking fire," he called into the microphone as a second barrage held him in place. "WATCHER—call for help. Five—on me."

The barrage ended. Milton heard the jangle of empty casings falling to the floor.

"You've been burned," he called out.

There was no reply. Milton crawled ahead on hands and knees.

"We know who you are and what you've done."

There was another volley of gunfire; this one was not aimed in his direction, though. Milton glanced around the doorframe. There was enough silvery light for him to see the fragments of broken tile and other debris on the floor next to the door to the dining room. Pope would have approached from that direction.

Milton aimed and fired, sending a fusillade in the direction of the target.

"Five," Milton said when the clatter of the rifle had faded away. "Come in. Over."

"The shooter saw me," Pope responded. *"I'm pinned down."*

"Go outside and come around the back."

"On my way."

He heard the buzzing of a motor and then a scraping noise from the direction of the annex. He knew what it was: the garage doors were opening.

He crawled forward and poked his head around the chewed-up doorframe.

Muzzle flash. The submachine gun fired again, and Milton jerked back into cover. The wall and balustrade behind him exploded, chunks of plaster and wood blowing out into the room as the hall was riddled with incoming fire. The plaster fell onto him, coating him in a fine white powder.

37

Nataliya had been taken by surprise. She had almost blundered into the kitchen, had almost run into the agent who had been waiting there. She had fired too quickly, the rounds going high and wide, but it had still bought time to get the passport and retreat. She was backing up when she saw another shadow in the doorway that connected with the dining room. She fired another volley.

She heard the sound of the motor that opened the garage doors and then, immediately after, the grumble of the Porsche's engine. That was her cue to move. The first man called out again, telling her to stay where she was, but she ignored him. She left cover, and, walking backwards so that she could continue to aim at anyone who might try to follow her through the doorway to the kitchen, she crossed the annex sitting room, then the bedroom, and finally returned to the garage.

The doors had just finished opening and, in the wide shaft of moonlight that they admitted, she could see that Mikhail was inside the car. Vincent was next to the armoury, the shotgun held in both hands. There was the body of a woman on the floor.

Vincent had pressed the dead woman's earpiece into his own ear and was monitoring their comms. "There are at least two more," he said, raising his voice so that Nataliya and Mikhail could hear him over the rumble of the engine. "And they've just called for backup. We need to leave."

MILTON FELT as if he was caught between reality and the dream. He was balanced on a precipice, teetering there; it would only take a little for him to fall. He moved through the annex, staying low, stumbling a little, the gun up and his finger held loosely around the trigger. He cleared the sitting room and then the bedroom, finally reaching the door to the garage. The door was closed; he slid next to it, pressing himself against the wall. His breath was coming in shallow gasps and he was sweating, drops rolling down his forehead and into his eyes. He wiped his face with the back of his sleeve.

He heard a car door open and close, took a deep breath, wiped his eyes again, reached for the handle and pulled it down. The door was unlocked. He opened it and, after waiting for a moment, he stepped back so that he could look through the doorway.

There was a car in the garage. The engine was turning over and the cabin lights were lit, casting a greenish glow over the silhouette of the man who was sitting in the driver's seat. He looked into the back and saw another person: a woman, perhaps the one who had just shot at him.

Milton raised his weapon and aimed at the driver.

He straightened his arm and started to tighten his finger

around the trigger, but before he could pull it all the way back, he caught the reflection of a second man in the window of the car. He had been around the corner, hidden, but now he moved into sight, a shotgun clutched in both hands. The man brought the stubby barrel around and fired; Milton fell farther back into the bedroom as the doorframe exploded. He was showered with another cloud of wood and plaster.

He heard the sound of a car closing and then the whine of the engine as the driver fed it gas. Milton rolled low out of the door as the car pulled out onto the drive. He fired a burst into the car, aiming for the engine and the driver's side window. The bodywork chimed with each impact and holes were punched through the glass, but the window held.

The car kept going.

"Targets are in a Porsche Cayenne," Milton said into the radio, his voice hoarse. "They're heading toward the gate. Over."

He saw the silhouettes of two people in the back of the car: the man with the shotgun had joined the woman. He heard the buzz of the hydraulic motor; the doors were closing again. The light from outside narrowed and dimmed as the doors drew together but, before the light was snuffed out altogether, he saw a woman's body on the floor. He recognised the jacket that Conway had been wearing.

"Ten is down. Repeat: *Ten is down*."

38

Pope retraced his steps and, the UCIW clasped in both hands, he ran back into the drawing room, into the hall and then out of the front door. He ran hard, reaching the corner of the building and poking his head around it in an attempt to scope out the garage. A car raced out of it and went by him, the brake lights flaring bright red as it slowed for the turn in the drive, and then the engine roaring loudly as it straightened out. Pope ran after it, making his way around the turn as the car started to accelerate toward the closed metal gates.

He raised the machine gun and pulled the trigger, five short bursts to stop the muzzle climbing on him. The gun chewed through the magazine, sending rounds slapping into the back of the vehicle. The rear window spiderwebbed as bullets punched through it. The car remained on course, the engine whining as it plunged into the dead centre of the gates. The metal screamed as it was torn apart; the gates were ripped from their hinges and spun onto the asphalt, clanging loudly as they slammed down hard. The car raced across the short fringe that separated the gates from the road, the brake lights showing again as it fishtailed right and then left, then winking out as the driver buried the pedal and raced away to the west.

Pope sprinted after it, ejecting and reloading as he ran. He came out of the gates just as the glare of a motorcycle's headlamp approached along the main road. Pope jumped out in front of it, waving his arms. The motorcycle was travelling slowly, and the rider brought it to a halt and put his foot down. Pope grabbed the man and dragged him off the bike, dumping him on the road. Pope caught the bike before it could fall, mounted it, shoved the UCIW around so that it hung from its sling across his back and twisted the throttle. He raced away from the house and sped after the fleeing spies.

BECK FOUND that he was biting his lip. The atmosphere in the car was tense. Nataliya had cursed as the rounds had punched through the rear window, and Beck had reached over to brush away the small fragments of glass that had fallen onto her. They had been lucky: most of the bullets had missed, and the rest had been stopped by the chassis of the car or the luggage in the boot behind them.

Mikhail was driving fast, hitting sixty as he raced out of the village and then squeezing up to seventy despite the narrow, twisting road. Nataliya had half-turned in her seat so that she could look back through the window for signs of pursuit. She was beautiful. Beck sometimes thought of her and Mikhail as the children that he had never been able to have. He had often daydreamed about what it might have been like if they had been allowed to return to Russia together. The two of them had been good enough to let him indulge his fantasy, and he knew that they would have stayed in contact with him even after their professional relationship had come to an end. It was unprofessional, but he loved them. He loved them, and, because he did, he knew what he had to do.

Mikhail glanced up into the rear-view mirror. "Someone's behind us," he said.

Beck craned his neck around and saw the glow of a single headlight in the distance behind them.

Mikhail turned the wheel to the right and swept into a minor road that ran to the north. He put his foot down, quickly racing up to sixty and then seventy. Beck turned around again and saw that the glow of the headlamp was still behind them. Mikhail swung the car onto another minor road and then immediately turned right, making a series of unpredictable manoeuvres that the vehicle behind would be unlikely to match unless it was following them.

They raced through the countryside. Beck turned back. The headlamp was still there.

"Pull over," he said.

"Beck—" Nataliya started to protest.

"I'll slow them down. The longer we wait, the more coverage they'll have. That's a motorbike. Maybe that's all they have now. You won't be able to get away if we give them the chance to bring more."

"But you're still coming?"

He turned to the front, said, "I am," and hoped that she wouldn't be able to read his face. "There," he said, pointing to a track on the right. "Stop there."

Mikhail braked suddenly, the seat belts biting and holding them all in place even as the wheels slithered across the dusty road.

Beck had rested the shotgun next to him. He took it, opened the door and stepped out.

"Go," he said. "Don't wait. Remember: Popham Airfield. I'll see you in Moscow."

He slammed the door before either of them had a chance to speak and waited until the car lurched ahead once more. He could see the glow of the headlamp suffusing the night above the meandering hills. He clasped the shotgun in both hands and walked out into the middle of the road to meet it.

39

Pope gripped the handlebars and gritted his teeth. The targets had a head start and they were driving aggressively and quickly. He knew that it would be impossible for him to follow them without them noticing, and that had been confirmed as the Porsche had taken two sharp turns and then accelerated away at high speed. They were going to try to shake him; Pope would have to try and stay on them until he was able to summon reinforcements. Control's preference that the operation remain limited to Group Fifteen looked fatuous now; they were going to need to call on the police to bring the car to a stop. Pope just had to stay on them until that was possible.

The road was straight for a moment; Pope took the opportunity to reach up to his radio and pressed the button to open the channel.

"WATCHER, WATCHER, this is Five. Can you hear me? Over."

"Barely. Speak slowly and clearly. Over."

"I'm in pursuit of the targets. They are driving a Porsche Cayenne, partial registration BL12. Repeat: partial registration is BL12. We are proceeding west out of Kings Worthy. Over."

"Five, copy that. Over."

The road curved to the right; Pope gritted his teeth as he bent the bike low to the ground.

"Request police assistance. Track my location and get them to close the road ahead. Out."

The road was narrow, with barely enough space for two cars to pass. There was open space to the left and right, with hawthorn hedges marking the boundaries. There was no light; Pope could see no farther than the glow of the headlamp. The wind rushed around him, pushing his hair back against his scalp and stinging his eyes.

A sharp left-hand turn approached. Pope drifted wide so that he could accelerate through the apex and, as he cleared it and straightened out, he saw the figure of a man standing in the middle of the road ahead of him. The headlamp bathed him in its golden glow and threw out a long shadow behind him; Pope could see that he had a shotgun braced against his shoulder and that it was aimed down the road at him.

He yanked the handlebars hard and leaned back. The bike slid through ninety degrees until it was almost parallel to the road. It bounced against the surface and then scraped along it. Pope travelled with it, then released his grip and allowed it to slide ahead of him. He felt the burn of the road's surface against his legs.

He heard the boom of a gunshot, but the lead passed harmlessly overhead.

The bike continued down the road. It started to spin and, as it did, the front wheel clipped the legs of the gunman. The man toppled face first to the ground, his head cracking off the hard surface, his body bouncing once before it crumpled and he lay still.

The bike crashed into the hedge and came to rest. Pope slid by the man, digging in with the heels of his boots until he had arrested his forward momentum. His trousers were ripped and torn, and the flash of pain said that he had abraded the skin on his thighs and calves. Those were minor concerns that he had no time to worry about now.

The road was dark without the glow of the headlamp to illuminate it. Pope waited a moment for his eyes to adjust and then approached, covering the shooter with the machine gun. There was enough silvered light from the moon for Pope to see that his assailant was male and seemingly well dressed. He was face down, his arms splayed above his head. Pope knelt down for a better look. The man was no longer armed; Pope couldn't see the shotgun in the darkness. He reached down with his left arm and turned the man over so that he lay on his back. It was too dark for Pope to see much, but there was enough light for him to recognise Vincent Beck. Blood was pouring out of a gash in his forehead.

Pope stood and gazed down the road. The bike was on its side, wrapped around the trunk of a small tree. The engine was still turning over, and the headlamp glowed through the vegetation. It wasn't going anywhere. He looked beyond it, into the deeper darkness as the road led away. The agents were gone. He doubted that he would have been able to find them now, even if he had transport to continue the pursuit. Beck had sacrificed himself to buy their escape.

Pope pressed the button on his radio.

"WATCHER, I've got PAPERCLIP. Please send pickup to my location. Over."

"Copy that, Five. The others? Over."

"Gone. Have you informed the police? Over."

"I have. But it's late. Minimal assets available. Over."

Pope knew it was a lost cause. Timoshev and Kuznetsov were in the wind. "Copy that, WATCHER. Out."

Pope ended the call and took his phone out of his pocket. He switched on the flashlight and shone the beam on the old man's face. The blood covered his face from his scalp all the way down to his chin, and more was still pouring from the gash. Pope opened the camera app, snapped off two quick photographs, and emailed them to Global Logistics. Then, he put the phone on the ground, the beam shining up, and frisked the man. He found a wallet inside his jacket and flipped it open. There was a driver's licence in the name of Vincent Beck. Nothing else of interest.

Pope looked down at the old man. It had already been a rough night for him. That was a nasty gash on his forehead, but it was just an hors d'oeuvre for what was coming next. Pope didn't envy him. His night was going to get much, much worse.

FARNBOROUGH

40

I t was two in the morning and the motorway was empty. Pope was driving the plain black Range Rover that had been driven to Winchester by one of the Group Three bloodhounds. Vincent Beck was in the back, his hands cuffed behind him. PAPERCLIP had regained consciousness not long after Pope had loaded him into the car. He had been groggy and had grunted and groaned in response to Pope's simple questions.

He followed the M3 northeast, approaching Farnborough on the way to Vauxhall Cross. Pope had pushed the speed up to a hundred and ten. The satnav suggested that they would be at their destination by three at the latest. There was no time to delay; Tanner had already relayed Control's orders that they debrief PAPERCLIP as quickly as they could. Timoshev and Kuznetsov—and any other agents for whom Beck was responsible—would not be in the country for long. If they wanted to stop them, they would have to find them in the next few hours.

"Where are they?" Pope asked, looking up into the mirror so that he could see Beck's response.

"Where are who?"

"Come on, Beck. This isn't going to help you."

"I'm sorry. I don't know who you are talking about."

"You know what's coming. When we get to London— you know, right? It'll be easier this way. Just tell me."

"I'm sorry, Mr…"

"My name doesn't matter."

"I'm sorry, sir, but I really do not know what you mean. I hit my head. I need to see a doctor."

Pope drove on, his knuckles whitening around the wheel. "You're going to have an awful morning if we get to London and you haven't given us anything."

"I'm sorry. I don't know what you're talking about."

What was the point in talking to him? Pope doubted that it would be fruitful and, anyway, there was something to be said for letting him stew in his own thoughts. If he was the agent runner responsible for the two sleepers, then he would know the gravity of the situation that he had found himself in. Despite that, Beck remained composed as Pope followed the motorway. His age suggested experience and he was probably old enough to have a realistic fatalism about what would find him eventually. Death or capture. It came to them all, one way or another. Pope was very aware of it. Not many made it out on their own terms.

They passed a sign for Fleet Services.

"I'm sorry," Beck said. "I need the bathroom."

"You'll have to wait."

"I can't. Please—I'm old. When I have to go… well, you know. I'm sorry, it's embarrassing, but there's nothing I can do. Please."

Pope told Beck to hold on, flicked the indicator and took the slip road off the motorway. He slowed down, turned into the car park and found a space next to the buildings. He got out, went around to Beck's side, and helped him to get down, too. The old man's hands were still behind his back. Pope stood him against the car and, for the second time, frisked him. There was nothing of concern. Pope took the key for the cuffs from his pocket and unlocked them.

Beck rubbed his wrists. "Thank you," he said.

Pope gripped Beck's elbow and led the way to the entrance. The car park was lit by the yellow sodium wash of the overhead lights and they could hear the occasional rush of cars on the motorway. Beck allowed himself to be led, reaching up to remove his spectacles as if to clean them. Pope paid no heed to it until Beck put one arm of the spectacles into his mouth and bit down on it. Pope reached for his hand and pulled it away from his mouth; the glasses fell to the ground and shattered, and, as Pope looked, he saw that Beck had chewed down hard on the arm so that a section of the plastic was missing.

Shit.

Beck was already gasping for breath. Pope manoeuvred him to a bench and lowered him down onto it. He grabbed the spectacles and examined them; the missing piece of plastic was a cap for the compartment that would have held a sodium or potassium cyanide pellet. The compartment was empty.

"You stupid fucker," Pope said.

Beck stared up at him. He was already frothing at the mouth. Pope had been trained on the use of cyanide and knew precisely how it worked. The chemical affected the haemoglobin in the blood, compromising its ability to transport oxygen around the body. Cyanide led to death by asphyxiation. He might have been able to reverse the process with amyl nitrate, but he didn't have any. Pope loosened the old man's collar, but it was hopeless. His lips were blue and, as Pope leaned over him, his breathing grew shallow and, finally, stopped.

LONDON

41

M ilton woke up. He lay on the damp sheets and concentrated on his breathing—in and out, in and out—until he found a point of balance, some equilibrium, something stable that he could build upon. He didn't feel nauseous any longer but, instead, he just felt washed out. His sleep had not been restorative; quite the opposite. It was as if the strength had been allowed to drain out of him, as if his resistance had been scoured away.

He opened his eyes. The bedroom was a mess. He had undressed down to his shorts, and his trousers and shirt were strewn over the back of the wooden chair in the corner of the room. He reached across to the bedside table to his right, scrabbling through the loose change, his cigarettes and lighter until he felt the links of his watch strap. He took it, holding the watch close to his face until he was able to focus on the time.

It was one o'clock in the afternoon. He tried to remember what had happened after he had left the property in Kings Worthy. He couldn't recall what time he had made it back to his apartment, but, he knew that he must have been out of it for several hours. He turned over so that he could look for his phone; it wasn't on the bedside table, which meant that it was probably still in the pocket of his jeans.

He sat up, and immediately wished that he hadn't. His head throbbed and he tasted vomit, stale cigarette smoke and alcohol in his mouth. He glanced around the room and saw the detritus of another lost night and morning. There was a bottle of gin on the floor, resting on its side; there was an inch of liquid still inside it, a damp patch darkening the carpet just beneath the mouth. He saw three crumpled tin cans in the wastepaper basket and a bottle of prescription sleeping pills, the contents spilled out over the floor.

He put his feet down and gingerly stood up. A fresh wave of vomit bubbled up his gullet, and he stumbled to the bathroom to lower his head over the toilet bowl, just in time. His vomit was thin and acidic, followed by mouthfuls of bile. He spat it all out, rubbed the sweat off his face with a hand towel and then ran the shower. He stripped and stepped into the cubicle, turning his face so that the water could splash off him.

He stood there for five minutes, scrubbing away the dirt of the previous day. A wave of guilt swept over him. He thought of the dream, of Callaghan, of the latest in the long line of victims whom he had murdered. He thought of all the others, the men and women, more than a hundred of them. They all visited him in his dreams, the things that he had done replaying over and over again: a knife slashed across a throat, the muzzle of a gun pushed against a head, a chokehold cinched until life drained away. They visited him more and more often. Milton thought of them and imagined all the others that he would be asked to kill if he continued working for Control. How many more victims? How many more dreams?

He felt dizzy and thought that he was going to be sick again; he spat out a mouthful of phlegm, but the moment passed.

He needed to get out of the Group. He had known it before, a thought that drifted through his consciousness like a phantom, but it was tangible now. He couldn't ignore it. He knew that it wouldn't be easy—that it might not even be possible—but he knew, with complete conviction, that his career spent murdering for the government needed to come to an end.

Milton towelled himself off and went back into the bedroom. He found his jeans, fished his phone out of the pocket, and checked the display. There were no missed calls. He didn't know whether that was a good or a bad sign, but he put it out of his mind. He opened the browser and navigated to the page that he had bookmarked, the one that showed the details of the AA meetings in London. There was one near Dalston in an hour. He found clean clothes in his wardrobe and dressed, putting on his shoulder holster with the Group-issue Sig. He hid it beneath his jacket, pulled on a pair of boots and made his way to the door.

42

Milton performed careful counter-surveillance on his journey. He took a bus from his flat in Chelsea, riding it for ten minutes before hopping off and getting another that headed back in the opposite direction. He hurried down into the underground and changed trains twice before boarding the eastbound East London Line train that eventually deposited him at Dalston Junction station. It was a classic dry-cleaning run and now, as he emerged from the station onto the street, he was confident that he was black. It felt ridiculous to have to assure himself that he was not being surveilled by his own people, but this would hardly have been the first time that Control had assigned agents to follow one of his own. Control was paranoid, his neuroses bred in the suspicions of a divided Berlin, and Milton knew that he had to be careful.

He walked east. St. Jude and St. Paul's Church was on Mildmay Grove, a pleasant road to the north of one of the main thoroughfares that passed through this part of central London. It was a warm afternoon and Milton unzipped his jacket a little. Milton could see half a dozen men and women ambling toward the entrance of the church and he felt the same mixture of anxiety and nervousness as he had felt at the hospital meeting last night. He delayed, pausing on the bridge to watch a train as it passed through the cut. The church was ahead of him, on the junction of King Henry's Road. There was a row of terraced houses beyond it that would once have offered accommodation to the workers who had made this part of London their home, but had now been forced out by rising prices that could only be afforded by the professionals who travelled into the city every morning. There were expensive cars parked in bays on both sides of the road, with a leafy canopy overhead. The tall spire of the church reached up high into the afternoon sky. Milton looked back to the entrance and watched as the men and women went inside. He looked at his watch: a minute before two. The meeting was about to start.

He had come all this way. He wasn't going to turn around now. He tried to rationalise it: he would go in and see what happened. He wouldn't speak, and if he didn't like it, he would never have to come again. There was nothing to lose.

The gates that separated the churchyard from the pavement were open, and the blue cardboard sign that had been tied to the railing fluttered in the gentle breeze. Milton reached up and took it between his thumb and forefinger: it was a blue circle with a white triangle inside it and, inside that, two white As. Milton released the sign, watched it twist in the wind, and then, swallowing down on a dry throat, he pushed the gate open and walked up the path to the door.

There was a lobby just inside. The church was built from stone, and it was cool here out of the sunshine. It reminded Milton of a crypt, but it also felt peaceful and calm. A table had been folded open and a large urn of hot water had been set up. There was a collection of dirty cups, a handful that were still clean, and a plate of biscuits. The table was unattended; the woman who Milton guessed had been responsible for the refreshments was making her way into a small hall to the right. Milton followed.

The hall wasn't large, and had rows of stacking chairs along the stone walls. The chairs were almost all taken; Milton guessed that there were twenty-five men and women here. They were talking quietly to one another, the meeting not yet started. There was a table with two chairs behind it. There was a lit candle on the table and a poster had been blu-tacked to the front of it. The poster was made to look like a parchment scroll, with twelve separate points running from the top to the bottom. The poster was headed THE TWELVE STEPS TO RECOVERY.

Milton had hoped to take a seat at the back of the room where he could melt into the background, but he could see that that would be impossible. The chairs were arranged so that they all faced into the middle; there was nowhere that Milton could go where the others would not be able to look at him. The arrangement spooked him, and he was about to turn around and leave when he felt someone behind him.

He turned.

"Hello."

It was the man that he had spoken to outside the meeting yesterday evening. He tried to remember his name, but couldn't.

The man saw Milton's confusion. "It's Michael. We met yesterday."

Milton definitely wanted to leave now. This was a bad mistake. He shouldn't be here.

"You want to sit over there?"

There were two chairs together on the opposite side of

the room. Milton was about to say no, to make his apologies and leave, but Michael was in the way and some of the others were looking up at them.

"Take your seats, please," a woman in the middle of the room said. "Hello. My name is Laura, and I'm an alcoholic. Let's get started."

Michael put his hand on Milton's shoulder. "Just stay and listen," he said. "You don't have to say anything."

Milton flinched at the touch of the man's hand, but he didn't try to leave. He flashed back to the dream again, and the drink and the drugs that he had abused in an attempt to keep his memories at arm's length, and he knew that he had to try something else. His method wasn't working. More than that, it was making things worse; he knew that he would kill himself if he continued on the same path. He was here now. He was black, no one knew who he was, and no one needed to know. Michael was right; he would sit down and listen. What harm could come of that?

43

Milton found, to his surprise, that he enjoyed the meeting. There was a formal structure to it, with the woman who had spoken first—Michael leaned over and whispered that she was the secretary—introducing the speaker who was going to share her story with the others. The speaker was in her forties, Milton guessed, and looked like any one of the women who could be seen with their babies in expensive prams outside the coffee shops in Highbury and Islington. Milton had expected that her story would be dull and have no correlation to his own and, at least in content, he was right. She spoke about a boring life, the tedium of looking after two small children, and a career that she had abandoned for her kids but that she now missed terribly. Milton's first conclusion was that she had nothing to offer him, but, as she spoke about why she drank, he started to see the points of similarity. She had guilt: she loved her children but didn't feel that she was a good mother, and drank a bottle of wine every night to push that toxic thought to the back of her mind.

She resented her husband for his career, his friends, and the normality that she feared that she would never see again.

Milton found himself nodding as she made her points.

Guilt.

Resentment.

Fear.

He knew them all.

The woman finished her story after half an hour and was applauded for it. The secretary opened the floor to those who wanted to share their own experiences, and Milton listened to them, too. He felt his phone buzzing in his pocket as the meeting drew to a close, but ignored it. After a moment, the buzzing stopped.

The secretary brought the proceedings to an end with housekeeping matters, and a plate was passed around for donations. Milton reached into his pocket for a crumpled ten-pound note and dropped it onto the plate with the coins and other notes as it made its way around the room.

He got up and waited for those ahead of him to filter through the door.

Michael got up with him. "How was that?" he asked.

"It was good."

"That was your first meeting?"

There seemed little point in lying. "Yes," Milton said.

"And?"

Milton paused.

"Did you get anything out of it?"

"I don't know. It was peaceful. I needed that. But anything else? I don't know. The speaker didn't seem like she got any answers. No one offered their opinions."

"It doesn't work like that. Can I give you some advice?" Michael paused for a moment, but Milton could see that he was going to give it no matter what he said and so he managed a nod of assent. "We share our stories here, but it's not a conversation. Cross-talk isn't allowed. You share your story, you spill your guts, and everyone else just listens. You reflect on what has been said and look for the ways that their experience is like yours. And then you thank them, maybe share your own experiences, you listen some more, then you leave. That's it."

"But no discussion?"

"It's a room full of drunks. Discussion can turn to argument before you know it, and arguments can lead to a fight. That's the last thing you want in the rooms. We want serenity. Peacefulness, like you said. It's like the best kind of meditation when it's at its best. You've got to come back—the more you come, the better you'll get at just switching off and absorbing it all."

"Are they all like this?"

Michael shook his head. "They're all different. The ones around here are like this: most of us are reasonably well off, professionals, decent jobs. But if you go to West Ham or Plaistow you'll get an"—he paused, searching for the right word—"an *earthier* crowd. I was at a meeting over there on Friday. The guy who was sharing was straight out of prison for armed robbery. Seriously. The man next to me said he was going inside next week. It varies. You've just got to find one that suits you and what you need. Try a few out. You'll get what you need eventually. One day at a time."

The crowd had shuffled out into the lobby. Milton made his way out, too, and Michael followed.

"We go for coffee now if you fancy it," Michael said.

Milton felt his phone buzzing again. He reached into his pocket and took it out. The call was from Global Logistics.

"There's a place down the road—"

"Sorry," Milton spoke over him, holding the phone up. "I've got to take this."

Michael held up both hands, smiled, and stepped back. Milton felt awkward and rude, but he didn't want to go for coffee and this was a good excuse not to. On the other hand, he didn't want to speak to Control either, but he knew that he couldn't ignore him forever. He took the call and put the phone to his ear.

"It's Tanner."

"Hello."

"Are you all right? I've been trying to get you for twenty minutes."

"I'm fine."

"You need to come in. The old man wants to speak to you."

"About?"

"Just come in, Milton. Soon as you can. He's not in a good mood."

44

Milton was sent straight up to Control's office. He remembered the first time that he had been shown up to the room. He had been much younger then, still in the Regiment and itching for a new challenge. He had worn his best suit, the one that he had last worn to the wedding of one of his old SAS muckers, and he had spent half an hour polishing his shoes until he could see his reflection in the caps. He looked down at himself now and could not fail to be disappointed by the comparison. His jeans and shirt had received the most cursory of irons. His boots were scuffed and marked and, as he reached up to rub his temple, his fingers ran through strands of hair that were long overdue a cut. Milton tried to pretend that he had allowed his standards to slip because it was easier to merge into the background when one looked like everyone else, but, although there was truth to that, it was not the reason. The enthusiasm that he had felt back then, and the desire to impress, had all faded away. He was going through the motions now. He had been for a while. He knew that something had to change.

Milton knocked on the door.

"Come," Control called.

Milton opened the door and stepped into the office. Control was standing behind his desk, facing the window with his arms clasped behind his back.

"Hello, sir," Milton said.

"Sit down, Number One."

Milton did. He could see in the reflection that Control had his pipe in his mouth. He took a matchbook from his pocket, broke off a match and lit it. He puffed in and out as he held the match to the bowl; it took thirty seconds to light the pipe, a process that Milton knew Control was prolonging in order to make him feel uncomfortable. It didn't matter; Milton was wise to all of Control's foibles. They had worked together for years. He sat quietly with one leg folded over the other and waited until Control was done.

He inhaled, held the smoke, and then blew it out. He turned to face the room. His expression was grim.

"What's going on, Milton?"

"What do you mean, sir?"

"Are you well?"

"I'm sorry?"

"You've been off the reservation all morning. Tanner couldn't reach you. Is there anything I need to know?"

"No, sir. I don't believe so."

"Penn said that you looked ill last night."

"He did?"

"When you left the property. He said you looked like you'd been sick."

"I had a migraine, sir," Milton said. "I've been suffering from them for the last few weeks."

"A migraine?"

"Yes, sir. They've been interrupting my sleep—I haven't

been well rested. I finished up at the Ryans' house and went home to sleep."

"I see," he said. "And are you better now?"

There was no compassion in the question; it was as if Control was asking a repairman if a domestic appliance had been fixed.

"Yes, sir. I am."

Control watched him shrewdly. "Nothing on your file about migraines."

"They've been recent."

"Have you spoken to the doctor?"

"No, sir."

"Why not?"

"My preference would be to deal with it myself."

Control stared at him for a beat. He was old school; you didn't let something as mundane as a *headache* interrupt your work. You'd need to be shot, or stabbed, or break an arm or leg, but even then, it would be a case of getting patched up and throwing yourself back into the fray. A migraine, though? That wouldn't do.

"See that you mention it next week," he said.

"Next week, sir?"

"I've referred you to Dr Fry. He'll want to speak to you. Make sure you tell him what he needs to know."

This was a black mark against his name; Milton knew it, but he didn't care. "Yes, sir," he said. "Thank you. I'll do that."

Control stood and started to pace the carpet behind his desk. "I need to update you on PAPERCLIP."

"Number Five apprehended him."

"Yes," Control said. "He did. But then he killed himself. Cyanide capsule hidden in the stem of his glasses. We lost Kuznetsov and Timoshev, then we lost him. You can understand why I'm unhappy with how the operation was handled. It's been a bit of a fuck-up, hasn't it? A comedy of errors—one thing after another. The government is going to want to know what happened and, frankly, I have no idea how I'm going to dress it up."

There was a knock on the door.

"You'll be glad to hear, though, that you have a chance to make amends. You and Five, actually. Come."

The door opened and Tanner came inside. "He's here, sir," he said.

"Send him in."

Milton turned in his chair as Pope stepped into the office. Tanner said he would bring in some refreshments and hobbled away.

Control rested the pipe in an ashtray. "Good afternoon, Five."

"Sir."

Control indicated the chair next to Milton and Pope took it.

"You two are going to have to cancel any plans you might have been unfortunate enough to have arranged. What happened yesterday obligates a strong response from us. You dropped the ball—the illegals are gone and PAPER-CLIP is dead. But we have another source of intelligence and we have another opportunity. I'm going to give you the highlights, and then I'm going to tell you what I want you to do."

45

Control puffed on his pipe. "We have a source of intelligence within the Center: the cryptonym is BLUEBIRD. We were told that Beck was a Directorate S handler, but BLUEBIRD didn't know about the operation against Aleksandrov until after the fact. We were fortunate that we had Beck under surveillance, and that he led us to Timoshev and Kuznetsov. We've confirmed that they murdered Aleksandrov and Geggel yesterday."

"Do we know why?" Milton asked.

"Why they did it?" Control shook his head. "BLUEBIRD suggests that Aleksandrov was in possession of a list of all the SVR's agents in Western Europe, and that he wanted to sell it to us. Aleksandrov approached Geggel to act as intermediary." Control blew smoke. "Geggel's phone records have been examined—it turns out that Aleksandrov called him last week. We don't have any record of what was said, but it was important enough for him to drive over from London to see him."

"And Geggel didn't tell anyone? Didn't call it in?"

"He did not," Control said. "And that's not surprising. I

knew him a little. He'd been around. He left SIS under a cloud. Made a mess of one of the files that he was handling —a source in the GRU was burned and it looked like he might have been to blame. He wasn't ready to retire and they rather pushed him toward the door. If you asked me to guess, I'd say he went to see for himself whether Aleksandrov had anything of interest and, if he decided that he did, he was going to be the one to bring it in."

"And we believe the intel?"

Control shrugged. "Aleksandrov was a nobody. He gave us decent intelligence when he was operational, but that was years ago. Something changed that made him a target. Offering us a list of active agents would be enough to put him in the crosshairs."

Control took another match and lit the pipe again.

"Where are Timoshev and Kuznetsov now?" Pope asked.

"On their way back to Russia. They were exfiltrated out of a private airfield after you lost them. They had a pilot fly them over the channel to France. ATC confirmed the vector —they took off from Popham and landed at Calais-Dunkerque at just after six. We've contacted the DSGE, but the odds of finding them now are slim. They will have picked up new legends as soon as they arrived. If it were me, I'd get them into the Netherlands and fly them out of Schiphol, but it could be anything. They're gone. We can't stop them getting home."

Pope crossed his legs. "So what do we do now?"

"We go after them. BLUEBIRD thinks he might be able to help us find them again. The two of you are going to go to Moscow and set up there. As soon as we know where they are, you are going to take them out." He got up again and walked to the window that overlooked the grey river. "They killed those two men to make a point. The Center is sending a message: they want any other dissident, inside or outside the motherland, to know that the SVR has a long memory and a long arm. And they were making a point to us, too. To the security services. To the country. It was an *insult*. They don't care because they don't see us as a threat. They are thumbing their noses at us, and we cannot allow that to stand. So that's what you're going to do. You're going to go to Moscow, you'll find the sleepers, and you'll kill them both. And then you'll find whoever it was who ordered the operation and you'll kill them, too. We're going to show our Russian friends that there are consequences to their actions. We won't be anyone's punchbag."

Milton sat quietly. An operation in Moscow would be difficult, to say the least. An operation in Moscow against two high-profile SVR agents would be something else entirely.

"There's an Aeroflot flight out of Heathrow at ten forty-five tonight. Pick up your legend from Tanner. You'll be briefed at Moscow Station at seven tomorrow morning. I want this taken care of as quickly as possible. No mistakes this time. *Absolutely* no mistakes. Understand?"

"Yes, sir," Pope said.

Control didn't take his eyes off Milton. "Number One?"

"Sir?"

"See that it gets done. Take them both out. Dismissed."

PART III

MOSCOW

46

Aeroflot flight SU 2585 was delayed on its departure from Heathrow, finally taking off at five minutes past midnight. The captain apologised, but said that he was confident that they would be able to make up the lost time en route. It was a standard flight for the carrier. The cabin crew were efficient but not particularly attentive and the late snack that was brought around was cold and unpleasant. Milton passed up the food, asking instead for a vodka and tonic. He drank it as he studied the legend that Tanner had supplied.

The name was his usual one—John Smith—but this time he was a diplomat in the British Embassy reporting to work in the Economic Section. He had been educated at Colchester Royal Grammar School and Trinity College, Cambridge, where he had obtained a BA and then a PhD. He had joined the Foreign and Commonwealth Office and was then posted to Bucharest where he had worked as Second Secretary for three years. Following that, he had been transferred to Ankara and then Rome and then, bringing the file up to date, he was moved to Moscow. He was single, had a flat in Highgate, enjoyed cooking and supported Arsenal. He went over the details again, committing it to memory. He had done the same thing many times before, and he knew it would stick.

Pope was several rows ahead of Milton in the cabin; he could see the back of his head. They would maintain a discreet distance until they met at the embassy for their briefing in the morning. They both knew that there was a good chance that there would be SVR agents on the flight with them, and they did not want to give them any reason to increase the surveillance that they would be subjected to upon landing. Milton didn't even know Pope's legend; he might be a diplomat, like him, but he could equally be a trade delegate or a cultural attaché. It made little difference.

The vodka slid down easily and Milton ordered another. He downed that, too, and then put his chair back as far as it would go, strapped himself in and allowed the drone of the engines to lull him to sleep.

THEY LANDED at Sheremetyevo at four in the morning. The terminal was quiet and they were able to disembark and make their way to immigration quickly. Milton made his way across the lines until he was in the diplomatic channel, and then breezed through the checks and into the arrivals lounge. The embassy had sent a car for him and the driver was waiting, holding a sign with his name on it.

"Hello," Milton said.

"Mr. Smith?" He was English.

"That's right."

"Come with me, please."

The man offered to take Milton's suitcase, but he shook

his head and said that he had it covered. Milton followed the driver through the airport to the parking garage.

"Pleasant flight, sir?"

"It was fine."

Milton looked around at the other travellers who were making their way to the garage. He saw a few whom he recognised from the aircraft, and others whom he had not seen before. He glanced at the ones following behind them —a young man with tattoos who was carrying a guitar in a case, an elderly couple, a middle-aged woman—and wondered which of them worked for the FSB, the domestic intelligence service. He saw the CCTV cameras positioned overhead. Those feeds would all end up in the Lubyanka and would, he knew, have already been examined by the clerks who were paid to scrutinise new arrivals and cross-check them with known intelligence agents. It was a long time since Milton had been to Russia, and the identities and likenesses of Group Fifteen agents were known to a vanishingly small cohort of senior staff. Milton did not believe that there was a file on him, but he knew not to take anything for granted.

They reached the garage, took the elevator to the second floor and reached a Mercedes with blacked-out windows. The driver opened the rear door for Milton and slid into the front.

"We've booked you into the Lotte," the man said as he pulled out.

It had been raining, with a fine drizzle still hanging in the air. A large municipal building faced them as they drove away, and, with its pink and yellow tiers, it reminded Milton of a Battenberg cake. An illuminated sign on the roof announced MOCKBA, the glow reflecting off rain-slicked asphalt. Milton stared out of the window. It felt real now. He was in Moscow, in enemy territory. He was naked, too, an agent operating without backup. He was always reminded of the espionage films and novels that had enthralled him during his youth, and the malign influence of the all-powerful KGB. That body might have been disbanded, but the change was little more than window dressing. The FSB was its successor, with a reach and malignancy that was every bit its equal. Milton and Pope were alone against it now, and if they were compromised, there would be little support.

He leaned back in the seat as they hurried through the quiet streets. He had grabbed an hour of fitful sleep on the flight, but that was all; his only rest since Friday had been his drunken stupor this morning, and he had an early start at the embassy today. It would just have to do.

THE HOTEL WAS on Novinskiy Boulevard and was one of the best in Moscow. It was a large building that curved around a bend in the road, the neon sign on the roof burning bright against the slowly lightening sky. The desk was staffed twenty-four hours a day, and, after Milton had checked in, he was escorted to his room by a polite and attentive porter. The woman spoke excellent English, and asked Milton about his trip and what he hoped to do during his visit to the city. Milton suspected that her good nature was not entirely genuine, and that he was being probed for information that might be passed along to the FSB division that specialised in counter-intelligence and the monitoring of foreign visitors.

"I'm going to be working at the British Embassy," he said.

They reached the second floor and the porter indicated that they should turn left to find room 261.

"We have many diplomats from the embassy," the woman said.

Milton knew that, of course; it was the reason the room had been reserved for him here.

"Is it close?" he asked.

"You haven't been before?"

"First time."

"Yes, it is close. You can walk there in fifteen minutes."

"Excellent," Milton said.

They reached the door. "What will you be doing there, Mr. Smith?" she asked him.

"Working on a deal to buy more Russian oil and gas. Not particularly interesting, I'm afraid."

Milton said that he was tired and how much he was looking forward to his bed. The porter shone a bright smile at him as she held a keycard to his door, said that she hoped that he would find the bed comfortable, and, after taking his tip, she left him alone in his room.

Milton checked his suite. There was a large marble bathroom and a similarly generous bedroom. He had no doubt at all that the room was bugged, but he made no effort to find the devices. That would be the behaviour of a spy, and John Smith was an economist. Milton didn't mind that he was observed. He undressed and got straight into bed. It was just after five. The briefing was at seven. He had an hour; not nearly enough, but it would have to do. He closed his eyes and was asleep in minutes.

47

Milton woke at six. He felt rough, with not nearly enough sleep in the bank, and had to stand under a cold shower for five minutes to wake himself up. He stood before the mirror and stared at his reflection. He looked tired. He needed a cigarette, but that would have to wait.

He dressed in the business suit that he had brought with him, pairing his white shirt with a blue tie. He polished his shoes with the kit he found in the cupboard and put his credentials, wallet and phone in his pockets. He looked down at the opened suitcase on the bed; he would leave it there. He knew that they would go through his things, but they would find nothing that contradicted his legend. He was an economist, posted to the embassy. He would leave his laptop, too. They would be able to crack the rudimentary password with ease, but all they would find would be a collection of spreadsheets and documents that related to the deal that he was here to work on. Milton did not anticipate needing the computer, but if he did, the encryption key that he carried in his wallet would enable him to use it without fear of his communications being eavesdropped upon.

He went down to the lobby, used his card to buy some roubles from the receptionist, and stepped outside. He purchased a packet of cigarettes from a vending machine he found on the street, tore off the cellophane wrapper, tapped out a cigarette and lit it. The embassy was to the west. He followed Novinskiy Boulevard, its eight lanes already thick with traffic, and then turned into the quieter Protochnyy Pereulok. It was obvious that he was being followed. He saw a man and a woman who appeared behind him as he made his way off from the hotel, and noticed a car with tinted windows that was parked near the junction of the main road. Milton made no effort to shake the surveillance. He made his way along the pavement, passing apartment blocks and cheaper hotels until he reached the broad highway that overlooked the river. There was suddenly a sense of open space; the water was wide here, with long bridges that crossed to the other side and the impressive buildings that made up the political district.

He arrived at the embassy and showed his pass at the front door. The guard looked down at it, checked that the photograph was correct, and asked him to confirm his name. Milton did. The guard wished him good morning and stepped aside. Milton removed his coat, watch, belt and shoes and passed through the scanner, collected his personal belongings and waited in the lobby for someone to meet him.

A MIDDLE-AGED WOMAN joined him after five minutes. "Mr. Smith," she said, maintaining his legend in the event that the intelligence services were listening in this unsecured part of the building. "My name is Susannah Jones. How are you?"

"Very well," Milton said. "Tired. I got in early this morning."

"We have some very strong coffee brewing. Come this way, please."

Jones led the way through an exterior courtyard and then up a set of marble steps to the attic. This was where the embassy held briefings when classified intelligence might be discussed. The stairs ended in a large metal door of the sort one might expect to find securing a bank vault. The door was open and, beyond it, there was the day door with the cipher lock, and then a wire gate that was opened by the entry of a code on the electric keypad that was fitted to the wall next to it.

Jones led Milton through all the layers of security until he was inside the briefing room. Pope was already there.

"Morning," he said.

"Won't be a moment," Jones said. "Help yourself to coffee."

She turned and made her way back outside. There was a tray on the table with a vacuum flask of coffee and half a dozen china mugs. Pope filled two of the mugs, gave one to Milton and then sat down next to him.

"How's your hotel?" Milton asked.

"Almost certainly bugged. Yours?"

"Same. And I was followed here this morning."

"Me too," Pope said. "We're going to have to be thorough when we're ready to move."

Milton nodded his agreement, and then looked around the room. It was bare, with just the table and chairs. There was a laptop on the table, fixed with a lockable seal that helped guard against unauthorised access; the machine would have been preloaded with a secure software suite at GCHQ and then pouched to the embassy to ensure that it was not tampered with. The room was lit by overhead fluorescent tubes that would also have been imported from London to remove the risk that units sourced from the domestic market might have been provided with bugs included. There was a line of small windows on either side that were guarded by bars, then steel shutters, and finally triple-glazed glass. The lack of natural light, combined with the harsh glow of the tubes overhead, made for an unpleasant space. The price of security, Milton thought.

"Who's briefing us?" he asked.

"Station Chief," Pope said. "Just waiting for a fourth person."

"He say who that is?"

"Station Chief is a *she*, actually," Pope said. "And, no, she didn't."

They had been given very little in the way of information, save that they should report to the embassy for an operational briefing. Milton didn't like to be unprepared, but he knew that the planning and execution of the operation would be left to him and Pope. Control had made it clear that speed was important, but Milton would balance it, so far as was possible, with careful organisation.

"Gentlemen," said a voice from the doorway behind them.

Milton turned around. A middle-aged woman in a black skirt and jacket was standing just inside the wire gate.

"I'm Elizabeth McCartney," she said, stepping inside and offering her hand. "I'm the chief here."

Milton shook her hand but, before he could respond, he saw a second person ascending the stairs.

It was a second woman. She paused at the doorway and her mouth fell open.

"You?" she exclaimed.

He shook his head in wry amusement.

Jessie Ross.

"Hello," he said.

"What the fuck?"

"Do you two know each other?" McCartney asked.

"We met on Sunday," Ross said. "Smith was assigned to the Southwold investigation. Military liaison."

"That's right," Milton said.

"What is it today? Still the same?"

Milton turned to indicate Pope. "We work for a government agency. I can't tell you what that is, but I can say that we've been sent here to find the agents who are responsible for the assassinations in Southwold."

"What government agency?"

"I'm sorry," he said. "That's classified."

Milton watched her face as he spoke. She looked from him to Pope and back again. Her eyes sparked with irritation, and there was blood in her cheeks.

"This is nuts," she said, throwing up her hands. "'Find the agents responsible?' What does that mean? Are you going to give them a good talking to? Tell them not to do it again?"

"No," Milton said.

"So I'm being partnered with a killer, then. A murderer. Yes?" She glanced over at Pope and corrected herself. "Excuse me. *Two* murderers."

"Is this going to be a problem?" McCartney said.

"I'm sorry," Ross responded, "but why am I here? I don't understand. Why do you even need me?"

"You agreed to come," McCartney said evenly. "You volunteered, I believe."

"Yes," she said. "Before I knew..." She threw up her hands. "Before I knew *this*."

"Raj Shah agreed with you because it made sense," McCartney said. "You're fairly new to the Russian desk. It's possible they"—she pointed to the one uncovered window, and the buildings that crowded the far shore of the Moskva —"won't even know who you are. And if they don't have anything on you, you'll find that movement is a little easier. Believe me—that's a benefit here, and it doesn't usually last long."

"So I'm new and they don't know who I am. That's it?"

"And you've been here before," McCartney added patiently. "You studied here. Your Russian is flawless."

The compliments mollified Ross a little. She turned to Milton and Pope. "And them? What do they do?"

"You're right," McCartney said. "We can't ask the Russians to put the bad guys on the first BA flight back to London. We need to draw a line. They're going to draw it."

48

P rimakov took the executive elevator to the fourth floor. He folded his arms and tapped his foot impatiently, glancing up at the shield of the SVR, the Star and Globe, that had been fixed to the wall of the car. The doors opened and he emerged into the gloom and silence of the corridor that led down the centre of the floor. The carpet was thick, muffling the sound of the footsteps of the men and women who worked here. No one spoke, the silence disturbed only by the clacking of keyboards in the typists' pool. Primakov looked left at the portraits of previous directors of the KGB, each man glaring down at him as he passed, as if disapproving of his illicit use of agency resources to further his own goals. The opposite wall was hung with the portraits of the directors of the 'reformed' SVR; a sick joke, he thought, knowing from personal experience that the current incarnation of the agency was at least the equal of its murderous forerunner.

Primakov went through into his office and sat down behind the grand desk, a slab of oak finished with a leather top. He swivelled his chair so that he could reach the credenza and picked up one of the telephones, buzzing his secretary to ask her whether Nikolaevich had arrived for the meeting yet. The woman said that he hadn't, and would he like her to contact the deputy director's office to see where he was? Primakov looked at the clock on the wall. Nikolaevich was already thirty minutes late, and it was he who had asked for the meeting. He knew this was one of his old comrade's favoured tricks, a not-so-subtle gesture designed to remind him that Nikolaevich was the more senior man. It irritated Primakov, and he would not normally have stood for it, but he knew that he might need Nikolaevich's help if his plan did not succeed, and so he decided to make a show of just how patient he could be. He told his secretary that there was no need; he would wait.

Primakov turned to look at the deep fringe of forest that encircled the building. He always found the view peaceful, and a little tranquillity was precisely what he needed now. Patience was one thing, but that didn't mean that Nikolaevich's game playing had no effect on Primakov's mood. Primakov hated having to rely on others at the best of times, especially when it came to a rival. The two men had known each other for twenty years, ever since they had met at the Academy, and their careers had mirrored one another. Primakov had been an agent in Madrid. Nikolaevich had served in Bruges. Primakov had been made the *rezident* in Caracas. Nikolaevich had been made the *rezident* in Rio. They had returned to the Center within three months of one another and had both been promoted: Primakov was placed at the head of Directorate S while Nikolaevich was made First Deputy Director of the FSB. Both knew that the other coveted the directorships of their respective agencies. Those were the very top rungs of the ladder, with the only report being to the president himself. Primakov had had designs on his advancement right from the start, and although Nikolaevich was less obvious in his covetousness, he wasn't fooling anyone; he most certainly wasn't fooling Primakov.

"Nikolai."

Primakov saw the reflection in the window and turned. Nikolaevich was standing in the doorway.

"Alexei," Primakov said. "I told my secretary to—"

"I told her I'd go straight in," Nikolaevich said. "I'm already late enough as it is. My apologies. The president wanted a report on a Chechen cell we've been keeping an eye on. The meeting lasted longer than I had expected." There it was: a casual reference to a meeting with the president. It was classic Nikolaevich. He loved to present an impression of humbleness, but it was a show; he wanted Primakov to know that he had been to the Kremlin, that he had the president's ear.

"You wanted to see me," Primakov said. "What can I do for you?"

Nikolaevich took a seat. Primakov went to the sideboard. He had asked Catering to prepare tea for them both, and they had delivered a silver salver with two antique tea-glass holders. He gave one to Nikolaevich.

"This is a little delicate," the major-general said.

Primakov opened his hands wide in a gesture he hoped would appear accommodating, and one that he hoped might mask the sense of foreboding he felt. "Please," he said. "How can I help?"

"You have a source in MI6."

It wasn't a question.

"We do," Primakov said.

"And this source—he or she is well placed?"

"Reasonably," Primakov fenced. "What is it, Alexei—how can I help you?"

Nikolaevich rubbed his temples. "I have a problem, and I wondered whether you—your source—might be able to assist."

Primakov felt a little twist of anxiety in his gut and took a sip of his tea to buy himself a moment. This had to be handled delicately. "Of course, but within reason. PROZHEKTOR is very valuable."

"That's the cryptonym?"

Primakov said that it was.

"Searchlight." Nikolaevich gave an approving nod. "Shining a light onto MI6's darkest secrets?"

The words sounded gauche when Nikolaevich said them, and Primakov felt a pulse of irritation. "Indeed," he said. "They have been an effective source, and they promise more. But, because of that, I wouldn't be able to agree to anything that might jeopardise their position."

"Their position," Nikolaevich mused. "Where is that?"

"You know I can't say, Alexei. Please—what is your problem? I'll help if I can."

Nikolaevich slumped back in the chair. "Very well. I hope we can keep this between ourselves." He waited for Primakov to indicate that he wouldn't share whatever it was that Nikolaevich was about to tell him.

"Fine," Primakov said.

"Thank you. Two British agents entered the country this morning. We picked them up at Sheremetyevo and we have surveillance on them, but I wondered if there was anything that PROZHEKTOR might be able to tell us about them. More specifically, what they are here to do."

It was early, but Primakov glanced over at the decanter of vodka on the sideboard and yearned for one to steady his nerves. He couldn't, of course; the last thing he wanted was for this cunning old fox to know that he was anxious.

"British agents come here all the time," he said. "Why are these two any different?"

"I'm thinking about the operation with Aleksandrov. I have my own sources, of course, and the suggestion is that they are from Group Fifteen. And that makes me nervous."

"I can't speak to that," Primakov said.

"I realise that. I suppose I'm a little embarrassed to know so little about them—ignorance will not be looked at kindly by the president if something were to happen."

"What could happen?"

"There are several possibilities. Your agents, for example. The ones who carried out the operation. They are in Moscow?"

There was no point in pretending otherwise; it was common knowledge. "They are."

"It crossed my mind that if the British knew who they were, they might try to take revenge. It would be the kind of thing that they would do. You are as familiar with Control's file as I am, I'm sure—his vengeful streak is well known."

"He wouldn't be so foolish as to do something like that."

"Why not? We killed one of theirs on their soil. It would be a *quid pro quo*."

Primakov stood, eager to bring the conversation to an end. "Thank you for mentioning it, Alexei. I will review the security arrangements for my agents."

Nikolaevich stayed seated. "And I will continue to watch the two of them. If, in the meantime, you felt able to ask your asset whether he or she knows anything about what they might be doing here, any information would be very gratefully received."

Primakov had to resist the urge to reach down and pull Nikolaevich to his feet.

"What about our own mole hunt?"

Primakov fought back a sigh. Nikolaevich wasn't finished. "Yes? What about it?"

"I had hoped that our colleagues in Line KR would have smoked out whoever it is by now."

"But they haven't. We must continue to be cautious."

"Until they have been found, we must assume that they are providing intelligence to the British—intelligence like the location of your two sleepers. That's why I am nervous about these two agents."

"But that presumes that the leak is in my department. And I'm confident that it is not."

Nikolaevich smiled and, finally, he stood. "It goes without saying that any help you can provide will be treated as a personal favour. It would be one that I would never forget; you would be able to call on it whenever you wanted and I would be honour bound to come to your aid."

"Thank you, Alexei," Primakov said. "I understand. I'll see what I can do."

LONDON

49

C ontrol was unhappy that his morning had been interrupted. He had received a call that he was urgently required to attend a meeting at head-quarters at ten. It was inconvenient, to say the least. He had scheduled a call with Moscow Station to discuss the operation against the Russian sleepers, and now he would have to postpone it. He queried the request with Tanner, but, after checking, his adjutant had reported that there was no way he could absent himself. Control asked for clarification on what was to be discussed, but Tanner was rebuffed and reminded that this was classified Strap Two-Level Secret. Eyes only.

It was only a short walk between the Global Logistics building and the monstrosity that had been foisted upon the Secret Intelligence Service as its new base of operations. It was a pleasant morning, but the good weather did nothing to brighten Control's mood. He made his way in through the main entrance, passing through the mundane ignominies of the security scanners, and made his way up to the executive floor. The meeting was being held in one of the bland conference rooms next to the offices of the senior staff. Control was evidently the last attendee to arrive and, after acknowledging the others around the table, he took his seat and looked around. It was a particularly high-powered meeting; perhaps it was important, after all.

There were eight others around the table. The government was represented by two ministers, together with their private secretaries. To his right was Harry Cousins, the defence secretary. Cousins was a stolid, reliable political operator, resilient enough to have enjoyed a long career under three different prime ministers and yet not devious or avaricious enough to progress beyond his current station. Next to Cousins was Christopher Younger, the foreign secretary. Younger was something of a media darling, derided by those in the intelligence community for his fondness for the limelight, his embarrassingly naked ambition and the occasional buffoonery that caused frequent embarrassment abroad.

Representing the intelligence agencies were Sir Benjamin Stone and Vivian Bloom. Stone was SIS Chief; he was in his mid-fifties, a reasonably large man with a middle-age spread that he seemed uninterested in arresting. Bloom was the most interesting of the other senior attendees. He acted as the permanent liaison between the Firm and the Government. His nickname within the building was the Reverend. This sobriquet was derived from a brief appointment as the sub-rector of Lincoln College, Oxford, and, perhaps, the unruly dress sense that put Control in mind of a bumbling rural vicar. His appearance was deceiving, though, and Control had seen many people make the mistake of underestimating him. He was in his late sixties and had worked in the intelligence business since the start of the Cold War. One did not manage that sort of tenure without ruthlessness. Bloom was well connected, unfailingly zealous and duplicitous to a fault.

"Thank you for coming, gentlemen," Stone said. "Particularly on such short notice. Shall we start?" Stone continued without waiting for an answer. "How much do you know about the Sukhoi-58?"

"The aircraft?" Cousins said. "Don't you mean the Su-57? The one the Russians are building with the Indians?"

"*Were* building," Stone corrected. "The Indians pulled out and the Russians mothballed it—officially, at least."

"But the 58?"

"Sukhoi has been working on two fighters. The Su-57 is the one that has been publicly acknowledged. Knowledge of the Su-58 has been restricted. We've only heard rumours up until now." Stone turned to the others. "I'm assuming no one else knows anything about it?"

"Nothing at all," the foreign secretary said. Control thought that ignorance was always a safe assumption where Younger was concerned.

"I can give you a short summary, Foreign Secretary," Stone said diplomatically. "The aircraft has been given the NATO designation 'Factor.' The Russians have known for years that they've got nothing in the skies that can get close to the Americans' fifth-generation fighters. It appears that Putin has decided that that state of affairs must be reversed, and has authorised a multi-billion-rouble design program that is much, much farther along than we thought it was. Our understanding from previous intelligence is that the Factor is a single-seat, twin-engine multirole fighter designed exclusively for air superiority and attack operations. The aircraft is stealth equipped with best-in-class front, side and rear radar. Thrust vectoring control, a top speed exceeding Mach 2.5 and advanced supermanoeuvrability. It will carry an extensive payload including air-to-air, air-to-surface and anti-ship missiles."

"Meaning?"

"Meaning, sir, that it will immediately be the most advanced fighter in the world. It will be more than a match for the F-22 and F-35. The assessment has always been that if the rumours were correct, the jump from the F-35 to the Su-58 would be about the same as the jump from the Tornado to the Lightning. Night and day."

Cousins shook his head. "Why didn't we know more about this?"

"No one knew," Stone said. "They've played it very cleverly. The focus was on the Su-57. They let us gloat when they pulled the plug on it, but it was just misdirection. The real work was in Komsomolsk. We knew they'd built two new factories in the Russian Far East. We thought they were to handle the mass production of the Su-57. We were wrong."

The foreign secretary knocked his knuckles against the table in a show of annoyance. "Might have been helpful to have had a little more intelligence before we paid the Americans £2.5 billion for fifty Lightnings, together with spending another half a billion at Marham so that we can fly the bloody things."

"Yes," Stone said. "That would have been wonderful, but I'm afraid they played us. Credit where credit is due. It's been an impressive counter-intelligence operation."

The atmosphere in the room had chilled. Control knew why: this kind of revelation would cause problems in lots of different departments and agencies, and the attendees were already working out how to deflect the blame and whom to scapegoat.

"What does this have to do with us?" Control said.

Stone steepled his fingers. "The Russians have been

flawless so far, but we may have enjoyed a stroke of good fortune. We came into possession of this document on Sunday evening."

Control, Younger, Cousins and Bloom leaned forward as the chief took a manila envelope from a sealed plastic document pouch. Stone slid his fingers inside and drew out two pieces of paper, which he placed on the table. The others stood up and leaned in so that they could see them. Control looked down at the documents: the first was an email and the second was a photograph of a schematic. It looked like part of a military jet.

"What is this?" Younger said.

"We retrieved it from the email account of Leonard Geggel. The schematic is the aft deck heating contour map of the Su-58. We believe that Pyotr Aleksandrov gave it to Geggel in Southwold before he was murdered. Geggel photographed it and sent it to himself—it's standard redundancy, in case anything happened to the original. Turns out he was very sensible. The original wasn't found on his body or in his car."

"Why did Aleksandrov give it to him?" Younger asked.

"We had no idea until this morning, when we received this."

Stone took out a third piece of paper. It was a copy of a handwritten note. He tapped his finger against it. "This was delivered to the front desk of the British Consulate in Vladivostok. A courier brought it in and left it. Nothing else. Control," Stone said, "would you do the honours?"

The document contained a paragraph of handwritten Russian text. Control's Russian was decent from the time he had worked at Moscow Station during the Cold War. He read it out loud.

'My name is Anastasiya Romanova. I am the daughter of

Pyotr Ilyich Aleksandrov, who was murdered by the Russian state in England two days ago. I am an aerospace engineer responsible for the development of the Sukhoi-58 aircraft. My father was attempting to arrange the terms of my defection to the United Kingdom when he was killed. I still wish to defect. I have extensive data relating to the Su-58 and I am prepared to give it to British intelligence in return for safe passage, protection for me once I arrive there and ten million pounds sterling. These terms are non-negotiable. If you are interested, I will be at the railway station at Komsomolsk-on-Amur at midday on Friday. Your agent should carry a copy of the Komsomolskaia Pravda. *I will introduce myself to them if I am satisfied that it is safe to do so. If I am not satisfied, I will return the next day. In the meantime, please find enclosed a further schematic from the Su-58 to demonstrate my good faith.'*

Stone held up a fourth piece of paper with another cutaway diagram. "This is the hard-point for a new air-to-air missile. We don't have a NATO designation for it. We didn't even know it existed."

"Is this all legitimate?" Younger asked.

"It's been checked," Stone said. "It's the real deal. You recall that we have a source within the Center?"

BLUEBIRD. They wouldn't reveal the cryptonym to civilians who couldn't be trusted to keep their mouths shut.

"Yes," Younger said. "I remember."

"We spoke with them," Stone went on. "Goes without saying that this is eyes-only classified." Stone took a sip from his cup and eyed them all for confirmation that they understood. They each nodded that they did, and he continued. "Pyotr Aleksandrov contacted Leonard Geggel and arranged the meeting in Southwold, after which they were both killed. What we didn't know was *why* Aleksandrov wanted to meet, and why they were murdered. Our source indicated that Nikolai Primakov, the deputy director of Directorate S, led the Kremlin to believe that Aleksandrov was trying to sell a list of active SVR agents to us, and had to be killed because of it. But that looks to have been a lie. It was the Su-58 on the table, not their agents."

Control knew of Primakov. They were of similar age and had been on opposing sides for years. "Why would Primakov lie about something like that? If Putin found out he'd been misled..."

"Quite," Stone said. "We don't know, but we are looking into it. For now, though, it would appear"—he tapped his finger against the letter—"that Aleksandrov was trying to sell the secrets his daughter has stolen."

"What do we know about her?" Younger asked.

"A good question, Foreign Secretary," Bloom said, taking over. "We've been busy investigating her, as you might imagine. We're still building the picture, but it appears that she works for Sukhoi, and has done ever since she graduated from AFA State Technical University in Moscow. She's thirty-nine and brilliant—she was given the Russian Federation Presidential Certificate of Honour for contributions to science. Our understanding was that there was a rift between father and daughter when he defected. Aleksandrov's file was full of it—he said that both Anastasiya and his wife were patriots, and that they disowned him after he was convicted of spying for us. It would appear that she has had a change of heart."

"Do we know why?"

"Our source reports that Anastasiya's husband was arrested and imprisoned a year ago. We believe he died in the gulag. Some disagreement with an oligarch who is close to the Kremlin—the usual. It seems likely that his death changed her view on the motherland. But it doesn't really matter. The schematic is authentic and Romanova checks out. There's more than enough here for us to take it seriously."

"Before you ask," Stone took over, "we are aware that this could be a trap. It's difficult to get any certainty out of Russia and we're being forced to move fast—that means there's a risk. On the other hand, our source thinks that this is legitimate. On balance, we think it's something we have to move on. The benefits are significant."

Younger gave an overly dramatic nod, his bouffant hair bouncing. "Assuming we give this the green light, what comes next?"

"That's what we need to decide. The operation against the two Russian assassins is ready to go ahead. Control?"

Control pursed his lips as he weighed it all up; he knew that he was about to be asked to change his plans. "I have two assets in theatre, and the intelligence on Kuznetsov and Timoshev has been passed to a cut-out. The cut-out will meet with my agents in"—he checked his watch—"two and a half hours. Assuming that everything is acceptable, the plan is to go ahead tonight."

"I propose a variation," Bloom said. "Benjamin and I have spoken and we believe there might be a way that this could be done. Does the operation against the Russians need two agents?"

"Ideally, yes," Control said.

"You have half a day—could you get another agent over there?"

"Possibly." Control looked at his watch; it was half-ten. He sighed. "Probably."

"Then that's what we should do. Split your agents up. Send one to Komsomolsk to meet Aleksandrov's daughter. The other one can stay in Moscow and do what needs to be done. It'll draw the Center's attention inward. Might be a distraction."

Control didn't object; he knew there was no point. The decision had already been made.

"Foreign Secretary?"

"Happy to defer to you chaps," he said.

Stone turned to Cousins. "Secretary of Defence?"

"This is your area. I'll go along with your recommendation."

"And the PM?"

"Yes," Cousins said. "We should mention it to her, yes. But I doubt she will have a problem."

"That's settled, then. Control—can I leave the arrangements with you?"

"What about local liaison?" Control said. "Moscow is one thing. We have support there. But Komsomolsk is something else altogether."

"Doesn't SIS have an agent runner with your assets? I don't remember her name."

"Her name is Ross," Stone said. "Raj Shah vouched for her. Says she's good. Excellent Russian, a cleanskin as far as the FSB is concerned—I've no objections with you borrowing her. She can go with whoever you choose to send."

Bloom looked across the table at Control. "You'll get onto it?"

Control stood. "I will."

"If you need anything—"

"Thank you," Control cut over him. "It's in hand. I'll report later, when it's done, but I need to get back to the office. I have a telephone call to make."

50

C ontrol stood at the wide office window that overlooked the Thames and tamped down tobacco in the bowl of his pipe. He clenched the stem between his teeth and puffed down as he held a match to the bowl. His mouth filled with the taste of the smoke and he held it there for a moment before angling his head and emitting it in a long, languid stream that would hang in the room for hours. It was midday, and the sun was directly over the buildings on the other side of the water. He looked down and saw the familiar swell of traffic on the road that followed the river. He stood there for a moment and watched, allowing his thoughts to settle.

There was a knock on the door.

"Come in," Control said.

Tanner opened the door. "Callan is outside, sir."

"Send him in."

Tanner stepped aside and, after a short pause, a new man stepped into the office. Christopher Callan was in his mid-thirties. He was tall and thin and elegantly dressed: he wore a dark grey suit with a faint herringbone pattern, his trousers neatly creased and his shoes polished to a high sheen. He undid the button of his jacket as he came inside and, as it fell open, Control saw two things: an understated lilac-coloured lining and the glint of a pistol holstered just beneath his left armpit. Callan would have been considered handsome by most people, but there was something a little alien in his appearance that Control found unsettling. His head was smaller than usual, crowned by a nest of tight curls that reminded him of the statues of da Vinci. His skin, too, was as alabaster-white as those statues.

"Sit," Control said, gesturing to the comfortable chairs before the table.

Callan sat. Control watched him. His lips were thin and pale. His eyes were pale, too, almost limpid. There was a natural cruelty in his face. Control had been alerted to the man's potential and, after studying his record, had decided that he was worthy of further investigation. He had served with distinction in the Special Boat Service until very recently. His father's business had collapsed and Callan had passed the naval scholarship examination to pay for his school fees. He had served in the SBS company in the Middle East and had commanded a Marine company in Afghanistan. He had been in Kabul when a Taliban suicide squad had commandeered a tower block overlooking the embassy district and started firing grenades and automatic weaponry. Callan had commanded the SBS team who cleared the building. None of the jihadis had walked out of that building alive.

Control took the teapot and poured out two cups, handing one to Callan.

"Congratulations are in order, Mr. Callan," he said.

"Sir?"

"One of my agents was killed in action yesterday morning. That means a vacancy has arisen. I'd like you to fill it—if you're still interested in working for me, of course."

"Yes, sir," Callan said quickly. His enthusiasm was obvious.

Callan had been subjected to the usual barrage of tests that awaited any potential recruit to the Group. He had been taken to the Group's facility at Trafalgar Place in Wiltshire where he had performed well. His recordable metrics were first rate, and he had returned an excellent score in the final assessment in the Brecon Beacons. He had been subjected to two days of brutal interrogation and his background had been given a forensic examination. There was nothing to cause concern: he was single, possibly homosexual, no close friends; his parents were dead; no obvious foibles or weaknesses that could be used against him; he lived for his work. In short, nothing had been uncovered that had warranted concern.

His physical scores were excellent and so, too, was his psychological report. The Group psychiatrists had reported a natural callousness and lack of empathy, together with a lack of concern for the feelings of others. They had suggested a possible inability to feel emotions deeply, together with an inability to acknowledge fear in others. There was an extremely high threshold for disgust, as demonstrated when Callan was shown pictures of battlefield fatalities. Control could diagnose that easily enough: these were all symptomatic of psychopathy. It did not concern Control at all. It was just a label, and, indeed, the qualities of a person whom society might deem psychopathic were useful in an agent, up to a point.

"Are you sure?" Control asked him. "You understand the gravity of your decision."

"Yes, sir. Absolutely. And I am sure—I would like that very much."

"Excellent. Then you are now Number Twelve." He put out his hand. "Welcome to Group Fifteen."

Callan took his hand and shook it. Control found his grip surprisingly loose. His fingers were long, almost feminine, and his flesh was cold. Control removed his hand. He needed to move things along.

"I have something for you to do today, as it happens."

Callan nodded, then sat quietly and listened.

"You're aware of the news, I'm sure."

"Southwold?"

"Indeed. An almighty mess, but we're getting to the bottom of it. Two Russian sleepers are suspected of carrying out the murders. We tracked them back to a property near Winchester, but they were able to escape. They've been recalled to Moscow where, I'm sure, the president will fête them as returning heroes. We can't have that, Number Twelve. We can't have that at all."

"What do you want me to do?"

"We intend to move against the assassins this evening. Number Five is in Moscow now, planning the operation. I want you to join him. There's a car downstairs that will take you to Heathrow. There's an Aeroflot flight to Sheremetyevo in ninety minutes. You're booked on it. Tanner will ride in the car with you to the airport and brief you on your legend."

"Yes, sir. Of course."

"The Russians killed Aleksandrov the way they did to send a message to us—to us and to anyone else who might be thinking of working against them. We're going to show them that we were listening."

MOSCOW

51

Milton, Pope and Ross had spent the morning preparing for the operation. Milton had planned to go ahead that evening. Pope was responsible for making contact with the cut-out and it was decided that Ross would accompany him to the rendezvous, leaving the embassy after lunch in order to allow for an extended SDR. In the meantime, Milton would make the preparations for the hit and their exfiltration immediately afterwards.

Planning the operation had made Milton uncomfortable. The dream felt close; he saw glimpses of Callaghan out of the corner of his eye, but when he turned to look there was nothing there. He would have to add two more victims to his tally. He didn't want to do it, but he knew he couldn't easily say no. He felt deadlocked, caught between his fear of the dream and the consequences of insubordination. He found, to his surprise, that he wanted to go to another meeting.

They had a working lunch of sandwiches and coffee and pressed on. Ross seemed to have come to terms with the nature of the operation and had stifled any further objections. Pope had spread a map out over the table and Ross helped him plan the SDR, a long route with extensive switches and double-backs that would bring them to a vegetable warehouse in the Biryulyovo district where the cut-out had agreed to meet. Ross was evidently familiar with the city from her previous time here, and she suggested an alteration to the dry-cleaning run that Pope approved.

"What do we know about the cut-out?" she asked.

"Nothing," Milton said. "That's the point."

"And you're okay with that?"

"It's just how it is," Pope said. "He's the only one who has contact with the source and with us. If we get into trouble, the only person we can give up is the cut-out. The same goes for the source. It's insulation."

"I know how it works," she replied. "It's just... wouldn't you rather go straight to BLUEBIRD?"

"That's never going to happen," Milton said.

"Do we know anything about them?"

"No. And I don't want to know. Neither do you."

COS McCartney had returned to the secure room. "How far have you got?"

"It's coming along," Pope said. "Depending on what we learn this afternoon, I think we'll be ready to go tonight."

She sat down at the table. "I'm afraid you're going to have to adjust things a little. There's been a development."

Milton looked up. "What?"

"Potential change of plan. We know a little more about Southwold."

"Go on," Milton said.

"Aleksandrov was killed because of his daughter."

"Why?"

"Her name is Anastasiya Romanov. She wants to defect.

She's offered British intelligence a cache of restricted information in return for safe harbour."

"Information?" Ross asked.

"Plans for a new Russian fighter aircraft. I'm no expert, but it's got everyone in the River House sitting up and paying attention. Aleksandrov was arranging the transaction, going through Geggel. The Russians must have found out what he was offering and decided that it was important enough to send two of their most valuable agents to deal with it. They killed them both for it."

"But not the daughter?"

"No," McCartney said. "Because she's still in Russia. That's where the plans need to change. We're researching her at the moment, but she's made contact directly. And we don't think the Russians know where she is."

"But we do?" Milton said.

"She couriered a package to the consulate at Vladivostok this morning. It was a message—the deal stands if we can get her out. She's going to be waiting at the railway station in Komsomolsk-on-Amur in two days' time, and then again on the following day."

"I don't know where that is," Pope admitted.

"No reason why you should," Ross said. "It's in the east. A thousand miles north of Vladivostok. It's the arse-end of nowhere. Not the sort of place you'd ever be expected to visit."

"But you've been?"

"I have," she said. "When I was a student. I did the Trans-Siberian. I wandered around when I got to the Far East. Komsomolsk has got to be one of the strangest places I've ever been to. It's basically two cities—one grew up around the shipyard and the other around the Sukhoi factory. And this is in a place that is minus-twenty in the winter and plus-thirty in summer."

Milton turned to McCartney. "What does London want us to do?"

"They want to get Anastasiya out, but it's going to have to be done quickly and discreetly. You're already on the ground. You can move fast. London wants you to go and collect her, then get her out of the country." She turned to Ross. "They want you to go, too, Ms. Ross. It's Smith's operation, but there needs to be a Russian speaker and you've been there before."

"A long time ago," she protested.

"You speak the language and you know the region. Smith will need assistance, and that's the best we can do at short notice."

Pope drummed his fingers on the table. "And what about the assassins? We forget about them?"

"We do not," McCartney said. "But we have to decide whether you can still make it work. Smith?"

Milton found, with a mixture of relief and shame, that he was relieved to have had the responsibility of eliminating Timoshev and Kuznetsov taken from him.

"Smith?"

Callaghan was in the shadows at the edge of the room. Don't think that you're getting away with it. This is just a reprieve. There's still more killing to do.

"Smith?"

Milton blinked the phantom away. McCartney was asking him a question.

"I'm sorry," he said. "I missed that."

"I need to know whether you think we can still go ahead with the operation."

"With just one man?"

"No. They're sending another to make up the team. He'll be here later this afternoon."

"Do we know who?"

"We don't," McCartney said.

Milton could guess: it would be one of the others from the Group.

"That doesn't matter," Pope said. "I'll meet the cut-out this afternoon as planned and then I can nail down the plan with." Pope turned to Milton for approval. "Agreed?"

"It can still be done," Milton said.

"What about us?" Ross said, glancing over at Milton.

"You need to be on your way," McCartney said. "London wants you to make contact with Romanova at the first available opportunity. That's tomorrow. And Komsomolsk is a long trip. We're going to need to work on new legends and get the travel documentation arranged. You're flying out tonight."

52

Primakov had been working on his plan all morning. He felt as if this sordid business was finally entering its end game. There were just a few loose ends to snip and then it would be done. He had to hold his nerve for just a little longer.

His intercom buzzed.

He turned back to his desk and pressed the button to speak. "Yes?"

"Major Stepanov and Captain Mitrokhin are here, sir."

Primakov looked at the clock on the wall: they were on time, punctual as ever. "Send them in."

Primakov sat down as Major Yuri Stepanov and Captain Boris Mitrokhin opened the door and came into the office.

"Good afternoon, Comrade General," Stepanov said with the usual combination of respect and deference.

"Good afternoon, comrades," Primakov said. "Please—sit."

The two men unbuttoned their jackets and sat down opposite him.

Stepanov tugged down on both cuffs until an inch of

creamy shirt showed beneath the sleeves of his jacket. He
was a fastidious dresser, although, when the situation
demanded it, adept at disguising himself so adroitly that he
could melt into his surroundings. He was in his early forties,
with an army buzzcut and thick, heavy features. Mitrokhin
was younger, mid-thirties, and a little rougher around the
edges. Both were more informally described as *chistilshchiks*,
or 'mechanics.' Stepanov had first come to the attention of
Primakov during the siege of School Number One in Beslan.
Stepanov had been assigned to Vympel, the Spetsnaz unit
that had been sent into the school to end the siege. He had
eliminated more than a dozen of the Chechen terrorists
who had been responsible for the atrocity, and had then
chased down the leaders of the conspiracy as they fled into
the hills and mountains of Ossetia.

Stepanov had then been reassigned to Department V of
the SVR, bringing his enthusiastic junior officer with him.
The Department's role was described as 'Executive Action,'
but that was a bland euphemism for the work that its agents
concerned themselves with: they were deployed by the
other Directorates when circumstances demanded a more
rigorous solution to problems. Of course, Primakov knew of
Group Fifteen, and Stepanov and the other men and
women who comprised the Department fulfilled a similar
function for the Rodina. The Department had existed in the
same form during the reign of the KGB and had stubbornly
resisted change during the KGB's metamorphosis into the
SVR. It seemed that there would always be a need for men
like Stepanov and Mitrokhin, regardless of the window
dressing and public relations nonsense that its mother
organisation might now be subjected to.

Primakov had recruited them both six months ago. He
wanted someone to whom he could turn when his illegals

needed a specialist to close out their operations. There had been operations in the Crimea and the Ukraine, and all of them had been carried out flawlessly. Stepanov was something of a throwback to the purer days of the Soviet state, and his dissatisfaction with what he saw as the excesses of modern Russia had been noted in his file. That might have impeded his upward trajectory if he had stayed where he was, but Primakov was a pragmatist; Stepanov was an expert, a consummate professional who could be relied upon to deliver excellent results, and, as such, Primakov was prepared to accommodate his opinions. Indeed, Primakov too was opposed to much of what he saw at the Kremlin; he would have been a hypocrite to have penalised him.

Mitrokhin was easier to handle: he did everything that Stepanov told him.

"How are you both?"

"We are well, Comrade General," Stepanov said, speaking for them both. "You have need of us?"

Stepanov was all business, just as ever. "I do." Primakov stood up and went around to the other side of the desk. "The British have sent agents to Moscow to assassinate two SVR officers. I would like you to stop them from doing that."

"Yes, sir," he said. "Who are the agents?"

"Two men from Group Fifteen."

If Stepanov was concerned about the pedigree of their targets, he did not show it. "When?"

"They will make an attempt on the lives of our agents this evening," he said. "We have a source within their organisation—they will be told where the SVR officers are staying. We believe that the attempt will be made there."

"Where?"

"The Four Seasons."

"Do the SVR officers know that they are at risk?"

"They do not. It's unnecessary. You will intervene before any action can be taken against them."

"What action would you like us to take, sir?"

"Follow them—I'll make a surveillance team available to you. They will be meeting a cut-out, and that might lead us to the traitor within the Center."

"And then?"

"Kill them both when they make their attempt and then disappear them. This is something that must stay between us. No one else is to know what we have done."

Primakov swivelled and reached down for the file on his desk, a manila folder with three sheets of paper clipped inside. It contained everything that Stepanov and Mitrokhin would need to know. Primakov handed it to the major.

Stepanov flipped through the pages, then closed the folder and stood. Mitrokhin did the same.

"Very good, sir. I'll see that it is done. Is there anything else?"

"No." Primakov looked at the silent Mitrokhin. "Captain? Anything to add?"

"No, Comrade General," Mitrokhin said.

Stepanov gave a sharp nod. "We will report tomorrow."

Both men saluted, turned on their heels and made their way out of the office. Primakov exhaled. Stepanov was a peerless operator, efficient and utterly ruthless, and Mitrokhin was the same. He had lost count of the number of files that he had passed to Stepanov for action—thirty, maybe more—and none of the men and women put in the *chistilshchiks'* way was still breathing. It was strange: they both made Primakov nervous, and yet there was a calming sense of finality that came with handing the assassins a file and knowing that the work would be done without any further need for him to be involved.

He thought of Natasha. It would all soon be finished. The only loose end was Anastasiya Romanova, but PROZHEKTOR would find her eventually, and when that happened, the whole sorry mess would come to an end. He would prepare another file and hand it to Stepanov and then, finally, he would be able to relax.

53

P ope was driven out of the embassy at five o'clock that afternoon. The sun was still shining down onto the city, and it was pleasantly warm. The driver had taken a route that followed the Moskva River before looping around and crossing it on Smolenskaya Ulitsa. He had waited until the last moment to leave it, hanging a sharp right that pointed them toward the park at Lesya Ukrainka. He turned right again and then, almost immediately, left onto the narrow street that skirted the park. The driver turned again onto another quiet side street and, holding up three fingers, started a countdown as he slowed the car. Pope opened the door and bailed out, throwing himself down behind a parked van as the driver sped up again. The unmarked FSB tail followed just behind, maintaining a discreet distance that had allowed Pope—so far as he could tell—to get out without being seen.

He stayed where he was, waiting for another minute to confirm that there was not a second car, and then, satisfied that there was not, he set off toward the tall, dilapidated apartment block that loomed over the park like a sentinel.

He took a cap out of his pocket and pulled it down so that the brim was tight around his forehead, and then put on a pair of dark glasses.

He walked north, caught a bus on Raduzhnaya Street and rode it for fifteen minutes before getting off at Otradnoye station and riding the Metro back in the opposite direction. He continued the game for four hours, covering miles of the city until his feet were aching and sore. By the time he finally reached out his arm to flag down a taxi he was as confident as he could be that he was black.

The taxi was an old Lada that had seen better days. The driver leaned across to wind down the window and asked him where he wanted to go. Pope told him the Annino Metro station; the driver grunted his approval and indicated with a jerk of his head that Pope should get into the back. He did, settling into a musty-smelling leather seat that was held together with strips of duct tape. He yanked the seatbelt across his chest and pushed it home. He had been driven in taxis all around the world, but he remembered his previous experiences on the streets of Moscow as being particularly concerning. This driver looked very much like the others that he remembered: surly, aggressive and, judging by the smell of alcohol that permeated the cabin of the car, quite possibly drunk. The car didn't look as if it would offer much by way of protection if they were to be involved in an accident, and so he resorted to crossing his fingers as the driver bullied his way out into the traffic and set out toward Pope's destination.

54

The warehouse district was open, with wide roads and lots of space within which the buildings had been constructed. Pope stepped out of the taxi, paid the driver the two thousand roubles he demanded, and then looked around in an attempt to gain his bearings. The streets around the station were broad, with three lanes of traffic passing in each direction. The sky looked especially large here, with clouds idling overhead on a gentle breeze.

Pope walked away from the Metro. He had been shown the route he would need to take before leaving the embassy, and he found it simple enough to match the landmarks around him with the images he had seen on Google Street View. He reached the warehouse that had been arranged as the location for the meet. The warehouse was a legitimate business, offering wholesale budget groceries to the city's traders. He passed through the open door and made his way along rows of well-stocked shelving. The interior was functional at best, the lighting provided by ugly strip lights that swung from the ceiling on old metal chains. Pope reached the rear of the warehouse and the plain door that he had been told opened into the office. He went inside, passing between two lines of racking before he reached a second door. He rapped his knuckles against it.

There was a pause. Pope looked up at the camera that had been fixed above the door and knew that he was being scrutinised.

"Come in," said a voice in heavily accented English.

Pope pushed the door open and stepped into the compact room beyond. It was evidently used as the office for the business. There was a desk with an old computer positioned on it, two green metal filing cabinets that had been dented and scuffed over the years, and a second screen that displayed the feeds from a number of security cameras that had been placed both inside and outside the property. There was a single window, little more than a slit in the wall, that offered an unglamorous view of the yard outside where industrial bins were stored in readiness for collection. The room was lit by an unmasked bulb that cast a harsh light on the man who was sitting on the chair behind the desk.

"Aleksey?" Pope said.

"Yes," he said. The man's name was Aleksey Varlamov. He was in his early sixties. The lines on his careworn face were deep, testament to the cold Russian winter and a life that was more than unusually full of stress. "I take it you have been careful?"

"I've been going around in circles for hours," Pope said. "My feet ache. If they're still on me, they're better at this than I am."

"Thank you," he said. "They have been more vigilant than ever in these last few months. The president is building up the security apparatus to beyond where it was during the Cold War. It is tiring."

The BBC's twenty-four-hour news channel was showing

on the monitor. The anchor handed over to an outside broadcast and the footage changed to a shot of the house in Kings Worthy where the Ryans had lived. The camera was positioned so that it could shoot up the drive. The house was invisible, but there were police officers in protective gear gathered around a plain white van. It was momentarily disorientating: Pope had been inside the house just thirty-six hours earlier.

Varlamov noticed that Pope's attention was on the news. "It is quite a story," he said.

Footage of Putin at a meeting in the Kremlin appeared on the screen. The old man waved a hand at the images. "Vova is making a point," he said, using the president's nickname. "It doesn't matter where you hide and who is protecting you. He has a long arm and a longer memory."

Varlamov leaned over, clicked a mouse and closed the window down.

"Shall we begin?" he suggested. "You are interested in Kuznetsov and Timoshev."

"Do you know where they are?"

"Our mutual friend has provided me with information," Varlamov said. "He says that they were debriefed this morning and that the sessions are expected to last for the rest of today and then tomorrow. The Center has a lot to ask them, no doubt."

"And now?"

"The source tells me that they are staying in the Four Seasons hotel. They are being presented to senior members of the Center at a reception this evening, and then, I assume, they will return to the hotel to rest."

"Where is it?"

"Ulitsa Okhotnyy Ryad."

"How easy is it to get in?"

"Simple enough. They are not being given special security. Why would they need it? We are in the heart of Moscow. The British would not be so foolish as to make an attempt on them here." Varlamov glanced over at Pope and smiled. "That you would be so foolhardy is what will give you your advantage. The Center has grown too arrogant. Perhaps you will teach them some humility."

"Afterwards," Pope said. "I'd prefer them to stay arrogant until I'm out of the country."

"Of course," Varlamov said.

"How do I get in?"

"We have taken measures to make that as easy as possible."

He opened a desk drawer and took out a small key.

"This opens a locker at Leningradsky railway station. The locker is number 537. You can get there from here on the Metro. Everything you need is there. There are two uniforms for the hotel and a keycard. You must go around the back of the building. There is a passage that leads to the staff entrance. The card will open the door. You will go inside, through a lobby area, and then you will find the staff canteen and bathrooms. You won't be challenged there. You and your colleague should get changed into the uniforms and then you will be able to make your way to their room without issue."

Varlamov had been working on the basis that there would be a two-man team and hadn't been updated since the recent change to the plan.

"What number room are they in?" Pope asked him.

"1022. The tenth floor."

"What about the equipment?"

"There is a bag inside the locker," he said. "It is all there."

Varlamov got up, taking a moment to stretch out his shoulders. "Is there anything else?"

The monitor flicked across to its screensaver: a horizontal tricolour of green, white and red. The Chechen flag. There was almost always a personal reason—a family reason—why men and women decided to take such great risks to work against the state. Pope guessed that Varlamov had plenty of reasons.

"No," Pope said. "That's all I need."

The old man leaned back against the wooden slats of his chair. "My people have a saying: *Oyla yocuš lettarg ka docuš vella.* Look before you leap. Be careful. They do not know you are coming, but Moscow is a dangerous city. They have eyes everywhere."

Pope took the old man's hand; his skin was leathery and the bones felt brittle beneath. "Good luck," he said.

"And to you."

Pope turned around and opened the door to the office. He slipped the key in his pocket and started for the street. He had plenty to do.

55

S tepanov was in one of the surveillance cars that was responsible for tracking the British spy. They were passing by the warehouse just as the man came out onto the street.

His driver reached down to the radio and opened the channel. "He is on the street again," he reported.

"Go around," Stepanov said to the driver. "He will go back to the Metro. I want one more look at him."

The operation had proceeded smoothly. The surveillance team was large; Stepanov had counted eight cars, and there were more agents on foot. Ground units were arranged in several layers, able to swap in and out seamlessly. Foot assets waited ahead of the British agent along likely routes, and teams matched his progress on parallel flanks. There was nothing to suggest that the target had noticed that he was being watched. Primakov would be pleased.

The driver spoke into the radio again. "Alpha team: stay on Varlamov," he said. "Find out where he goes. He is to be kept under twenty-four-hour surveillance. Beta team. Stay on the British agent."

"Understood," the leader of the second team radioed back. "What are the rules of engagement?"

Stepanov took the microphone. "This is Major Stepanov," he said. "Follow him, but you are not to intervene under any circumstances. You only move against him with my express permission. Is that clear?"

"Very clear, Comrade Major."

Stepanov was careful. He had advanced to his present position through a combination of planning, political acuity and ruthlessness. He was not old enough to remember the days of the KGB, but he had heard stories of how it had been from his uncle and his father, both of whom had served with distinction. He knew that he was as guilty of romanticising the agency as the ex-spooks who recalled it with such fondness, but he liked to think that advancement then had been more honourable and straightforward than had been the case during his own rapid rise to the top. The Kremlin today was a nest of vipers. The desire to please the president had bred an atmosphere of poisonous treachery, of risk assessments, of "optics" maintained by duplicitous press secretaries, an environment that favoured promotion by way of back-stabbing rather than merit. It was not what it once was. That was a cause of regret for him. At least the comrade general had given him the opportunity to indulge the strategies that had served his predecessors well for so long.

The driver looped around and they went past the warehouse in the opposite direction. It was a short drive to the Metro, and Stepanov saw the Englishman making his way along the sidewalk toward the entrance to the station. The man had conducted an impressive counter-surveillance routine; he wouldn't have risked the meet unless he was satisfied that he was clean, and that assumption was reasonable. But the surveillance team was expert and they swarmed around him like bees around a honeypot. There were enough of them that they could duck in and duck out, varying the followers so that the subject continued to be blissfully ignorant of the true situation.

Stepanov expected him to return to the city and meet with his colleague. They would equip themselves and then prepare to put their plan into effect. Timoshev and Kuznetsov would be oblivious, nothing more than the bait used to lure the enemy into the trap.

Stepanov was confident that he could leave the surveillance detail to maintain their coverage. He told the driver to provide regular reports, and then indicated that he should stop alongside a cab rank. He got out of the car and then slid into the back of the taxi at the front of the queue.

"Where do you want to go?" the driver asked him.

"The Four Seasons," he said, and settled back as the car pulled out. He took out his phone and sent a text to Mitrokhin, telling him to meet him at the hotel in an hour.

Stepanov closed his eyes and started to work through the list of things that they needed to do. They were going to be busy for the next few hours.

56

Pope rode the Metro to Leningradsky station. He spent the journey thinking about the operation, and the alterations that had been rendered necessary by the change in priorities. It would have been a straightforward job with Milton; they had worked together before, and Pope trusted him implicitly. But Twelve was different. He was new to the Group, stepping up from the reserves to replace the unfortunate Ten. Pope had known nothing about the agent—even his or her gender—until Tanner had forwarded him a brief précis from his file. Twelve's history was impressive, but it didn't carry the same weight as would personal experience gained in the field together. Pope would proceed with more caution than usual.

The train arrived at the station and Pope disembarked. He took the escalator up and into the station, made his way to the left luggage facility and found locker 537. He took the key from his pocket, put it into the lock and opened the door.

There was a leather backpack. He opened the backpack inside the locker so that he could examine it without being observed. There were two bundles of clothes, neatly folded, jackets and trousers that looked like the uniform one might expect a hotel porter to wear. Pope saw the logo of the Four Seasons on the lapel of one of the jackets. There were two Sig Sauer P224s, together with two boxes of ammunition and two suppressors. There was an envelope. He pushed his finger inside the flap and slid it along, opening it. The envelope contained a keycard that was also marked with the Four Seasons logo, a wedge of high-denomination banknotes, and two wallets with bank cards and other IDs in the name of two fresh legends, one for him and one meant for Milton. There were passports in the same names, with their pictures on the photo pages.

It all looked to be in order; Pope put the envelope back, zipped the bag up, took it out of the locker, unhooked the garment carrier and closed the door. He put the bag over his shoulder and, instinctively checking the aisle in both directions, made his way back to the entrance and the concourse outside.

Pope made his way to the Romanovsky Obelisk in Alexander Garden, close by the walls of the Kremlin. The monument had originally been erected to commemorate the Romanov dynasty, but Lenin's propagandists had altered the obelisk so that it now paid homage to revolutionary thinkers: Marx, Engels, all the others.

Pope recognised Number Twelve from the description that Tanner had given him. He was waiting for him on the steps near the obelisk. He was in his mid-thirties, tall and thin and dressed in jeans, a shirt and a light jacket that he wore undone in the pleasant weather. He had a rucksack slung over his shoulder.

Pope nodded at Twelve as he approached. Twelve drew alongside and matched his pace.

"Good evening," Pope said.

"Evening."

It was a short ten-minute walk to the Four Seasons. They set off through the gardens. Pope glanced over at Twelve. He was looking left and right, eyes open for possible repeats that might suggest that one or both of them had brought surveillance with them. Pope had been watching, too, and had seen nothing. He saw nothing now, either.

Pope glanced over at him. "Do you have an update?"

"The operation is authorised. They want it done tonight. Do you know where they are?"

"The Four Seasons," Pope said. "It's not far."

"Did you get the equipment?"

"I did. A keycard to get in, two uniforms for us, two pistols."

They passed a couple sitting on a bench and Twelve was silent until they were out of earshot.

"Is this your first operation?" Pope asked him.

"Yes," he said. "But I have experience."

"I'm sure you do," Pope said. "But this is *my* job. I'm the senior man. That going to be all right?"

Twelve looked across at him, his face impassive. "Of course."

There was something about Twelve that Pope did not like. His tone, his coldness; it was difficult to put his finger on it, but he decided that he would need to be careful with him.

57

Primakov and Natasha had met at the safe house earlier that evening. Primakov had made them cocktails and then they had retreated to the bedroom for an hour. Primakov had fallen asleep and, when he awoke, it was to the smell of cooked liver. He showered, dressed, and padded through to the kitchen on bare feet.

Natasha was preparing a midnight snack of toast and pâté. She was an excellent cook, and it was his favourite of the dishes in her repertoire.

"Are you well rested?" she said, smiling at him.

"I am," he said. "I needed it. It's been a long week."

"I'm sorry about that," she said. "I know it's my fault."

"No, no," he said, worried that she might think that he had rebuked her. "I don't blame you, not at all. You were unfortunate."

"And yet fortunate that I had you to take care of it for me."

He stepped behind her and massaged her neck. He was happy to accept her gratitude. He stepped closer now so that her back was pressed against his chest and watched over her shoulder as she worked. She had caramelised chicken livers and pancetta, and then deglazed the pan with a slug of brandy. Now she was chopping parsley, capers and shallots, the knife slicing down with impressive speed and accuracy as she prepared the ingredients.

"Where did you learn to do that?" he asked.

"YouTube," she grinned.

"Smells good," he said.

She reached up with her left hand and held his hand on her shoulder. "Thank you, Nikolasha," she said, using the diminutive that he liked so much.

"For what?"

She turned her head so that she could kiss him on the lips. "For helping me. Thank you for everything."

She added the chopped ingredients to the pan and then added lemon zest, lemon juice and a tablespoon of oil. The aroma deepened and Primakov's mouth began to water.

"Five minutes," she said.

He had left his phone on the dining table and he heard it buzzing with an incoming message. He went over to it, saw that it was an encrypted text, and waited for the algorithm to decrypt it.

He frowned. It was a message from PROZHEKTOR.

WE NEED TO MEET. USUAL PLACE. MIDNIGHT. PLS CONFIRM.

"*Chyort wozmi*," he said. *Shit.*

"What is it?"

He looked at his watch. Eleven-thirty.

"Nikolasha? What's the matter?"

"It's work," he said. "I have to go."

"*Now?* Why? What's wrong?"

He didn't want to tell her that it was PROZHEKTOR, and that this was likely to do with the British and his attempt to clean up the mess that she had made with Anastasiya Romanova.

"I can't say," he deflected. "It's probably nothing—nothing that you need to worry about. Will the pâté keep?"

"I can put it in the fridge," she said, pouting a little. "But don't be long. I'm tired. I want to go to bed."

He put on his socks and shoes, took his coat from the back of the sofa and shrugged it on. "Give me an hour," he said. "I'll be back as soon as I can."

58

Pope and Twelve found the hotel and split up so that they could scout the area independently of each other. The Four Seasons was next to a colourfully decorated arch that opened onto a neat communal square. The street was busy, despite the hour, with cars hurrying in both directions. There were a few pedestrians out and about, although Pope saw nothing to suggest that he was being surveilled.

They had agreed to meet at eleven-thirty. Pope found the entrance that led into the hotel garage and then, in turn, to the hotel's staff entrance. Twelve was waiting for him there.

There were no security staff posted at the garage and they were able to enter without being seen. They found their way inside until they reached the staff door. Pope took out the keycard that he had been given and held it against the reader next to the door; the device emitted a satisfied beep, a light shone green and the lock clicked open. Pope pushed the door and they both made their way inside. There was an antechamber inside the door with a notice board and a vending machine with drinks and snacks. A corridor led away from the antechamber, and, as Pope tested the doors to the left and the right, he found male and female toilets and a small canteen. There were two women in the canteen, smoking cigarettes through a window that opened onto a fetid corner where the big industrial bins were kept.

Pope backed away from the door before the women noticed that he was there and made his way back to the male toilets. There were two rooms for men and two for women, each with a toilet and sink and a storage locker. Pope stepped into the first men's room. Twelve came in after him and Pope slid the bolt in the lock.

Pope opened the rucksack and took out the hotel uniforms. They both changed. One jacket had been intended for Milton, and Twelve was slenderer than him; the jacket was a little baggy, but it would still serve. Pope took out the pistols and handed one over. Pope put on the shoulder rig, double-checked the load on his weapon and pushed it into the holster, checking in the mirror to ensure that the jacket covered it. It did. Twelve did the same.

Pope took their clothes and stuffed them into the rucksack. He opened the storage locker and left the bag inside.

"Ready?" he asked.

Twelve nodded.

Pope checked his watch: half past eleven. He took a deep breath, slid the bolt back and opened the door. The two women he had seen in the canteen were loitering outside the door to the women's toilet; Pope nodded as he went by and, before they could speak to him and expose the fact that he spoke no Russian, he was past them and on the staircase that led to the hotel's public spaces. Twelve followed close behind.

59

There was a service elevator in a separate shaft adjacent to the elevators that the guests used. Pope summoned the car and then he and Twelve stepped inside. The car needed to be authorised before it would move, but all it took was for him to press his keycard against the reader and the buttons for each floor changed from red to green. Pope pressed the button for the tenth floor and stood back to wait for the doors to close. He heard a man's voice, a shouted request in Russian, and then, even as he willed the doors shut, a hand shot between them and pressed them open again. The man who stepped into the car with Pope was wearing the uniform of hotel security, with faux-military epaulettes and piping along the shoulders of his shirt.

"*Zdravstvujtye*," the man said.

Pope had been staring down at his feet; now, though, he glanced up and saw that the guard was looking at him.

"*Zdravstvujtye*," Pope said, knowing that his pronunciation was terrible.

Twelve stood there, quietly, and Pope could feel the violence emanating out of him like woozy summer heat.

Pope waited for the man to say something else. He wouldn't be able to understand him or reply without making it obvious that he did not speak the language – and that, as a staff member in the glitziest hotel in Moscow, would not have been credible. He felt the shape of the gun tucked against his body and knew that there was a good chance that he would have to use it. That would lengthen the odds of successfully completing the operation to such an extent that he would most likely need to abort. And if he did that, if the alarm was sounded, then how would he—

His increasingly gloomy train of thought was interrupted by a chime as the elevator reached the seventh floor.

"*Proshchay,*" the man said, smiling guilelessly as he stepped through the open doors.

Pope found that he was holding his breath; the doors closed, the lift started to ascend again and Pope exhaled in relief.

"Lucky," Twelve commented.

Pope knew that he didn't mean them.

It was a temporary balm. The numbers ticked up through eight and nine and then reached ten. The lift chimed again and the doors parted. Pope and Twelve stepped out. There was a generous lobby, with a lit water feature burbling musically in a sconce, and a corridor stretched away in both directions. The carpet was deep and luxurious, and the door numbers looked to have been inscribed on pieces of polished slate.

Pope followed the signs for room number 1022. His palm itched for the weight of the Sig and he felt the first drops of nervous sweat running down his back. It wasn't unusual for him to feel anxious at a time like this, and this operation, unlike almost all of the others that he had undertaken since he had joined Group Fifteen, had not received the same degree of planning. Indeed, it was quite the contrary; it seemed as if it had received very limited consideration, and then Twelve had been foisted on him at the last moment and what planning they had done had been disregarded. Intelligence had been received and it needed to be acted upon quickly and decisively; that might have been acceptable if he had been able to take out the targets at arm's length with explosives or a ranged weapon, but that was not the case. The mandarins wanted to put on a show, to make a point that their counterparts at the Center would not be able to ignore or mistake. It was Pope's job to make that point, and hang the consequences.

He was nervous.

60

The rendezvous was in Park Presnenskiy, near the children's playground. It was just before midnight when Primakov arrived, and the only people he saw as he made his way inside were a couple who were evidently the worse off for drink, staggering together arm in arm. He paid them no heed and walked quickly, following the path between a line of oaks to the bench.

PROZHEKTOR was waiting for him.

He sat down.

"My dear Jessie."

"Hello, General," she said.

Jessie Ross was fidgeting with her phone, the screen washing blue light up over her face. Primakov had been personally responsible for her recruitment and had kept her file as a project even after his promotion to deputy director. She had been twenty when he had recruited her. They had been fortunate to find her when they did. The recruitment pool for possible Directorate S agents was large: foreign government representatives, businessmen looking to broaden their interests in a country that was encouraging inward investment, scientists, academics, military personnel, and students. It was in this last category that Ross had been found. Her professor had worked for Directorate RT, the KGB's fore-runner to Directorate S, and had continued to work for it after Putin had reincarnated the KGB as the FSB. He had identified her as politically active with socialist leanings and had suggested that she might be ripe for an approach. Directorate S almost always used native Russians; they were more malleable, could be motivated by patriotism and, when things went bad, could be influenced by threats to loved ones who were still at home. One had to be more careful with recruiting foreigners, and the process for bringing Ross aboard had been long and meticulous. The network of agents known as the *agentura* had become involved in a process of get-acquainted chats. She was studied via agents at the university, by adminis-trative and professorial staff who were friendly to the cause. It was determined that she had the necessary aptitude to facili-tate a career in a sensitive area on her return to her country.

Only then had the approach been made. Her professor had been responsible for it and, over the course of a month, he had reeled her in. She had not been won over by politics or ideology; she had shown no interest in either. Rather, she was a product of capitalism in its basest, most brutal sense: she had named her price, and Primakov had decided that they could pay it. The price had gone up over time, but so too had her performance.

She had received additional training that went beyond the curriculum of her course and had been returned to London with the tradecraft necessary to keep her beyond suspicion. Her subsequent application for work at Vauxhall Cross had been accepted and, to Primakov's delight, he had found himself with a live asset in the heart of the enemy's intelligence apparatus. She provided regular reports, using an SRAC relay that was buried in Epping Forest. She had developed an interest in mountain biking and would visit the forest under the pretext of indulging it. The trail she followed passed within fifty feet of the relay, allowing her to transfer her reports without incurring even the slightest scintilla of suspicion. Ross had already more than justified the time it had taken and the expense that had been invested in her recruitment.

Primakov had made the educated guess that Anastasiya Romanova would reach out to her father once she had gone into hiding. Ross had already been assigned to the department responsible for babysitting the traitors who had fled to the United Kingdom, and she had been able to pass Aleksandrov's file to Vincent Beck. She had lobbied to be added to the trip to Moscow—it was an easy yes given the circumstances—and she had alerted Primakov to the two Group Fifteen headhunters who had arrived in the city ahead of her and the plan that had been conceived. She had given him the opportunity to prevent the assassination attempt on Timoshev and Kuznetsov. She had given him the chance to arrest the headhunters and hand a public relations coup to the president.

He turned to her. "What is it?" he asked.

"You have a problem."

"With what? The operation—it's still going ahead?"

"It is," she said. "But that's not the problem. There's been a change of plan." She took a moment to gather her thoughts. "I only have ten minutes. I'm supposed to be at the hotel. They think I'm getting ready to leave."

"I don't understand. Leaving? Where to?"

"Anastasiya Romanova has been in contact with Vauxhall Cross. She couriered a letter to the consulate in Vladivostok."

Primakov clenched his fists. "Saying what?"

"That she wants to defect. She said that she had asked her father to help, and that the Russians killed him. But she hasn't given up. She proposed a meeting the day after tomorrow and said that VX should send someone to get her out of the country."

"Where?"

"Komsomolsk," she said.

Primakov dug his nails into his palms. "She's been there all the time?" he said.

"It seems so."

"What will the British do?"

"They're sending one of the agents to go and get her —John Smith."

"Alone?"

"No," she said. "That's why I can't stay. Smith doesn't speak Russian, so they're sending me, too."

Primakov felt the buzz of anticipation; this was better news. "When?"

"We're booked on a flight in the morning."

"When and where has she proposed to meet?"

"The railway station. Saturday, at midday."

"Well done. You must go back to them now. They must not suspect you."

"What will you do?"

"I will send a team," he said. "Two of my best men will lead it."

"What do I do?"

"Whatever they've told you. Will you be going to the rendezvous?"

"I don't know," she said. "I expect so."

"We will be there. We will arrest them both. If anything changes, you must contact me. Do you understand?"

"Of course," she said, with a little bite in her voice.

Primakov knew that the British had consistently underestimated her, and that she hated it; he reminded himself not to make the same mistake. She had already demonstrated tradecraft well beyond what he would have expected in one so young and so inexperienced.

"What about me?" she asked him.

"You'll need to get away. Smith won't be able to expose you. He will be locked up. They will have given you an emergency exfiltration route—what is it?"

"It hasn't been mentioned. That might be down to Smith. I have a lot of time with him until the meet."

"Follow it," he said. "I'll see to it that you can leave the country. Tell them that there was an ambush and you managed to escape. They know they have a leak. They will suspect that it is you. They will interrogate you, and it won't be pleasant. You will have to win back their trust when you return."

"I can do that," she said.

"Go back to the hotel," he said. "We will be waiting at the rendezvous."

She started to leave, but paused. "Be careful," she added.

"Of what?"

"Smith. There's something about him. He makes me uncomfortable."

"Don't worry, Jessie," Primakov reassured her. "He is here, in Russia, far from home. He might be dangerous, but he will be outnumbered. There will be nothing that he can do—you have seen to that."

She nodded her agreement and, again, he marvelled at her composure. She had the potential to be the most important Russian agent since Philby and the others. She was young and already embedded within the institutions of British intelligence. There had been early successes, most notably her seduction of the private secretary to the foreign secretary, a coup that had delivered strong results before it had been brought to an abrupt end by the politician's wife. Even with that, Primakov knew that she hadn't even started to deliver everything of which she would eventually be capable; she could provide him with years of gold-plated intelligence. It would not be a simple thing to protect her now but, even given her potential future value, he was prepared to take the risk that she would be blown. There would be an inquest in London, but Ross was good and Primakov concluded that she stood a decent chance of continuing to fool them.

"Your flight—is it through Vladivostok?"

"Yes," she said.

"I will send my man to speak with you there. There is a business lounge there—the Laguna Lounge. Two hours before your flight, tell Smith you intend to take a shower. He will meet you then, once you are alone. Yes?"

She nodded.

"Good luck, Jessie. You are doing valuable work. I am grateful—we're all grateful."

"Be sure that shows in my next payment," she said, and, from her expression, Primakov knew that she was serious. She was driven by avarice; Primakov could ignore that when her production was so good.

Ross headed in the direction of the Metro and Primakov went to his car. He took out his phone and called Stepanov.

"Good evening, General."

"Report, please."

"The agents are in the hotel."

"Who?"

"One of the men we have been following and another I don't recognise."

"Listen carefully, Major. I need you to abort."

Stepanov couldn't hide his surprise. "Sir?"

"Abort the mission. Do not interfere."

"I don't understand, sir. They will kill our agents."

"I know that," Primakov snapped. "How many men are with you?"

"Just me and Boris."

"Good. You are not to mention this matter to anyone. Come to Yasenevo once it has been done—tonight. I have something very important that I need you to do for me."

He ended the call and put his phone back into his pocket.

He knew that he had just signed the death warrants for two Russian heroes, but, at the same time, he knew that it was the right thing to do. The British couldn't know that they had been compromised, and they would if his *chistil-shchiks* killed their agents before they could carry out their orders. It was a bitter pill to swallow, but swallow it he must. Natasha's future depended on him silencing Anastasiya Romanova, and Ross had given him his chance to do that. He would salve his conscience with Smith. He would bury him in Lefortovo Prison and let Stepanov have his way with him. They would squeeze every last drop of intelligence out of him, try him for espionage and then inter him in the foulest, most unpleasant camp that they could find.

And then, in time, they would take him outside, put him against the wall, and shoot him.

PART IV

MOSCOW

61

Stepanov had been waiting in the hotel all evening. The surveillance team had reported that the British agent had collected a bag from the locker at Leningradsky station, and then met with another man at the Romanovsky Obelisk. It was clear that the two agents would make their move tonight; as far as they knew, Timoshev and Kuznetsov would be moved elsewhere in short order, and their new location might be more difficult to access.

Mitrokhin had called him two minutes earlier. He had been in the elevator with both of the British headhunters. They were headed to the tenth floor. Mitrokhin was on his way up via the stairs. The plan was for him to wait in the stairwell until the British were inside the room, and, once they were, he would make his way over.

Stepanov was in room 1020. Timoshev and Kuznetsov were in 1022. They had no idea that he was here, nor did they know about the miniature camera that he had installed outside their room while they had been glad-handing the Security Council at the Kremlin that evening.

Stepanov had told Mitrokhin that they were standing

down, and that he was not to engage either man. Mitrokhin had asked him to repeat the order, but had not questioned it. He was well trained and loyal, although Stepanov knew that he would be as confused and disappointed as he was. They were abandoning two patriots to their fates. None of it made any sense. He trusted that Primakov would explain himself at Yasenevo.

Stepanov was alone. The room was as neat and tidy as when he had checked in earlier. The bed was still made, the sheets undisturbed, and the glasses on the bedside tables still wore their paper tops. Stepanov's pistol—an MP-443 Grach—was on the bed, together with his shoulder holster. Mitrokhin carried his own pistol. There were also two SR-3 Vikhrs, short-barrelled carbines fitted with suppressors. The SR-3 was a Spetsnaz mainstay and offered all the firepower they would have needed to take the British agents out.

The feed from the camera was displayed on a screen that had been installed on the bureau where the television used to be. Stepanov saw motion on the screen, and, as he watched, two men came into view. They exited the elevator lobby, made their way down the corridor and paused outside the door to 1022. The man whom Stepanov had seen that afternoon knelt down and started to work on the lock. He was efficient, and it didn't take him long; he stood, opened the door slowly and carefully, and went inside. The second man followed.

≈

THE CURTAINS WERE DRAWN and the room was dark. Pope pulled out his supressed Sig and took a moment to allow his eyes to adjust; it was a suite, with a bathroom off to his left and a sitting area ahead and to the right. The bedroom was ten paces ahead of him. He could hear the sounds of breathing, the rhythmic ins and outs suggesting that Timoshev and Kuznetsov were fast asleep.

Twelve pulled his own pistol and, before Pope could stop him, stepped around him and went farther into the room. Pope could see the shape of two people in the king-size bed. Twelve aimed the pistol at the nearest body and pulled the trigger twice. The body jerked, enough to wake the second sleeper, but too late. Twelve aimed and fired two more times. The second body spasmed and then it, too, was still.

Pope wanted to curse, to rail at Twelve for his presumption, but he gritted his teeth. Not now. Later. He switched on the bedside lamp, took out his phone and took quick photographs of the man and woman so that their identities could be confirmed later. He nodded to Twelve, and they made their way back to the door. Pope reached for the door handle, pulled it down and checked that the corridor was empty. He stepped outside, held the door for Twelve, then closed it with a quiet click. They made their way back to the service lift.

"What the fuck?"

"I was following orders," Twelve said.

"Not *my* orders. I told you I was the senior—"

"No, not yours," Twelve said. "Control's. The job's done. Take it up with him if you have a problem."

Twelve stood quietly and, as Pope looked at him in the mirrored wall of the car, he thought he saw a smile playing at the corner of his mouth. Pope intended to take it up with Control. It was all he could do not to punch Twelve out.

They went down to the staff entrance and made their way to the men's room. They changed back into their street clothes, took the hotel uniforms with them and then exited onto the street. Twelve zipped up his jacket and headed south, crossing the road and slipping into a side street. Pope found a taxi and told the driver to take him to Domodedovo. He was booked on the 07.15 JAL flight to Narita where he had a connecting ticket on the Emirates flight to Heathrow. He would have a few hours to kill at the airport. He doubted that Timoshev and Kuznetsov would be found in time to trace either him or Twelve before they had left, but he knew that he would have to be careful. He would only be able to relax once he was on his way.

62

The taxi pulled up in the drop-off area outside the terminal at Vnukova International Airport. Milton paid the driver, stepped out of the car into the early morning chill, and held the door for Ross.

"Ready?" he asked her.

"How long do we have?"

"The flight leaves in an hour. Plenty of time."

They made their way into the terminal. It had been a busy few hours, and there had been no time for much more than a few snatched moments of sleep. A small team had been assembled to put together their legends and itinerary. The embassy's travel department had assessed their options for getting to Komsomolsk-on-Amur. The city was in the Russian Far East and was not a simple task to reach from Moscow. It was possible to take a train, but the eight-thousand-kilometre journey would have taken six and a half days, and they knew that they didn't have the luxury of time. Driving was out of the question for the same reason, and it had been decided that they had no choice but to fly. SAT

Airlines flew direct from Moscow to Komsomolsk, but that route was only twice-weekly and the next flight was two days away. The best that they could do was to fly on an Aeroflot 777 to Vladivostok, put up with a twelve-hour layover and then take the Aurora flight to Komsomolsk. It would take a day to complete the trip. They would be in time to make the meet with Anastasiya Romanova, but there would be precious little time for preparation. Ross had asked if that would be a problem; Milton said that it wasn't ideal but assured her that they would be able to manage.

Their new legends had them as a married couple: Richard and Amy Burns. They were photographers visiting the Far East after being commissioned by an architectural magazine to shoot the Neo-renaissance buildings that were still present in the city centre. The legends were impressively thorough, especially given the limited time the staff had had to adorn them. They were presented with phones that had been carefully preloaded with evidence to back up their stories: there were full email histories, including copies of the correspondence with the commissioning magazine, and photographs from the other stops on their trip, including touristy shots that showed them standing outside the Kremlin and St Basil's Cathedral and the Winter Palace in Saint Petersburg. Their contract with the magazine was given extra ballast thanks to payments that had been made into their fake bank accounts to represent their fee and expenses. They knew it was possible that the authorities would access their accounts if they conducted a full check, and, if they did, they would find transactions that evidenced the couple's flight from Paris to St Petersburg and then on to Moscow, payments for their hotel stays, and the meals and drinks that they had enjoyed.

Their legends were tested for the first time as they passed through security. An officious-looking functionary examined their passports and tickets, asked cursory questions about the nature of their trip, and then waved them through. The guards at the security booth were similarly inquisitive, and asked Milton to open their carry-on after it had slid through the scanner. He did, taking out the cameras that the embassy had provided. The guard insisted that he hand them over, and Milton made a show of his anxiety as the woman roughly examined the kit. She grunted her satisfaction, dumped both cameras on the metal bench and left Milton to repack them.

There was a bar in the departure lounge and Ross led the way across to it. She ordered two bloody Marys, and, without asking if Milton wanted one, slid a glass across the pitted surface of the bar and waited until he picked it up.

"Cheers," she said. "Here's to unexpected trips to places no one should be asked to visit."

There were no other travellers within earshot, and Milton forgave her the indiscretion. He touched his glass to hers, put it to his lips and knocked the drink back in one thirsty gulp.

Ross did the same, then set the glass back on the bar and wiped her mouth with the back of her hand. "Another?"

They had forty-five minutes before they needed to go to the gate and Milton knew that a drink would help him to sleep on the plane.

He was tempted, sorely so, but raised his hand. "Too early for me," he said, thinking back to the meeting in Islington and knowing that there was no way on earth he could ever share with them the circumstances of this latest temptation. And then, thinking about that, the prospect of another became difficult to dismiss and, with the surety that this would be the last, he changed his mind, told her "Why not?" and waited for the bartender to prepare a second round.

AEROFLOT FLIGHT SU 6281

he Aeroflot flight took off on time. Ross put on her eye mask, reclined her seat and went to sleep.

Milton was tired, too, but not quite ready to follow her example. He opened his carry-on and took out his tablet. He opened his mail server and selected the encrypted file that he had requested from Ziggy Penn before they had left the embassy. It was Jessie Ross's MI6 personnel file. Milton was uncomfortable that he knew so little about her. They were travelling to an isolated area with limited consular assistance, and he wanted to understand her better. He would have preferred to travel alone, but, despite his misgivings, he could see the good sense in having her along. She spoke perfect Russian and had experience travelling in the area. Just as importantly, being part of a couple with reason to be there made it slightly less likely that he would attract the attention of the authorities.

He read. Ross had been born in Portsmouth. Her father was a gas fitter and her mother worked in the reception of a local accountancy firm. Ross had studied at a local comprehensive, where she had developed a particular aptitude for languages which had, in turn, led to her taking a degree in Russian. She reported that she had enjoyed the course, and especially the year she had spent at the British Council in St Petersburg. The year had allowed her the latitude to travel across the country, from east to west; her Russian had become more natural and she had learned about the culture and expectations of Russia that were to become important later in her career.

She had graduated and taken a job as a researcher at Cambridge University. Transcripts of her interview with the SIS recruiter were appended to the report. She had said that she found academic work to be too dry for her tastes, and she'd found it difficult to acquire the funding to make the trips back to Russia that would enable her to further her practical research. After she had been turned down for a grant that would have allowed her to study for a year in Moscow, she had decided that she would leave and look for a job in management consultancy. It was a fortunate coincidence that she had seen the advertisement for SIS intelligence officers as she was looking around. She had applied, and, after a comprehensive background check—the fruits of which Milton was reading now—she had been accepted.

Her first posting had been as a report officer with responsibility for Russia and the former Eastern Bloc countries. R-Officers were tasked with meeting agent runners, often in the field, to discuss the intelligence that had been provided by their agents. She was required to assess the quality of the intel, corroborate it by way of second sources, and contextualise it for onward delivery to her superiors and politicians. She had developed a solid reputation and was quickly fast-tracked and given responsibility for briefing ministers on Russian affairs.

Milton flicked on and found, to his surprise, that there

was a blot on her otherwise immaculate copybook. It was reported that she had had an affair with the private secretary of the foreign secretary. The man was married, and, it was reported, had chosen his wife over his mistress. The wife had found Ross and had instigated a brawl that had led to the wife's eye socket being fractured. The police had been called and Ross had been arrested. Her career, although tarnished, was her saviour: she was heavily involved in analysis of a failed Islamic plot to bomb the New York subway and it was decided at a 'senior level'—Milton knew that euphemism most likely meant the management tier at VX, perhaps even Benjamin Stone himself—that she should be released so that she could continue her work. The story of the affair had been kept out of the newspapers and Ross had been put back to work.

Milton flicked on. Ross had applied to become an agent runner. The psychiatrist who had assessed her suggested that the reasons for her desire to switch roles were obvious: she wanted the chance to prove herself after the reprimand that she had earned thanks to the affair. Furthermore, her former lover was now being groomed for high office, with much of his success being attributed to his reputation as a loving husband and doting father. Ross was asked about her feelings for the man during her psych evaluation and had replied that she was disgusted by his duplicity and the willingness of the government to cooperate in the pretence. She said that she wanted to get as far away from him as possible, and that "Russia was a long way from Whitehall."

Ross had been given a diplomatic legend and was assigned to Moscow Station. She had taken over the running of existing agents and developed new ones, including several promising leads into the lower levels of the Kremlin. And then she had returned to London. The affair had left her pregnant; she had given birth to a son and said that she wanted to bring him up at home. She had replaced Leonard Geggel, taking on the responsibility of looking after the defectors who had come to the United Kingdom for sanctuary during and after the fall of the Wall.

Milton was impressed. He glanced over at her, sleeping in the seat next to his. She had only just turned thirty, and she had packed a lot into her career so far. This, though, was something that she had never done before. Running agents was one thing; not without danger, but nothing compared to the risks that the agents themselves took. Ross didn't have the insulation of diplomatic protection now. She was not riding a desk at VX, nor even in the protected environment of Moscow Station. This was an active operation, conducted in one of the most heavily surveilled countries in the world, against an opponent with thousands of agents in the field, an enemy that already had blood on its hands. This was real, and dangerous, and with an outcome that Milton could not predict.

VLADIVOSTOK INTERNATIONAL AIRPORT

64

R oss stretched out her legs. She and Smith had found two empty seats in the Laguna Lounge. They had already been waiting for four hours, and there was another eight still to go. There was a TV on the wall and it had been tuned to RT, the Russian state broadcaster that could be relied upon to run the government line. They had watched three hourly bulletins so far, and each had opened with footage from Southwold. Ross had translated for Smith, explaining that the anchors were decrying the slanderous accusations being made by the British government, and suggesting that they look nearer to home for the guilty parties. Smith gave a weary shrug, said that he wouldn't expect anything else and then concentrated on the copy of Dickens' *Martin Chuzzlewit* that he was reading on his phone.

Ross looked at her watch and then levered herself off the bench, stretching out the kinks in her back. "I'm going to freshen up," she said, pointing to the sign for the showers.

"I'll be here," Smith said.

Ross made her way to the cabanas.

ROSS PAID for a cabana and went inside. She turned on the shower so that it would be audible from outside and waited. Two minutes passed and then she heard a light tap at the door. She slid the bolt and opened the door; a man was standing there. He was nondescript, wearing jeans, a t-shirt and a light olive jacket. He stepped inside, closed the door behind him and then slid the bolt through the lock.

"My name is Stepanov," he said. "I work for the deputy director."

"We need to be quick," Ross said. "The man I'm with is sharp. He'll be suspicious if I'm away for too long."

"It won't take long. Just a few questions." He spoke quickly and quietly, the sound of his voice muffled by the hissing of the shower.

"Go on."

"The rendezvous with Romanova. Are the details still the same?"

"As far as I know. Tomorrow at midday at the railway station. What's going to happen?"

"I will be there," he said.

"Not on your own?"

"There will be two of us."

"And then? What will happen?"

"We will wait for Romanova to show herself, and then we will arrest her and the British agent." He paused. "But you must get away. As soon as you see us, start to run."

"Primakov explained. I get it."

"There is a river terminal in Komsomolsk, at the end of Oktyabrskiy Prospekt, right by the beach. You can take a hydrofoil to Nikolaevsk. It will take twelve hours. There is a small airport there. Get a flight to Sakhalin, then south to Japan."

She committed the route to memory. "Is there anything else?"

"The agent must not suspect anything. You must—"

"I've been fooling men like him for years," she said, cutting across him. "It's not going to be a problem."

"Of course," he said.

He was carrying a small bag. He unzipped it and took out a lipstick.

"What is this?" she asked.

"This is an *elektricheskiy pistolet*," he said. "A lipstick pistol. It has been in use for many years, but Line T have improved the design. It is a single shot pistol, with one 4.5mm Makarov round. You twist the base, here, and it will fire. It is accurate to two metres. We think you should carry it. You will need to defend yourself if something goes wrong."

"Nothing is going to go wrong," she said. "And if he goes through my purse and sees this—"

"He will see a lipstick," Stepanov interrupted. "Please. You are a valuable asset. We do not want you to be undefended."

"Fine," she said, dropping the lipstick into her bag. "Anything else?"

"No," Stepanov said.

She looked at her watch. "I need to shower. He's sharp, like I said. If my hair doesn't look wet he's going to be suspicious."

Stepanov went to the door, slid the bolt, opened the door a crack and looked out.

"Good luck," he said, turning back. "I will see you tomorrow."

He opened the door all the way and disappeared into the corridor. Ross closed the door behind him, locked it again, and undressed. She stepped under the tepid water and scrubbed it over her skin, tipping her head back so that it could run through her hair. She took a moment to assess how she felt and found—still—that she wasn't nervous. It was true what she had said: she had been doing this, working under the noses of Raj Shah and everyone else at the River House, for years. None of them suspected her. They underestimated her; they always had. They had no idea.

She twisted the tap to turn off the water, stepped out of the cubicle and towelled herself down. No, she thought. No idea at all. Smith might have been sharp, but she knew that she was more than his match.

PART V

KOMSOMOLSK-ON-AMUR

65

K omsomolsk had two airports due to the presence of the Sukhoi factory. Milton looked out of the window and saw the city laid out like patchwork below him. The city and its suburbs stretched out for over twenty miles along the left bank of the Amur, a large watercourse that looked particularly wide as they circled above it at five thousand feet. Milton had read the Wikipedia entry for the city during their layover; the city was spread out in two distinct sections: the central area, which housed the shipyard and the Dzemgi, an area that had coalesced around the Sukhoi factory. The central, older area featured the Stalinist architecture that they had nominally come to photograph, while the area around the factory was composed of modern, bland apartment blocks.

Their flight was scheduled to land at Khurba airbase, the second of the two airports. The pilot came over the intercom and delivered an update in Russian that Milton did not understand.

"We'll be on the ground in ten minutes," Ross translated for him.

The flight attendants started to pass along the aisle to prepare the cabin for landing.

"Any other ideas how we're going to play this?" Ross asked him.

Milton had been thinking about that. He knew that tomorrow was going to be difficult and dangerous. They would be operating in a city where they would have no consular assistance, and they were not travelling under a diplomatic passport. There would be no immunity if they were arrested. They would be alone and vulnerable.

"She wants to meet at midday," he said. "We'll scout the area in the morning and, if it looks safe, we'll wait for her like she asked."

"And then?"

"We get her out," he said.

Milton thought that she was going to ask him how they were going to do that, but, instead, she checked her seatbelt and looked out of the porthole window as the ground rushed up to meet them.

She turned back again. "But that's tomorrow," she said. "How about today? What are we going to do?"

"We look around the city and take pictures," Milton said, "just like we're here to do."

66

The embassy had booked them a room at the Hotel Voskhod, on Prospekt Pervostroiteleya. It was a new building, seven storeys tall and soulless. It had not been chosen for its amenities, but rather for its location: it was within walking distance of the railway station, and well placed as a hub from which to explore the rest of the town. There was a supermarket on one side of the building and a nightclub on the other.

They went into the reception area and Ross went up to the desk. A clerk was fiddling with a computer and looked up disdainfully when Ross cleared her throat. The conversation proceeded in Russian and Milton understood none of it; he heard the surname of their legends—Burns—and waited as the clerk took Ross's credit card for incidentals and then printed off two keycards for them.

"Fourth floor," Ross said once the process was complete.

She led the way to the elevators, summoned a car and stepped inside. Milton followed.

"Everything all right?" he asked.

"Fine," Ross said. "It all checked out."

"Two Westerners in a place like this," Milton said. "We won't go unnoticed."

"Probably not. She asked me why we were here. I told her we were taking photographs. She seemed to buy it."

Milton guessed that the hotel would be required to alert the local FSB office that they had two Westerners staying with them, and wouldn't have been surprised if they were checked out, perhaps even put under light surveillance. He was relaxed at the prospect. They were a long way from Moscow now, and even the FSB, with all its manpower, wouldn't be able to bring a big team to bear on them at short notice. He doubted that they would see it as a necessity, especially once they established their legends, and even more so given that they would be leaving town in the next day or two, depending upon when and if Anastasiya Romanova made an appearance.

The lift stopped and Milton made his way to room 404. He opened the door with his keycard and went inside. The room was pleasant enough: there was a double bed, a large bureau and two cheap leatherette armchairs. The curtains and carpet were burgundy-coloured and the ceiling seemed to have been made from vinyl; the room was reflected in the polished white surface. Milton had no idea whether the FSB's reach would extend to being able to bug a room like this, so far from anywhere Westerners might be expected to visit, but he had no wish to take chances; he went over to the radio, turned it on and then went to Ross.

He leaned in close, as if to kiss her on the cheek, and whispered, "It might be bugged."

She nodded and, before Milton could react, she twisted her head and kissed him on the lips. Milton could taste the mintiness of the gum that she had been chewing. He kissed her back, thinking about the possibility of bugs and cameras, telling himself that he was just playing the part that had been asked of him. She disengaged first, laying the palm of her hand against his cheek. She trailed her fingers across his stubble and gave him a wink. Milton was reminded how attractive she was. Pretty, but, more than that, she had an unruliness to her, an edge that made her different and interesting. This was just business, he told himself. It was all for show.

"What's the plan?" she asked.

Milton collected the camera bags and held them up. "Shall we go and take a look around?"

THEY DECIDED TO WALK. The city was laid out with a central hub that was then surrounded by a number of spokes that radiated out from it. Ross bought a guidebook and led the way to the unofficial symbol of the city, the 'house with a spire' near Lenin Square. They visited the Cathedral of the Holy Prophet Elijah, stopping in its wide square to take photographs of the five golden bulbs that sat atop its tower. They made their way along Lenin Avenue and Mira Avenue and took pictures of the buildings constructed in the style of Stalin's neoclassicism. They visited the History Museum, the Exhibition Hall of the Union of Artists and the Zoological Center. They took a taxi to Silinsky Forest, five hundred hectares of virgin pine, spruce and larch within the city limits.

They took photographs as they travelled, both of them carrying the Nikons they had been supplied with on straps around their necks. Milton kept an eye on their surroundings, looking for any sign of surveillance. There were no cars following them, either directly or on parallel streets; no leapfrogging surveillants; no watchers salted ahead of them to pick up their tail; no one with cameras trained on them; nothing. He glanced at Ross, who was seemingly absorbed in her surroundings and either didn't notice Milton's occasional distraction or didn't comment upon it.

Milton led the way to the railway station, heading across a wide parking lot to the main building. It was large, with a central section and two long wings, all of it painted an incongruous pink and white. There were rows of neatly planted trees, a paved area and then a wide space where cars had been parked. Milton had timed their arrival for midday so that he could get a sense of how busy it would be tomorrow. It was quiet, with just a handful of people waiting for their trains.

"What do you think?" Ross said.

"I'd rather it was busier. We're going to stand out."

"She'll be able to find us."

"And so will the FSB."

"You think they're following us?"

Milton looked out into the parking lot. As far as he could tell, they were alone. "I don't know."

They walked back outside and set off again toward the river.

"Have you thought how we're going to do it?" Ross asked him.

Milton looked again; there was no one near them. "We passed an Avis near the hotel," he said. "I'll hire a car later and we'll use that. If she's here tomorrow, we'll pick her up and go."

"Where? How are we going to get her out?"

"We'll drive south, back to Vladivostok. It'll take a day—when we get there, we'll take the ferry to Japan."

They came upon the embankment. It was the most

scenic part of town. The ferry terminal was here, and there was a park laid out around it with a fountain and statues. One statue stood out: four workers holding hammers and shovels and waving their hands as if greeting the party apparatchiks who might have visited to inspect their work. The official story was that a town had first been constructed here by patriotic members of the Komsomol—the Soviet youth league—who had landed on the shores of the Amur and set about building a communist utopia with wide avenues lined with trees, a modern transport system and comfortable housing for all. Milton knew that it was all lies. The region had been turned into one of the most voracious of the gulags during Stalin's purges, and it was the tens of thousands of political prisoners and Japanese prisoners of war who had really laid those first foundations. It was a city of lies, built atop thousands of unmarked graves.

They took pictures of the statue and then climbed the steps to the ferry terminal. It was an ugly building and was next to a brutal concrete pier that jutted out into the water. The view from the top was impressive, a broad panorama that took in the river—half a mile wide at this point—and the snowy hills on the opposite bank. The embankment itself was a grey and pink stone walkway, and they followed it to the east. They passed an area that was under construction, with large LED screens showing images of the river during winter, with locals wrapped up in heavy coats skating on the ice. It was warm today, as it had been for the duration of Milton's time in Russia. Steps led down to the water where a stretch of sand had been revealed by the retreating tide, a space for children to splash in the shallows while their parents lay back and enjoyed the sun's warmth. The temperature would plunge by forty or fifty degrees

Fahrenheit between now and the winter; it was difficult to credit.

"My legs are killing me," Ross said. "How far do you think we've walked?"

"Ten miles?" Milton offered. He was tired, but the fresh air had done him good.

She took out her phone and looked at the time. "It's five o'clock. Can we go back to the hotel?"

Milton could do with sitting down, too, and he was happy that they had wandered enough so that anyone who might have been watching them would be able to report that they had behaved as might have been expected from their legends. "Yes," he said. "I think we're done."

She linked her arm through his. "What are you doing tonight, Mr. Burns?"

He looked over at her; she was smiling mischievously back at him. He remembered the kiss. "Not much," he said. "Why?"

"Want to get dinner with your wife?"

67

They took turns to freshen up. They had each been provided with the kinds of clothes that travellers might carry in their packs, but, in both cases, the clothes had been chosen for their utilitarian qualities rather than for a night out. Milton showered first and, while he waited for Ross, he dressed in a pair of jeans and a black crew neck. He regarded himself in the room's mirror; he didn't care much about how he looked, and this outfit was never going to do him any favours. He went back to the bedroom.

"All yours," he said.

Ross regarded him. "Very nice, Mr. Burns."

Milton shook his head and smiled. "I'm going to get some ice."

"Don't mind me," Ross said. She went to the bathroom, allowing the towel to drop before she closed the door. Milton caught a glimpse of her in the mirror, turned his head away and went to the table. He collected the plastic ice bucket, left the room and walked along the corridor to the ice machine. He placed the bucket beneath the chute and pressed the button for ice; the machine chugged and grumbled and, eventually and rather resentfully, ejected a few dirty-looking cubes.

Milton took a moment for himself. He couldn't drink tonight. He wanted to, very badly, but he knew that it would be unwise. He needed to be careful with Ross and, more than that, he needed to be on his game tomorrow. He was wired tight, all the usual nerves and anxieties amplified now that they were close to the moment of action that might bring the affair to a close. He was as confident as he could be that his planning was good. He had done his best with limited information and an abbreviated timeframe, but their reconnaissance today had been satisfactory and he had discovered no threats that would give him cause to abort.

He knew why he was more nervous than would normally have been the case: it was Ross. He had grown to like her despite—or perhaps because of—her spikiness and unpredictability. He didn't know how much he trusted himself, and tomorrow was going to offer another, bigger challenge.

THE RECEPTIONIST RECOMMENDED L'GOLD STAR, a restaurant that specialised in Russian food with Chinese influences. It was on Ulitsa Alleya Truda, a mile and a half from the hotel, and, on Ross's insistence, they took the hire car that Milton had rented when they had returned to the hotel from their day's reconnaissance. The place was small, with fifty covers and basic decoration; it wasn't much more than a café.

"You take me to the nicest places," Ross said after the waiter had rather peremptorily shown them to their table.

Milton looked around and saw that there was only one other occupied table. The couple sitting at it had been there before them and, judging from the fact that they were enjoying dessert, it seemed that they had been there for a while. They couldn't have been FSB surveillants. Milton was satisfied that they were not being watched.

The menus were in Russian, and Ross offered to order for them both. The waiter came back and, without looking up, scribbled down the items that Ross selected, collected the menus and disappeared.

"What did you pick?" Milton asked her.

"You don't trust me?"

"I didn't say that."

She grinned. "Cantonese pork ribs and crispy sea bass. We can share. You want a drink?"

"I do," he said, "but I'm going to pass. So should you. We need to be clear-headed in the morning."

"Spoilsport," she complained.

The waiter came back with a tray and two bowls. He grunted something as he deposited the bowls before them; Milton looked down and saw borscht. There were spoons on the table. Milton's was dirty, but he decided it would not be politic to complain and wiped it on the back of his sleeve. He spooned up a mouthful of the soup.

"Good?" she asked him.

"Very good," he said, spooning up another mouthful. They hadn't eaten properly today and he was hungry.

Ross gazed at him across the table as she ate. "How much of what you've told me about you is the truth?"

"I can't remember what I've told you."

"I know the military liaison thing was a line."

"No," he admitted. "That's not strictly true."

"So what *is* true?"

"That almost everything is classified."

"And the bits that aren't?"

He paused, wondering how much he should tell her. "I was a soldier for a long time."

"That's obvious."

"It was years ago."

"You can still tell. Did you see any action?"

He smiled weakly; memories flickered like distant flashes of lightning. "Enough for me," he said.

"Special forces?"

"Eventually. Royal Green Jackets first, then the SAS."

"And then whatever it is you can't tell me about."

Milton nodded, keen to move the conversation away from himself. "What about you? How'd you end up working for SIS?

"None of it was very unusual," she said. "I'm not that interesting."

The self-deprecation struck a bum note. Milton guessed that she would enjoy the opportunity to talk about herself. "Go on," he said. "Tell me."

She ran through her career highlights, including her recruitment and early years. Milton remembered what he had read in her file and found it more interesting to see which parts she omitted. He wasn't surprised that she ignored the disgrace of her affair and her child.

"You've got secrets too, then?" he said when she was done.

"What do you mean?"

"You left some of it out."

She eyeballed him. "Meaning?"

"You didn't say anything about when you got into trouble."

"You know about that?"

"I've seen your file."

If she was irritated, she did not show it. "Yes," she said. "I ended up making a series of catastrophically bad choices and sleeping with the secretary to the minister I was responsible for briefing. That was probably the biggest one."

"But you're still here," he said.

"Because I'm fucking good at my job. And who else has got the sort of messed-up private life where no one cares if they jump on a plane to go to a dump like this at the drop of a hat?"

"And there I was," Milton said, "thinking you were having a good time."

"Are you kidding?" she said. "This is about the most fun I've had since this whole sorry mess got started."

The waiter collected their empty bowls and replaced them with their main courses. Milton took the sea bass and Ross took the ribs.

"You make any mistakes?" she asked as she chewed on a forkful of pork.

"Too many to count," Milton said.

"Any like mine?"

"With a woman, you mean?"

She nodded.

"I was married once. It didn't last long. We were both too young and my career meant too much to me. I was a bad husband."

"Same," she said. "Career comes first."

"Things would've been different now," Milton said. "*I'm* different. My priorities are different to how they were back then. I'm older. Seen more."

He stopped. He hadn't meant to be so frank. He rarely mentioned his ex-wife; it was so long ago that he hardly thought about his failed marriage at all, and, whenever he did, it always triggered a moment of wistfulness.

"Go on," she said.

He took a drink of water. "Life is all about choices. Every now and again, we have a decision to make that determines how things might look further down the line. The jobs we apply for. The people we meet. I was married before I got into the thing that I do now. I think if I had chosen her instead of my work, I would have been a very different person today. Life would definitely have been different."

"You wouldn't have been here?" she said.

He shook his head. "Not a chance."

"And you wouldn't have met me."

She looked at him as she said that, and, as Milton looked up, she held his eye and reached her hand across the table. She slid it over his and left it there for a long beat. Milton found that he was holding his breath; he exhaled, moved his hand away and forked another piece of fish, sliding it into his mouth. He looked up and saw that she was still looking at him. She held his gaze again, her eyes sparkling, and then smiled.

Milton smiled, and then looked down at his plate. He started to think about tomorrow.

MILTON KNEW that he shouldn't, but he couldn't stop himself. They kissed in the car as soon as he parked it in the lot next to the hotel, both of them hungry for the other. They hurried inside, running their hands over one another in the lift, their mouths pressed together, each drinking in the smells and the tastes, oblivious to the impatient buzz as the elevator reached the fourth floor. They reached the room and tumbled onto the bed, tearing at their clothes, their hands clasped together as she rolled atop him, then sliding underneath the crew neck and pulling it up and over his head, revealing the litany of scars that covered his body.

"Jesus," she breathed, her nails tracing the raised edges of stab wounds and bullet holes, injuries that told the story of Milton's career. She laid her palm on his mouth, stifling his retort, and then leaned down and kissed the point where a thug in Macedonia had shivved him. She kissed the burn beneath his left breast and the puckered entry point of the 9mm slug that had just missed his liver. She kissed down and down and Milton closed his eyes, loathing himself, knowing that he was betraying her and hating what he knew he was going to have to do.

PART VI

KOMSOMOLSK-ON-AMUR

68

Milton slept lightly, and when he awoke, it took him a moment of staring up at the ceiling before he remembered where he was. He felt the warmth of a body next to him, and when he turned over, he saw Jessie Ross lying there. She was on her front and had pushed the covers away from her body at some point in the night. Milton reached for his watch and checked the time: six. He got up as quietly as he could, padded across the room and, checking that Ross was still asleep, collected his clothes and took them into the bathroom. He took out his phone, opened the encrypted messaging app and sent a quick message. He showered and dressed with a pulse of anxiety in his gut. That was to be expected. There was no way of telling how the morning would go. He reminded himself that he had no choice, and that he should have no sympathy, either. Jessie had brought all of this on herself.

A return message buzzed onto his phone. He opened the door to the hotel hallway. A plastic bag containing a newspaper had been left on the handle. He took the bag—it felt heavier than it ought to have done—and replaced the Do Not Disturb sign. He closed the door as quietly as he could and edged back into the room.

"Morning."

He turned to the bed. Jessie was awake, watching him through heavy-lidded eyes.

"What time is it?"

"Six fifteen," he said.

"What's that?" she said, nodding at the plastic bag.

Milton took the newspaper out of the bag. It was *Komsomolskaya Pravda*, the paper that Anastasiya Romanova had said he should be carrying when he went for the meet. He sat down and laid the bag on his lap; it wasn't empty. He reached inside and took out a Beretta 92 with two spare, fully loaded magazines. He placed all three items on the bureau and watched as Jessie's eyes were drawn to them.

"Where did you get that?" she said.

"I know, Jessie."

"You know what?"

"Everything. I know it all."

Ross sat up, reaching down to wrap the sheet around her body. "What the fuck are you talking about?"

"Where do you want me to start?"

"How about by making sense?"

"You've been working for the SVR." He gave her a chance to confirm it, but she said nothing. He ignored her truculent silence. "Directorate S? It doesn't really matter— you'll give us all the details later."

"I don't know what you're talking about."

"Just listen—" Milton began.

She ignored him, surging up out of the bed and trying to pass him on the way to the door. Milton got to his feet and stepped across to block her way. Ross tried to shoulder her way past but he was too strong for her; he grabbed her by the shoulders and held her in place.

"Get off me," she spat.

"Calm down," Milton said.

"Get your fucking hands *off* me!" She shook his hands off, raising her hand to strike him. Milton grabbed her wrist with his left hand and then used his right to take her arm at a point three fingers down from her elbow. He dug his thumb into the pressure point. Her face crumpled with pain and Milton used the moment to guide her back over to the bed and down onto it once again.

"Relax," Milton said, releasing the grip.

"I'll scream," she threatened.

"I wouldn't do that. Think about your parents, Jessie. Your son."

Milton hated to have to threaten her like that, but he had no choice. He had to get through to her quickly, and she had brought everything on herself. Her face slackened as the anger drained out of it. She gaped for a moment, but then her eyes burned again.

"You bastard," she said.

"That's what happens when you play the game and you get caught. What do you expect?"

"My son—where is he?"

"He's with your parents. They haven't been approached, not yet, and the preference is that they won't be. But that's up to you. You get to choose what happens next."

"Really?" She shook her head derisively. "Do I?"

"You're lucky." He ignored the resentment shining from her eyes. "You can offer valuable service—valuable enough, perhaps, to balance out what you've done. You have two choices. One is more palatable than the other."

"Let me guess: one choice is bad for my son?"

Milton hated himself for what he had to say. "He'll be placed into care. And life will be made difficult for your parents, too. Your father's business will lose its export licence, for example. It will find itself in legal trouble, and then it'll be bankrupted. It would be a simple thing to wipe them out—all it would take would be a word from the people I work for. They'd do it without thinking twice. You've pissed them off, Jessie."

She stared at him, daring him.

"It's not a bluff—none of this is a bluff."

"And what about me? What if I don't agree?" She looked at the gun. "You going to use that?"

Milton's throat was dry, and he feared that if he replied he would betray the nausea that bubbled in his stomach. He hoped that Ross would see sense, and that he was not in the business of making baseless threats. His palms began to sweat.

"The other choice?" she asked.

"You work for VX—properly, this time, against the Russians."

"Just like that?"

"It doesn't need to be difficult. You just follow through with the operation as you planned it. We go to the rendezvous with Romanova. There will be an incident. I know that the Center is using us to get to her. They'll have agents waiting, but I'm going to take care of them. We take Romanova and leave the country, just like we planned."

"And then?"

"And then, once you're back in London, you signal the Center that you're fine, you haven't been compromised and that you're awaiting instructions."

"And the Center wouldn't think that I've been blown? Or that I tipped you off?"

"Why would they? You've never played them before. You're an agent at VX, in the heart of the secret service. They'll look for reasons to believe that you're clean. You're the golden goose. They'll hate even the thought that they might have lost you. And why would they think you've been blown? They have no reason to think that you've been exposed. You did your part—you led them to Romanova, just like you promised, but we were wise to it. They know we have a source—they'll think BLUEBIRD tipped us."

"As simple as that?"

"It can be. It's up to you—you just need to be yourself, as if nothing has happened."

Milton knew how that would be done: she would be provided with a stream of legitimate intelligence that she could leak, nothing too compromising, yet valuable enough to keep the Center's interest piqued. A promotion would follow, placing her in a more senior role, putting temptation in front of Russian noses, everything sharpened with the promise of more to come. The Center would be greedy, rapacious, and fed enough intelligence to ignore the nagging feeling that perhaps they should be more circumspect with their once golden girl. She would have to be convincing, but she had already demonstrated that she could do that; she had fooled British intelligence for years.

"They're not stupid, Smith," she said.

"You need to be persuasive. You do that, maybe things start to look a little better for you and your family."

"What's this?" she said, her lip curling. "A carrot to go with the stick?"

"No. SIS is going to be hard to win over. Raj Shah is unhappy. The mandarins had to be persuaded that I shouldn't just plug you here and now. You've got a lot to do before they think about rewarding you. But the status quo can be maintained in the meantime. You can go home to your son. Your parents get to keep their house. The account in Zurich, the one the SVR has been paying into—VX might even consider the possibility that you can keep that. But that's all up to you."

She looked away and clenched her jaw. "How did you know? About me—how did you find out? Who told you?"

"Does that make any difference?"

"Was it BLUEBIRD?" she asked.

"Did the Center ask you to find him?"

"Or her," she corrected. "They asked. But I never could."

"How you were found out doesn't matter," Milton said. "You were found out." He looked at her. "What do you want to do?"

"What choice do I have?"

Milton shook his head. "You don't."

She stood, gathered the sheet around her, and sat back down again. All the warmth from last night was gone now, replaced by bitterness and resentment. Milton wondered whether she ever had liked him, or whether she was just an accomplished and convincing actress. He knew: she was playing him. He was old enough and jaded enough not to take it personally, but, despite that, he still felt a tinge of regret.

"Fine," she said quietly. "What do you need me to do?"

"I have some questions about the rendezvous this morning," Milton said. "I need to understand what the SVR is planning to do."

"There's a man," she began. "His name is Stepanov. He works for Primakov—I think he does the kind of thing you do. He's going to be waiting. He said that he'll have a small team. They have orders to arrest you and Romanova."

Milton sat down in the chair opposite her. He needed to get all the information he could as quickly as possible. What happened next—whether they went ahead or bailed— would depend upon what he learned.

69

Stepanov and Mitrokhin sat in the car, both of them staring through the windshield at the men and women who made their way to and from the railway station. It wasn't a busy station, stuck at the end of the line in a district of Russia that had very little to offer unless one worked in aviation. Stepanov was alert, fortified by a cup of strong coffee that he had bought from a vendor as he scouted the terminus on foot half an hour earlier. He watched as a family made their way through the tall doors and into the pink-painted building. Others dawdled, perhaps surprised by the heat that was unusual for this part of the country. Stepanov had started to sweat the moment he had stepped out of the air-conditioned cocoon of the car, and now his shirt was wet and perspiration ran down his forehead. It felt like bathing in warm water. He was glad to be inside again.

He looked at his watch. "Five minutes," he said.

"Do you think she will come?" Mitrokhin asked him.

"They will," he said. "If not today, then tomorrow.

Perhaps she just watches today. Either way, if she is here, we will take her."

Both men were armed. Their MP-443s were on the backseat, but they had chosen to carry the two SR-3 Vikhrs. The carbines offered the mix of power and portability that they needed. They did not know if the British agent was armed, but it didn't matter; he would be badly outgunned.

Stepanov looked out of the windshield again. He picked out the other agents that he had selected for this detail. They were from Directorate S, their discretion assured. The old man in the cloth cap sitting on the bench was a retired agent. He had been picked because he had worked for Stepanov for years and because his age meant that he could blend into the background without arousing even the first shred of suspicion. The couple sitting on the grassy knoll listening to music? They had flown in from Moscow yesterday. The bum slumped against the building, seemingly drunk? He had served in the Directorate as an illegal in Greece and Macedonia. There were six of them in total, heavy coverage on the location that Romanova had chosen for the rendezvous.

Stepanov looked at his watch. Two minutes to midday.

"Come on," Mitrokhin said under his breath, unfolding the buttstock of the Vikhr and flipping up the rear sight.

"Be patient," Stepanov said. "She will come. We just need to wait."

He looked at his watch again.

Milton drove the hire car to the railway station. Ross was next to him, staring out of the window and saying nothing. Milton knew that he was taking a risk. And not just a small risk. The RV point would be heavy with SVR or FSB agents, a trap waiting to snap shut as soon as Anastasiya Romanova raised her head above the parapet. His fate was now tied to Ross's and, more specifically, to the mole within the SVR who had exposed her. He was relying on the hope that the information that had been supplied to him was accurate, and that the plan that had been concocted would work. If it did not—if BLUEBIRD had been compromised, or if Ross was preparing something unexpected—then Milton's future would be bleak: weeks of interrogation in the Lubyanka, a show trial to demonstrate Britain's perfidy, and then a short and unpleasant existence in a Siberian camp.

He glanced across at Ross now. She was still staring out of the window, biting down on the corner of her lip. What was she thinking? Was she weighing up the choices, assessing the benefits and disbenefits of one of them over the other? There was no way of knowing, and that made Milton uncomfortable. Ignorance was dangerous.

The Russians had mounted an elegant operation, and Ross had been at the heart of it. She had been persuasive and Milton had harboured not even the faintest suspicion that she might have betrayed them. She had shown nothing to suggest it, and the intelligence that he had received from BLUEBIRD during their layover in Vladivostok had taken him completely by surprise. But that intelligence was categorical: she had been a Directorate S sleeper ever since her recruitment as a student in Moscow ten years before. BLUEBIRD had only just learned of Ross's treachery and he had taken a significant personal risk to deliver it in person. He had waited for Ross to leave Milton; it was ironic that Ross had chosen that moment to meet with Stepanov.

Milton thought back to the brief airport rendezvous with BLUEBIRD. No one at VX had ever seen the agent before and Milton had been surprised by his appearance; he was much younger than he would have expected for someone with the access to both the FSB and the SVR that, Milton understood, BLUEBIRD had demonstrated during the years that he had worked as a British asset. There had been no time for a conversation, and Milton would not have asked in any event, but he wondered whether it was BLUE-BIRD that he had met or an emissary. His suspicion complicated matters—he would report it in due course—but, for now, there was nothing for it other than to continue as planned.

He looked back to Ross. Her hands were in her lap, her right hand massaging the joints of her left. It was difficult not to be impressed by her assiduousness. She had been working them all along. There had not been enough time at the airport for him to have been fully briefed, but Milton could read between the lines: he could see how Ross had put her head down and built up her career, how she had ensured that she was in position to take over the running of the dissidents and defectors once Leonard Geggel had retired. He knew that Geggel had been put out to pasture thanks to errors in his handling of an agent; Milton wondered whether Ross had been responsible for that, opening up a vacancy that she had been able to fill. It would all come out eventually.

Milton read the newspapers and knew about the deaths of Russian dissidents in recent years. The diplomat who had died before meeting prosecutors to discuss Russian activities in Italy; the oil tycoon and friend to a jailed dissident who had died of a suspected embolism; the oligarch who was found hanging from a cupboard rail in his Berkshire mansion; the ex-spy who had died beneath the wheels of a Tube train. Those deaths now looked much less like the unfortunate accidents that the police had categorised them as being and more like the assassinations that SIS had always suspected. Some of those men, and others who had died in similar circumstances, had been hidden from the SVR with fresh identities, supposedly put out of reach. Just like Pyotr Aleksandrov had been put out of reach. Ross had killed Aleksandrov, just as surely as if she had put a gun to his head herself. She had marked him for death, and perhaps she had marked the others, too. She had found herself in a compromised position, but she was evidently smart and ruthless. He wondered, again, whether there was another card that she still had to play.

70

They rolled into the parking lot outside the railway station. It was empty, and Smith drove across it so that he could park nearer to the buildings. Ross ran her palm over the hip pocket of her trousers. She had taken the lipstick that Stepanov had given her and dropped it inside; she could feel the hard metal tube against her leg. Using it was an option. Stepanov had said that it would be effective up to two metres. She just had to point it and twist the end and the single round would fire. Smith had no reason to suspect it; she could shoot him in the back and run. But what then? What of her son? She would never see him again. She couldn't do it.

"Come on," Smith said. "Let's go."

Ross opened the door of the car and stepped outside. Smith did the same, then reached down and collected the newspaper that had been delivered to the room with his gun. Ross looked at him and gritted her teeth at how comprehensively they had outmanoeuvred her. She had had no idea that they knew about her. She wondered how long he had hidden the knowledge. When had he been told about her? And by whom? It must have been BLUEBIRD. She knew that it was an academic question, at least for the moment. They had her on a hook now, ready to dangle her in front of Primakov and Stepanov and the rest of Directorate S, the bait to lure them into a trap that would unravel the work that she had done for them for so long.

It wasn't that Ross's beliefs were offended by what had been forced upon her that morning. She had no political leanings in either direction. The professor who had recruited her into the SVR had known her well enough not to try and persuade her with philosophical or ethical arguments, had not tried to sell her on the evils of the west, the purity of Russia or the benefit to the world of levelling the geopolitical playing field. No, Ross had been persuaded to work for the SVR because of a more practical motivation: money. They had offered to pay her handsomely and, as she delivered more and more valuable intelligence, they had reacted with correspondingly larger amounts. She knew that she was one of their most valuable assets, buried deep within SIS and marked for a significant career there, and, true to their word, they paid accordingly. Her Swiss account contained nearly a million pounds, and the flow of money had included the largest payment yet after she had located Pyotr Aleksandrov for them.

So, no, it wasn't her beliefs that had been offended. It was her pride. She was upset because she had been duped. The stuffed shirts at VX had made her look like a fool, and it was that that she found so hard to swallow.

Smith left the keys in the ignition.

"Ready?" he said.

"This isn't going to work," she muttered.

"You'd better hope it does."

"Or what? My life is over whichever way this goes."

He stared at her; his eyes were the coldest, most piercing blue. "It doesn't have to be. Make up for what you've done and things can be as they were."

"Really?" she said. "You'll excuse me if I'm not overcome with enthusiasm."

"I don't really care. You brought this on yourself. You've been given a chance to fix it."

"Or I could give the signal and have you arrested."

"You could. But you know what that would mean for your family. I don't think you'll do that."

She shivered in his stare, but ignored him. Perhaps she could make him a little apprehensive. She had almost no influence now; she held onto the small amount that she had left.

Smith led the way across the parking lot toward the station building. Ross looked around. It was a wide space, and it was almost completely empty. There were five cars and a dirty white van parked near to the building, but that was all. There were a few men and women outside the station: a man on a bench, a couple talking animatedly to one another. She didn't recognise any of them, although she knew that she wouldn't. They would be FSB or SVR, trained in surveillance, practiced at hiding in plain sight, giving nothing away.

Smith walked on, and Ross turned to glance into the cabin of a car that had been parked twenty feet away from them. Stepanov was inside. He looked at her, and, for a moment, their eyes locked. She knew that all she would need to do was touch her ear and he would bring his agents out into the open, weapons drawn. Smith would be arrested but she would be blown; her usefulness to the Center would be at an end and her family would suffer. She would have her money, enough so that she would never again have to work, but she would have no life. Her usefulness to Deputy Director Primakov would be at an end. And she would be stuck in Moscow forever, a prisoner in a gilded cage.

She didn't know whether she would be able to do it.

71

M ilton held the newspaper in his hand and led the way across the parking lot. Ross followed alongside him.

"Do you see anyone?" he asked Ross.

"No," she said.

"Are you sure?"

"I don't see anyone," she said.

Milton felt an itch in the centre of his back, right between his shoulder blades, a sensation of exposure and vulnerability. His skin was clammy and sweat started to bead on his scalp. It was hot, but that wasn't it.

It was the dream.

It wasn't far away.

MICHAEL POPE WAS in the back of the van. It was a GAZelle, a commercial van made by Gaz in Nizhny Novgorod. It bore the livery of a local wholesale grocery business, the logo and script barely visible beneath a layer of dirt and crud. The vehicle was parked with its rear end facing the entrance to the station, and the filthy windows in the double doors offered a view of the steps, the pedestrianised area and some of the cars that had been parked nearby.

Bryan Duffy was sitting in the driver's seat. He had stolen the van earlier that morning. Duffy was Number Eleven. Pope had worked with him before, but knew very little about him beyond his name—Duffy had revealed it at a bar in Vienna while they worked an operation two months earlier—and his designation.

Pope and Duffy had tipped the crates of produce out of the back of the van before they had driven to the station, and now there was enough space for him, their equipment and three or four others. Pope was dressed in black, with a black balaclava covering his face. He had a UCIW on a sling that he wore over his shoulder, the automatic cradled in front of his body. The gun had the shorter barrel and Pope had screwed a suppressor onto it. He had two spare magazines in the pouches of his combat trousers and a full magazine in the weapon.

Pope saw Milton and Jessie Ross arrive in a hire car. He watched as they stepped out and made their way to the station. He scanned the other vehicles and checked out the men and women who were gathered in the vicinity of the station. He knew, of course, that some—perhaps many—of them would be SVR agents waiting to snatch Anastasiya Romanova should she dare to show her face. How many? He had no idea.

"*You think she'll come?*" Duffy asked over the radio.

"I don't know."

"*Midday,*" Duffy said.

"Check," Pope said, and then, before Duffy could speak again, he saw her. "Coming out now."

He reached for his radio and depressed the broadcast switch two times.

Here we go.

THE RADIO SQUELCHED TWICE in Milton's earpiece and then he saw her. He recognised Anastasiya Romanova from the photograph that he had been shown. She crossed the station concourse and stepped outside, coming down the broad steps that led into the pink-painted building. She was wearing jeans and a plain white t-shirt with a sunhat shielding her eyes from the glare of the midday sun. A train wheezed as it pulled away and Milton wondered whether she had arrived on it. That would have been clever; the SVR would have expected her to arrive from the town itself, to make her way into the station rather than coming out of it. It wouldn't have made a difference—they would have recognised her either way—but perhaps she was thinking, acting cautiously, and that would be a good thing.

She paused on the steps, looking left and right.

Milton took Ross by the elbow. "Stay close to me. Do what I tell you and I'll get you out alive—you have my word."

Ross didn't reply. Milton spared her a quick glance and saw that she was pale, sweat beading on her brow. No time to worry about that now. She was resilient—a survivor—and he had no option but to hope that she had calculated her odds and come to the conclusion that she was better off with him.

Milton set off again, headed for Anastasiya. The woman saw him coming, squinting in the sunlight despite the hat. She looked down at the newspaper, then back up at him.

Her face flickered with fear and uncertainty. Milton smiled at her, as if that might make a difference.

"Hello," Milton said in English when he was close enough for Romanova to hear him.

"Are you...?" Her English was halting, and the words trailed away.

Milton spoke slowly and firmly. "I'm here to get you out. Do you have the data that you want to sell?"

She looked confused. "My English," she said. "Not good."

Ross spoke in Russian. Milton didn't know what she had said, and had no choice but to hope she was playing straight. He watched Anastasiya's face and saw understanding, and then a nod. She replied in Russian.

"She has it," Ross said.

"Tell her we're going to get her out," he said to Ross.

Ross started to speak, but, before she could finish, Milton saw movement all around them. It happened at once, on command, a coordinated response. The SVR thought that their prey were in the trap, and now they were rushing to close it. An old man wearing a cloth cap stood up from the bench that he had been sitting on. A couple sitting on the grassy knoll away to the left stood up, too, the woman taking a weapon from the cloth bag at her feet. The bum slumped against the building, playing drunk, now stood up straight and took a pistol out from the folds of his rags.

Milton counted four of them, with the man in the Mercedes making five.

"*Don't move!*"

The order was barked out in English and Milton turned to face the speaker. He was out of the car, a pistol in his hand aimed straight at them.

Milton raised his hands.

"Do as they say," Milton said quietly, his instruction intended for both women. "Stand still and put your hands above your head. It'll be all right."

STEPANOV GAVE the command and Mitrokhin knew that it was time to move. He opened the door and stepped out into the midday heat. Stepanov was out of the car, too, his carbine aimed at Smith and the two women.

"Don't move!" Stepanov yelled out.

The others swept into action now, abandoning their disguises as they pulled weapons and aimed them toward the entrance to the station.

Mitrokhin lowered his Vikhr, took out the Beretta that he had been given and took a step forward so he could aim over the hood of the car. He slid his finger through the guard, sighted, and fired three times.

He couldn't really miss. Stepanov's body jerked as the bullets punched him in the back. He stumbled ahead, his arms splayed out wide, and then he fell to his knees.

72

M ilton had seen BLUEBIRD get out of the car and knew what was about to happen. He reached out for Romanova and Ross and held onto their shoulders, drawing both closer to him as BLUE-BIRD aimed his pistol and drilled Stepanov in the back. His shirt bloomed red as the bullets punched out of his chest and he fell to the ground.

Milton had seen the other SVR agents: the tramp, the old man, the couple on the knoll. The shock of the gunshots froze all of them in their tracks, their attention drawn to the body of Stepanov and then to the man who had shot him.

Distraction was what their plan had demanded. Now they had it.

Pope came out of the parked van wearing a UCIW on its sling. He aimed at the SVR agent dressed as a bum and fired a burst. The volley stitched the man in the torso and he stumbled back against the wall, sliding down it until he was slumped back against it once again. Pope swivelled and sighted the old man who had pulled a pistol from his jacket and fired again, another three-round burst. Two shots cracked into the wall, blowing out puffs of mortar and brick dust, but the third drilled the man in the cheek. His head snapped back and he went down, poleaxed, and didn't move.

The dirty white van jerked away from the parking space, leaving rubber as the driver swung the wheel, smoke spilling out of the wheel arches until the tyres gripped and the vehicle rushed ahead. Milton held onto Ross and Romanova and moved them ahead. The van slithered to a stop; Milton opened the back door and bundled both women inside.

There was a rattle of automatic gunfire and a jagged line of holes appeared in the flank of the van. Milton ducked, drawing his Beretta and swivelling in the direction of the inbound fire. The sun was low and in his eyes, and he couldn't make out the shooters. He ducked as the automatic rattled again, more rounds slamming into the side of the van, one of them punching through the windshield and spiderwebbing it.

BLUEBIRD had moved away from the car. He aimed at the shooter on the knoll and fired, two contained bursts, and drilled the man in the back before he could fire again. The female agent who had been part of the couple moved down the slope away from BLUEBIRD and, as a cloud covered the sun, Milton was able to draw a bead on her. He fired, two careful shots, aiming into the mass between her head and waist. Both shots found their mark. She dropped onto her back, her hands pressed against her gut.

BLUEBIRD was ten feet away.

He dropped the Beretta to the ground. Milton collected it.

BLUEBIRD's face was calm as he gave Milton a single nod of his head. Milton raised his pistol, aimed low, and shot him in the leg. He fell to the ground, his hands instinctively clutched around the wound, blood already running between his fingers.

Milton pulled himself into the back of the van. Light spilled into the interior from the bullet holes that jagged up in a long diagonal. He slapped his hand on the side of the van and the vehicle jerked away, the doors still open. Eleven slammed on the brakes and Pope pulled himself inside. Milton closed the door as Pope yelled out that they were ready to go. The engine revved loudly, the rubber squealed against the asphalt, and Milton braced himself against the wheel arch as the van swung left and right, picking up speed. They roared across the parking space and onto the road. Milton looked back through the tinted window at the confusion in their wake, bodies scattered across the ground like ninepins.

Milton turned back to the interior. Anastasiya Romanov was sitting against the wheel arch, her legs bent and her arms around her knees, clutching them tight. Ross was next to her, her eyes wide. Neither of them spoke.

"Where are the change-ups?" Milton asked.

"Two minutes away," Pope said.

Milton turned back to the window and looked for any sign of pursuit. There was none. The agents had no other support, just as BLUEBIRD had suggested would be the case. The SVR had allowed arrogance to get the better of them. That had been their undoing, together with the closed nature of the operation that had been insisted upon by whomever it was in the Center who wanted Anastasiya Romanova for him or herself. Milton didn't know anything other than what BLUEBIRD had told him in the lounge at Vladivostok: that Jessie Ross had been turned and that he would be at the RV and would do his best to assist.

Milton had been given only a few hours to put the operation together, and most of his time had been circumscribed
because he had been with Ross. Pope had taken the JAL
flight to Narita after the assassination of the Ryans, but,
instead of continuing to London, he had taken the next
flight to Vladivostok where he had collected the arriving
Eleven before driving north. The two of them had handled
the detail, including sourcing the weapons and arranging
for their exfiltration. The biggest risk was that BLUEBIRD's
involvement, although valuable, would lead to him being
blown. Someone might have seen him firing on the
Russians, but, Milton thought, the scene had been so disorientating that any testimony would be unreliable. The men
that BLUEBIRD had killed were shot with 19mm Para-
bellum ammunition, rather than the Russian 39mm
cartridges that the Vikhrs fired, and Milton had collected
the Beretta that he had used. And then BLUEBIRD had
required that he be shot in order to lend weight to the story
that he would tell. Milton didn't know whether there would
be witnesses, and hoped that he had been convincing.

Milton called to Pope over the sound of the engine.

"How many cars do we have?" Milton asked.

"Two."

"You take Romanova."

"And Ross?"

"I've got her. Take Eleven, too. Romanova's the prize. I'd
rather you had the extra manpower."

Pope looked at him quizzically, as if wondering whether
to object, but he knew Milton well enough to know that he
wouldn't change his mind. "There are extra weapons in both
cars. Guns and explosives. We probably won't need
them, but..."

"What's the route for exfil?"

"Drive to Svetlaya. It's on the coast—twenty hours if you don't stop. There'll be a trawler waiting there. It'll take us out into the Sea of Japan. HMS *Sutherland* will pick us up and we'll be transferred from there."

"I'll go first," Milton said. "Follow a mile behind. If they stop me, you might be able to turn around."

Pope put out his hand. "Good luck, Milton. See you in Svetlaya."

"Good luck," Milton said, clasping Pope's hand.

73

Ross was jostled and buffeted as the van raced away from the station. She was sitting next to Romanova. The Russian was terrified, her knees pressed up to her chest and anchored there behind locked arms. Romanova had the wheel arch on one side and Ross on the other, bumping left and right as they progressed. Ross was frightened, too, but there was more to it than that. She had seen everything: Stepanov ordering them to be still, the man behind him—she didn't know him, but knew it had to be BLUEBIRD—opening fire, the other agent they had left behind at Moscow Station appearing from the back of the van with an automatic rifle. Ross was frightened, but she was also angry and embarrassed.

The van swerved sharply to the left and then skidded to a stop. Smith opened the doors and hopped down. They were in a parking lot near the river terminal. There were half a dozen vehicles scattered around the lot. The others disembarked the van and the driver led the way to two scruffy rentals parked next to each other. Ross looked left and right and saw no cameras or any other security; an elderly man made his way up the steps to the terminal, but he was staring at his phone and didn't look as if he had noticed them.

Romanova was taken to a BMW.

Smith took Ross by the wrist and led her to a Volvo.

"How lovely," she said. "A nice drive together, just the two of us."

"It'll be much more pleasant if you spare me the attitude," Smith said. "You'll be back home in a day or two to see your son and your parents."

"You think? We'll never get out of here."

Smith opened the door. "Get in."

He held the door open for her and then went around to the driver's side. She lowered herself into the seat and stared out of the windscreen into the bright blue sky, a wide canvas over the river and the town beyond. She put her finger to her lips and chewed on a nail. Her trousers were tight against her thighs and she could feel the lipstick in her pocket. Smith thought he had power over her. He thought that he had taken away her ability to choose. He hadn't. She still had the *elektricheskiy pistolet.* She could decide what happened next.

Smith started the engine and pulled out. "You might want to get some sleep," he said. "We've got a long drive ahead of us."

MOSCOW

74

P rimakov was close to panic. The rendezvous had been an hour ago and he had heard nothing from Stepanov. He had tried to call him, but his phone rang through to voicemail every time. Stepanov was usually so punctilious and now, in the aftermath of a particularly sensitive operation, to have heard nothing? It was out of character. He tried Mitrokhin's number with the same results.

He had tried to distract himself with a new operation that he had been planning. Yehya al Moussa and Sameera Najeeb were scientists who had, until recently, been employed by the Iraq Atomic Energy Agency. They had been swept up by the Iranians following the fall of Saddam and had contributed to the recent progress that the Ahmadinejad regime had made toward the production of the first Islamic bomb. The Center had been directed by the Kremlin to provide assistance to the Iranians, and, as a part of that, a meeting had been arranged with a corporation that would be able to provide them with the zirconium they needed for their reactors. The meeting was to be in the

French Alps and Primakov had activated a local sleeper to provide security. He had a pile of papers on his desk that he needed to review and he was already late.

His intercom buzzed. He reached back to the credenza and took the office phone.

"What?"

"Sir," she said. "Major-General Nikolaevich is calling."

He swallowed. His throat was suddenly dry.

"Sir?"

"Put him through, please."

There was a pause and then a fizz of static as the call was connected.

"Alexei?" he said, trying to keep the uncertainty from his voice. "What can I do for you?"

"I've just had a report from my chief in the Amur *oblast*," he said. "There's been an attack there—four men and a woman have been shot and killed at the railway station at Komsomolsk."

Primakov felt sick. "Really?"

"Nikolai—please. Are you telling me you don't know?"

"No," he said. He put his hand on the desk to steady himself.

"The dead haven't been identified yet. No papers on them. One man was still alive—Boris Mitrokhin. He's been shot in the leg. I remembered his name. Didn't he transfer from Vympel to work for you?"

"Yes," Primakov said. There was no point in lying about it.

"He's in hospital—not life threatening. I'm waiting to speak to him. But I don't understand. What was one of your men doing in Komsomolsk?"

Primakov's breath caught, as if a metal band had been slipped around his chest and then cranked tight. "I cannot say," he replied, unable to think of anything that he could do other than to stonewall.

"The others? Were they yours, too?"

"There was an operation, but it is sensitive."

"What kind of operation—"

"I have to go, Alexei," Primakov said, interrupting him. "Thank you for bringing me the news. I need to find out what has happened. I'll speak to you when I know more."

"Nikolai. The president is—"

"You'll get a full report. Goodbye."

Primakov slammed the phone down, grabbed his jacket and put it on. He swept the al Moussa and Najeeb papers into his briefcase, stepped out of the office, told his secretary that he was going out and that he would be back later in the day, and hurried down to the garage.

He didn't know what to do. All of his meticulously constructed plans were collapsing. His mind started to race: there would be an enquiry into whatever had happened in Komsomolsk, why Stepanov and Mitrokhin and the others had been sent there, and he was going to have to work hard to keep ahead of it. What could he say? Honesty was impossible; it would expose his lies and his attempts to cover up the consequences of Natasha's mistakes. That would bring them both down. He would have to think of another reason for the operation, and an explanation as to why it had so evidently been bungled. And Mitrokhin... he didn't know him as well as Stepanov, didn't know how well he could be trusted when the investigators of Line KR got their hands on him. What would he say? He knew a lot. Too much.

Primakov took a deep breath. He could do it. It wasn't too late. He just had to keep it together until he could get on top of the facts. He needed to speak to Mitrokhin, find out what had happened.

He saw the man as he walked toward his car. He didn't recognise him. He was slender, in his mid-thirties, with tight curls of blond hair. He was wearing a pair of jeans and a leather jacket and he had a rucksack over his shoulder. He came out from between two parked cars and turned into his path.

"Excuse me," the man said in lightly accented Russian.

"Yes?"

"You are Deputy Director Primakov?"

Primakov took a step back, a sickly bloom of fear welling up in his bowels. The man followed and, as he did, he took out an aerosol. Primakov noticed the smaller details: the branding on the aerosol looked like it was a deodorant and the man was wearing flesh-coloured latex gloves. He aimed the aerosol and pressed down on the dispenser, sending a jet of liquid into Primakov's face. It was cold and wet and oily and it got into his mouth and eyes and nose. It had a metallic taste, not overpowering but distinctive: the taste of copper pennies.

Primakov bumped back against the hood of the car behind him, setting off the alarm. He tried to wipe the liquid away, but there was too much of it and he only succeeded in smearing it about.

"*Proshchay*," said the man.

"What?" Primakov grunted.

"Control says goodbye."

The man put the aerosol into his bag and zipped it up.

Primakov suddenly felt unwell. He could feel his heart beating faster, and then faster still, quickly racing out of control. He started to sweat and, as he leaned back against the car, his muscles began to tremble. He reached into his pocket for his phone, thinking that he could call his secretary to send someone down to help him, but his hand was shaking so badly that he lost his grip on the phone and it dropped down onto the concrete. The man stamped on it, breaking it into three pieces. Primakov's heart raced faster still and he felt warm drool as it gathered in his mouth and then ran down his chin and onto his shirt. He tried to stand, lost his balance, and toppled down onto his front, scraping his face. His arms and legs spasmed helplessly.

The last thing Primakov remembered was watching the man with the pale skin and blond curls crouch down to pick up his briefcase. The man raised himself up and crossed the garage to the service exit that led out onto the street beyond. The door opened, the man passed through it, and the door swung closed once more.

EPILOGUE

MOSCOW

1

Boris Mitrokhin got out of the taxi, collected his crutch and leaned on it as he hobbled into the restaurant. Mesopotamia was an up-and-coming establishment that served Turkish food. It was busy, with most of the tables taken. Mitrokhin made his way inside, passing through the restaurant until he reached the private dining room at the back. There was a single table there; they could close the door and ensure their privacy against prying eyes.

There was a man waiting for him.

"Hello, Boris," First Deputy Director Alexei Nikolaevich said.

"Hello, sir."

"How are you?"

"I'm well."

"And your leg?"

"It's healing. Thank you."

"Please. Sit."

Mitrokhin pulled a chair back and lowered himself into it. His leg was more painful than he liked to admit; the bullet had been well aimed, slicing through the fleshy part of the thigh, but that did not mean that it hadn't been excruciating and debilitating. It had been a necessary inconvenience, though. The wound had bought him credibility with the FSB investigators who had questioned him following the botched operation in Komsomolsk.

"You did very well, Boris. Thank you."

Mitrokhin nodded, happy to accept the gratitude of his patron.

"The investigators were not too thorough, I hope?"

"Thorough enough," Mitrokhin said.

He was underplaying it. He had been taken to the cellars beneath the Lubyanka and questioned for two days and two nights. Primakov's secret operation to protect his sweetheart's reputation had been uncovered, as had the fact that it had been compromised by a source within the Center. The Director was furious that he had been deceived by his deputy, but that was only part of it. Mitrokhin knew that the real concern was the leak: the president would not stand for it. Someone had sold Primakov out and they wanted to find out who.

"They have filed their report," Nikolaevich said. "You are not suspected."

"That's good to know."

"What did they ask you?"

"They wanted to be sure that I was not compromised."

"And?"

"We spent many hours discussing my love for the Rodina."

"I can only assume that you were persuasive."

Mitrokhin stared at the general, watching, ready to assess. "They asked about you, sir."

His face flickered with concern. "Really?"

"The investigation into the leak is broad. They know that there is a problem and they are intent upon fixing it. They wanted to know about Deputy Director Primakov. They were interested in his malfeasance—that he had lied to the Security Council and misled the president—but they were more interested in how the British agents were able to disrupt his operation against Romanova."

"Of course," Nikolaevich said.

"They asked about you, sir. They said that you had been in contact with Primakov."

"And that is true."

"They said your contact was more frequent than usual."

"And?"

"I think it is likely that they will want to speak to you."

Mitrokhin watched Nikolaevich, looking for a reaction. He was good at observing people. He had developed the skill during interrogations, the ability to spot the smallest tells that would give away someone's true feelings: the way a man might rub his wrist when he was lying; the inability to hold eye contact; a glance up and to the right, the classic sign of dissembling. He looked at Nikolaevich now and saw a muscle twitching in his neck and a bloom of blood suffusing his cheeks.

"I'm the Deputy Director of the FSB," he said, summoning indignation. "Are they really going to accuse me?"

"I thought you should know," Mitrokhin said placidly. There was no sense in aggravating Nikolaevich, but his mind was made up.

The Deputy Director changed the subject. "Your meeting with Smith at the airport. What happened?"

"I told him about PROZHEKTOR, as you requested, and gave him the means to contact me. The others met me in

Komsomolsk. There were two of them. They told me what they were intending to do and gave me the weapon that I was to use. I explained that they would need to shoot me once it was done."

"What did you think of them?"

"Professional," Mitrokhin said. "They worked quickly and efficiently. I was impressed. Can I ask if they were able to exfiltrate the women successfully?"

"They did. I imagine Romanova is being debriefed now."

"And PROZHEKTOR?"

"We won't hear from her for months," Nikolaevich said. "The British will try and turn her back against us. It may work. The SVR see her as a valuable asset, and they will want her to be clean—it will blind them."

There was a bottle of raki on the table. Nikolaevich opened it and poured out two measures. He held up his glass, Mitrokhin raised his and the two men touched them together. Mitrokhin drank his, the unsweetened aniseed flavour sticky on his tongue.

Nikolaevich poured again. "The deaths of Primakov and Stepanov opens a rare opportunity for you, Boris. Once you have been cleared to return to duty, you will assume Stepanov's position. And Primakov will be replaced as First Deputy Director next week. Do you know Sharipova?"

"The *rezident* in Athens."

Nikolaevich nodded. "She's dour and uninspiring and close to retirement, but the Director wants a safe pair of hands after what has happened. Sharipova will keep the seat warm for you. I will see to it that you are well placed to assume the Deputy Directorship when she decides that the time is right to move on—that'll be a year, two at the most."

"Of course, sir. Thank you."

"Your new position will allow you to furnish me with

intelligence on foreign operations. You'll have access that you don't have now. That information will be valuable—for both of us."

"Yes, sir."

Nikolaevich made no mention of what the operation meant for him, but Mitrokhin knew. Primakov had been a rival ever since the Academy, and, now that he was out of the way, the way was a little clearer for Nikolaevich to climb the ladder. Perhaps he was eyeing the Directorship of the Federal Security Service or the Foreign Intelligence Service. Mitrokhin didn't know his plans other than that he was determined to do everything possible to scupper the president's intention to resurrect the corpse of the Soviet Union, and that the higher he could climb, the better he would be able to do that.

Mitrokhin did not share his patron's reforming zeal. Indeed, he found it childish; Nikolaevich might be able to inconvenience Vladimir Vladimirovich, but he could no more stop him than he could hold back the tide. He was wasting his time and, eventually, there would come a time when he himself was blown. Mitrokhin was concerned that day was approaching.

Nikolaevich looked at him and smiled. "I realise you haven't been paid," he said. "I wanted to wait until the investigation was complete."

"And now it is," Mitrokhin said.

"The money has been transferred," Nikolaevich said. "It has been deposited in your Swiss account. And I've added a small bonus for a job well done. You performed flawlessly, Boris, and I feel bad about your leg."

∽

NIKOLAEVICH'S DRIVER took him back to his house on Mokhovaya Street. It was a grand property and had cost him more than €1.5 million when he had purchased it two years previously. It had reminded him then of a small castle, with façades built from limestone and brick and covered with Virginia creeper that changed colour with the seasons. He loved the different aspects of the property; from the river, it still looked to him like a castle on the top of a cliff, surrounded by a wall with towers and battlements; from the street, it looked more like a cosy mansion with a collection of outbuildings. There were six bedrooms, seven bathrooms, a spacious living room, a music room, a billiards salon, a bar and a sauna.

"Here we are, sir," his driver said.

"Thank you," Nikolaevich replied, opening the door and stepping out onto the street.

He watched the driver pull away, climbed the steps to the front door, unlocked it and went inside.

The house was quiet. His wife would normally have the television on, but he couldn't hear it tonight.

"I'm home," he called out.

There was no response. That was strange. Maria was not due to be out this evening.

"Hello?" he called again.

There was still no reply.

Curious, he took off his jacket and made his way into the living room. The house was silent, with just the dripping of a tap from a nearby bathroom. He dropped his jacket over the back of his armchair and went to the bar. He took down his favourite bottle of vodka, opened it and poured out a measure into a crystal tumbler.

He was about to sip it when he sensed movement behind him.

Too late.

Hands reached over his head and pulled back hard, a wire garrotte biting into the flesh of his neck. He tried to struggle, but it was no use. The person behind him was stronger, and the more Nikolaevich fought, the tighter the wire cut into his skin.

The tumbler fell from his fingertips and smashed on the floor. Nikolaevich stumbled backwards, and, as he looked up into the mirror behind the bar, he saw the face of his assailant.

It was Mitrokhin.

Nikolaevich reached up and tried to slide his fingers between the garrotte and his throat, but it was impossible. The wire was too tight. Blood was running down his neck, dripping over his shirt front and onto the floor where it spattered onto the crystal shards.

Nikolaevich tried to speak, but all he could manage was a hopeless gargle.

"I'm sorry," Mitrokhin said, his voice calm despite the effort he was expending. "You are compromised. I can't take the chance that you will compromise me, too."

Nikolaevich felt the strength ebbing away from his legs, and he fell down onto his knees. Mitrokhin followed him, maintaining the pressure on the wire. Nikolaevich tried to speak again, tried to get his fingers beneath the garrotte, but his breath was almost all gone. As darkness began to gather at the corners of his eyes, he felt his arms go limp and then there was nothing.

LONDON

The psychiatrist assigned to Group Fifteen had an office on the top floor of the Global Logistics building. It was a pleasant, if uninspiring, space: two sofas that faced one another; a table with a vase of flowers between them; bookshelves that held medical texts; a standard lamp that cast a warm glow from the corner of the room. Milton was sitting on one of the sofas and the psychiatrist, Dr Fry, was sitting opposite him. Milton had made an effort this afternoon. He had visited a barber in Chelsea and enjoyed a shave with hot towels and a trim. He was wearing one of his better suits, together with a polished pair of leather brogues and the Rolex Oyster Perpetual watch that he had inherited from his father. Fry, on the other hand, was a little shabby. His suit was shiny at the knees and elbows and the caps of his leather Oxfords were scuffed.

"Thank you for coming, Captain Milton."

Milton nodded.

"You know why you're here?"

"Control sent me."

"Yes. But do you know why?"

Milton sighed. "It's unnecessary."

Fry looked down at his notes. "Headaches, isn't it? I understand you've been suffering from them?"

"Now and again," Milton said. "It's nothing, really."

"That's probably right, but I don't think it'll hurt to have them checked out. There's no mention of headaches on your file. It's probably tension, but it could be something else. Do you feel tense?"

"No more than usual."

"Your job can be stressful."

"But I've been doing it for a long time."

"How about depression? That can cause a headache. Do you feel depressed?"

"No," Milton said. "Couldn't be happier."

Fry looked up at him, gave a chuckle to indicate that he knew Milton was joking, and jotted a note in his file.

"How's everything else?"

"Fine."

"Drink?"

Milton flinched. "No more than usual."

Fry looked up. "Really? Your last three toxicology tests all came back with elevated blood alcohol levels."

"As you say, it's a stressful job. I have a drink at night sometimes to help me switch off."

"*A* drink?"

"A couple of beers."

"Every night?"

"No, not every night. I don't have a drink problem, Doctor, if that's what you're asking."

"How about drugs?"

"You know—you prescribed them."

"Yes. Gabapentin for nerve damage and oxycodone for general pain relief. Not them. I meant recreational drugs."

"Of course not. Please—move on. Ask your next question."

He looked down at the notes and made a show of reading them; Milton knew that Fry would be familiar with everything, and that this was all part of the show. "Your last assignment, in Russia. How do you feel you performed?"

"I met both objectives. Romanova and Ross were both exfiltrated successfully."

"They were, but not without a surprise or two along the way. Let me ask you about Ms. Ross."

Milton spread his arms. "Fine."

"You spent a lot of time with her. You didn't suspect she was working for the Russians?"

"No," Milton said. "Are you saying that I should have?"

"I'm just asking—"

"I didn't notice, and neither did anyone else. And she'd been playing us for a lot longer than I knew her."

"What about the *elektricheskiy pistolet*?"

"Sorry?"

"She had a lipstick pistol in her pocket. They found it when they debriefed her. Single shot, with one 4.5mm Makarov round. You didn't know she had it?"

Milton frowned and shook his head.

"Don't you think you *should* have known? She could have shot Romanova. Or you."

"I was more concerned with getting out of the country."

"Yes, I'm sure. But, still—don't you think you were lucky? You were alone in the car with her for hours. It would have been easy for her to take that out and shoot you."

"But she didn't."

"Do you think you would have noticed that five years ago?"

"Maybe. What are you saying? I'm losing my touch?"

"No, not at all. Your work is generally excellent." Milton heard the qualifier and let it go. "I'm just concerned that there's something that's bothering you. Your drinking—"

"I don't have a problem with drink."

Fry ignored the interruption and went on. "The mistakes at the house in Kings Worthy—losing the two Russian illegals—and then the errors with Ms. Ross. Those are not the sort of mistakes that I would expect of an agent with your operational experience. You're Number One for a reason, Milton. You've reached that plateau precisely because you *don't* make mistakes."

"Then I'll have to make sure I try harder," Milton replied with a truculence that he couldn't resist.

Fry held up a manila folder. "I understand Control has given you another file to action."

"He has."

"Two targets this time. A husband and wife." Fry opened the folder and took out a copy of the briefing that Milton had received yesterday. "Ah, yes, here we are. Yehya al Moussa and Sameera Najeeb. An atomic research scientist and an expert in microwave technology. You're due to action the file in France."

"That's right. In four days' time. And I'd like to be on my way as soon as I can. I have to prepare."

Fry ignored the not-so-subtle hint. "What do you feel about them?" he said. "How do you feel about them as targets?"

"Do you mean will I be able to do my job?"

"Yes."

"You don't need to worry about that."

"But one could argue they haven't done anything wrong. They have jobs to do, after all."

"I have no opinion on the rights and wrongs of it. A decision has been made that they need to die. The file has been given to me to action, and that's what I'll do."

"You don't think about them beyond the fact that their names are in this file?" Fry tapped his finger against the sheet of paper. "You don't think about the fact that they might have families? Loved ones who would miss them? You don't consider that they aren't traditional combatants? That they have no idea that they have just a few days left to live? That they'll be unarmed?"

"No, I don't. Let me put it to you like this: I'm a weapon, Doctor. That's all I am. I'm pointed at a target and I take that target out. I leave the soul-searching to those who give the orders. It isn't my concern."

"I see," Fry said, scribbling on the file. He looked up. "What's your Jewish folklore like, Captain?"

"I'm sure I could always stand to learn a little more," he said.

"There's a famous story," Fry said. "The golem of Prague. There was a rabbi in the sixteenth century—Judah Loew ben Bezalel—who created a monster made out of clay from the banks of the Vltava River and brought it to life through rituals and incantations. He instructed the golem to defend the Prague ghetto from anti-Semitic attacks and pogroms. But the rabbi worried that he would lose control of his monster, and eventually he took away the golem's power until it fell to pieces." Fry stared at Milton across the table. "I know that is a clumsy metaphor, but some people would see you and the others as golems. There is the worry that something might happen that would mean we might lose control of you. I've seen it happen to your predecessors, Milton.

Your work is toxic. There's only so much of it you can take. And that's why it is important that we have these regular discussions."

Milton stood. "Thank you, Doctor. Is that all? I have a train to catch."

"For now. But I would like to schedule regular meetings for when you get back from France. My secretary will be in touch. We'll spend a little longer next time. There are some things I'd like to discuss with you in more depth."

He stood and extended a hand. Milton shook it; Fry's grip was limp.

"Happy hunting, Captain."

MILTON TOOK a cab across London to St Pancras. He was travelling on the Eurostar, and his train was due to depart in an hour. He had time to kill and found himself drifting into Searcys, the restaurant on the upper concourse that boasted the longest champagne bar in Europe. It ran alongside the Eurostar platform for nearly a hundred metres, separated from the trains by a glass partition. The platform dropped away to afford guests a spectacular view of the trains as they rolled by. There were smart wooden booths and stools for a hundred and twenty people. Milton took one of them and beckoned to the bartender.

"Yes, sir? What can I get for you?"

"A glass of Krug Grande Cuvée, please," he said.

"Certainly, sir."

Milton dropped his bag on the floor next to his stool. It contained the things that he would need for his trip to France: his legend, a change of clothes, directions to the chalet in Chevaline that had been rented for him. His legend cast him as a tourist visiting the area for a cycling holiday; it would give him the opportunity to scout the area and the spot that had been selected for the assassination. He had asked for an HK53 for the operation, and the quartermaster had arranged to leave the carbine and its ammunition at the dead drop in three days' time.

"Here you are, sir."

The bartender put the flute down on the bar. Milton took a long sip as a train rolled out.

It had been a long day. He had been debriefed by Tanner before his meeting with the psychiatrist. Anastasiya Romanova had provided the data that she had promised and early analysis by scientists at the Ministry of Defence and the contractors who worked closely with the military suggested that it was at least as good as they could have hoped for, and perhaps even better. It had been decided that the information would be kept classified for now, but the intention was to share it with the United States and other NATO partners in due course. It was an intelligence coup of the highest order, and Tanner had reported that everyone—from the senior staff at VX to the mandarins in Whitehall and even Control—had been happy with the outcome of the operation. Milton trusted that was correct; indeed, he was counting on it. He knew that he had given Control reason to doubt him—the appointment with the shrink was evidence of that—and he hoped that some of the glow from the success of the exfiltration would distract from his own failings. He needed time to work out how he was going to leave the Group. He knew it would be difficult—dangerous—but, just the same, he knew that it was inevitable, too. He had made up his mind.

The bartender returned with the bill hidden in a small leather folder. Milton opened it, saw that it was for thirty pounds, took out his wallet and slid three ten-pound notes into the folder.

He felt someone next to him. Milton looked up and saw that a woman was standing there, smiling at him. "Is this stool taken?"

"No," Milton said. "Help yourself."

She sat down. "Getting the train?"

"Yes," he said.

"Me too. Shopping in Paris. Haven't been for years."

Milton nodded and smiled.

"What about you?" she asked.

"Cycling holiday," he said, slipping into his legend.

"Really? Where?"

"Around Lake Annecy."

"Beautiful," she said. "I've driven through there before. Stunning scenery." She put out her hand. "Laura Wood," she said.

"John Smith."

She ordered a glass of champagne and talked at Milton while she drank it, a stream of pointless anecdotes about France, her life in Kensington and her job in Soho as an agent for film and television actors. She was monumentally self-absorbed and spoke relentlessly; all Milton had to do was make the occasional affirmative noise and she would continue on with another inane story. She finished her glass and, with a final air kiss that missed Milton's left cheek by a clear two inches, she went to do a little shopping before the train departed.

Milton watched her go. The scent she was wearing had reminded him of Jessie Ross. Tanner had barely mentioned her during the briefing. She had been swallowed up by SIS, and would, he guessed, be interrogated for every last scrap of information about her recruitment by the SVR and about how she had worked for them for so long. They would want to know how much damage she had caused. Aleksandrov was just the most recent betrayal. They would want to know who else she had fingered for Timoshev and Kuznetzov's malign attention. Milton had no idea what her future would hold. She would have to persuade her superiors that she could be trusted to work against the Russians, and that was assuming that she was able to persuade the replacement for the slain Primakov that she was still a viable source. Even if she was able to prove that she was worth the risk, she would still be kept on the shortest possible leash. The fates of her son and her parents would forever be held over her as she started to record entries on the opposite page of the ledger and begin the work to remedy the damage that her betrayal had caused.

Milton drained the flute, looked at his watch and changed his mind. He signalled the bartender.

"Sir?"

"I'll have the bottle, please."

The bartender was discreet, as if it were commonplace for a single traveller to order a two-hundred-pound bottle of champagne for himself. Milton didn't know; perhaps it was. The man returned with an ice bucket and the champagne, and took the bill away so that he could update it. Milton finished the glass and poured himself another. He had a long trip ahead of him, and then he had to prepare for his assignment.

He turned and Callaghan was sitting on the stool. You think this is it? You think you can get out? They'll just let you leave? Come on, Milton. Doesn't work like that. You know it doesn't. They'll never let you go. You're in this for life. You belong to them. You're theirs.

Milton emptied the glass in one draught and poured

again. The phantom disappeared, but Milton could still hear his voice, whispering in the spaces between his thoughts. The whispers were right, but Milton didn't care. He was done. Finished. He would honour this file but no more.

He was going to get out.

AFTERWORD

It's a standard question when I tell people that I make my living as an author: where do you get your ideas? I've never had a problem with finding something interesting for my characters to do. It's often just a case of opening the news-paper or going to the cinema. The genesis of this book has been a little different, though. More immediate. Closer to home, and, once I started investigating and writing, much more difficult to stop.

I live and work in Salisbury. I had made good progress with my new novel when Sergei and Yulia Skripal were found on a bench in the Maltings, a shopping precinct in the centre of town. It's a two minute walk from my office to that bench, and, as the story changed from a suspected drug overdose to an attempted assassination that then became an international story, it was something that I simply couldn't ignore. More recent developments, in which Dawn Sturgess and Charlie Rowley were also poisoned (with Sturgess tragi-cally passing away) have added another, more frightening, dimension.

Life has imitated art. I was writing about a defecting spy who comes to the attention of his previous employer, and local events added relevance that would have been hard to credit if they were not true. My research has unfolded around me. I've watched the media helicopters hovering over the spire of the beautiful cathedral. I've seen forensics tents erected around suspected crime scenes. I've observed soldiers in Hazmat suits shutting down a homeless shelter. I've spoken to the police officers who have been guarding the cordons. I know the restaurant and pub that the Skripals visited before they became unwell. My daughter was playing in the park that was closed after the two subsequent victims were poisoned. And I live close to the hospital where all the victims were treated. As the story developed, so too did my compulsion to write about it.

If you ask around on the streets you will find plenty of people who don't believe the official narrative. That's not surprising. The authorities have revealed very little, for good reason. An official narrative that is so full of holes offers licence for conspiracy theories, and you'll find no shortage of them if you ask around. It also makes it possible for an author to take the lines of a story that has been sketched out and then to colour in the blanks. Why was Skripal targeted? Who targeted him? Why was an exotic nerve agent used, rather than a more prosaic – but more effective – method? How did Sturgess and Rowley find the poison? Why – if reports are true – did the would be assassins ditch the bottle rather than dispose of it more carefully?

It's been a challenge to take these starting points and turn them into a work of fiction while also remembering that this is an on-going story, with a human cost to those who have been unfortunate enough to have been affected by it. It has also been an interesting and exciting project, and one that I hope you've enjoyed.

Mark Dawson
Salisbury, September 2018

JOIN THE READERS' CLUB

Building a relationship with my readers is the very best thing about writing. I occasionally send newsletters with details on new releases, special offers and other bits of news relating to the Milton, Beatrix and Isabella Rose and Soho Noir series.

If you join my Readers' Club I'll send you this free Milton content:

1. A free copy of Milton's adventure in North Korea - '1000 Yards.'

2. A free copy of Milton's tussle with a Mafia assassin in 'Tarantula.'

3. An eyes-only profile of Milton from a Group Fifteen psychologist.

You can get your free content by visiting my website at markjdawson.com. I'll look forward to seeing you there.

ABOUT THE AUTHOR

Mark Dawson is the author of the breakout John Milton, Beatrix and Isabella Rose and Soho Noir series.

For more information:
www.markjdawson.com
mark@markjdawson.com

§ 3/2020
0 1/18/21
€ /22

Made in the USA
Monee, IL
07 January 2020